CW00554750

THE TALE OF H
DISTURBER OF THE PEACE

TRANSLIT
PUBLISHING

THE TALE OF HODJA NASREDDIN
DISTURBER OF THE PEACE

Leonid Solovyov

Translated by Michael Karpelson

To Alhairi
with my best
wishes!

Дмитрий
01. 04. 2013

TRANSLIT PUBLISHING

Translit Publishing

Copyright © 2009 Michael Karpelson

All rights reserved. No part of this publication may be reproduced, stored in a retrieval system, or transmitted, in any form or by any means (electronic, mechanical, photocopying, recording, or otherwise) without the prior written permission of the publisher.

ISBN 978-0-9812695-0-4

Contents

Part Two

Part Three

Biographical Note

 Leonid Vasilyevich Solovyov was born in 1906 in the city of Tripoli, Lebanon, where his parents had been working for the Imperial Orthodox Palestine Society. In 1909, the family returned to Russia; in 1921, it moved to Kokand, Uzbekistan. Solovyov worked for several regional newspapers and, during his travels in Uzbekistan's Fergana Province, studied regional folklore.

In 1930, Solovyov left for Moscow and enrolled in the literary and screenwriting program at the Institute of Cinematography, graduating in 1932. While living in Moscow, Solovyov wrote a number of novels, short stories, and screenplays. *Disturber of the Peace* – the first part of Solovyov's best known work, *The Tale of Hodja Nasreddin* – was published in 1939. During the Second World War, Solovyov served as a war correspondent and produced several wartime stories and screenplays.

In 1946, Solovyov was accused of conspiring to commit acts of terrorism against the Soviet state. He was interred in several prison camps until 1954, when he was cleared of all charges and released. The second part of *The Tale of Hodja Nasreddin*, subtitled *The Enchanted Prince*, was written in the camps and completed around 1950.

After his imprisonment, Solovyov settled in Leningrad. The two parts of *The Tale of Hodja Nasreddin* were published together for the first time in 1956 and enjoyed a very favorable reception. However, the author's health began to decline, and he passed away in 1962.

Translator's Note

Although rooted in the many stories and anecdotes about the traditional Sufi figure Nasreddin, Solovyov's character is unique. A tireless champion of the downtrodden and a thorn in the side of the powers that be, Solovyov's Hodja Nasreddin inspires the reader with his intelligence, wit, defiance of authority, and love of life. The occasional presence of Soviet overtones in the text does not diminish the reading experience in the least.

The two books of *The Tale of Hodja Nasreddin* have something to offer to readers of all ages – adventure for the young, philosophy for the more mature, and humor for everyone – and yet they are virtually unknown in the English-speaking world. I hope that this translation of *Disturber of the Peace* will help introduce Solovyov's creation to a wider audience.

Dedicated to my family.

THE TALE OF HODJA NASREDDIN
DISTURBER OF THE PEACE

"'And I said to him: 'For the joy of those who live with me on earth, I will write a book – may the cold winds of time never blow on its pages, may the radiant spring of my poems never yield to the mirthless autumn of oblivion!…' And – look! – the roses in the garden have not yet shed their petals, and I still walk without a cane, while the book 'Gulistan,' which means 'The Rose Garden,' has already been written by me, and you are reading it…"

Saadi

"This story has been passed on to us by Abu-Omar-Ahmed-ibn-Muhammad from the words of Muhammad-ibn-Ali-Rifaa, in reference to Ali-ibn-Abd-al-Aziz, who referred to Abu-Ubei-da-al-Hasim-ibn-Selam, who spoke from the words of his tutors, the last of whom cites Omar-ibn-al-Hattab and his son Abd-Allah – may Allah be pleased with them both!"

Ibn-Hazm, The Dove's Necklace

To the memory of my unforgettable friend Mumin Adilov, who died on the 18th of April, 1930, in the mountain kishlak of Namai from a treacherous enemy bullet, I dedicate this book, in reverence of this pure memory. He had many, many characteristics of Hodja Nasreddin – a selfless love for the people, courage, an honest slyness, and noble cunning – and when I was writing this book, I imagined more than once, in the quiet of the night, that his spirit was standing behind my chair and guiding my pen.

He is buried in Kanibadam. I visited his grave recently; children were playing around the hill, overgrown with spring grass and flowers, while he lay in eternal sleep and did not respond to the summons of my heart…

Part 1

"They tell also of a simpleton who walked along, leading his donkey by the bridle."

The 388th Night of Scheherazade

Chapter 1

Hodja Nasreddin met the thirty-fifth year of his life on the road.

He had spent more than ten years in exile, wandering from city to city, from one country to another, crossing seas and deserts, and spending the nights where he could – on the bare earth by a shepherd's meager fire, or in a packed caravanserai, where the camels scratch and pant in the dusty darkness till morning, jingling their bells quietly, or in a smoky, sooty chaikhana[1], among water-bearers, beggars, and camel drivers lying side by side, along with other poor folk who routinely fill the bazaar squares and narrow city streets with piercing shouts at the break of dawn. Quite often, he managed to spend the night on the soft silken pillows of some Iranian dignitary, who was meanwhile scouring all the chaikhanas and caravanserais with a detachment of guards, searching for the vagrant and blasphemer Hodja Nasreddin in order to have him impaled… A thin strip of sky would appear through the window grating, the stars would turn pale, a morning breeze would ruffle the leaves gently and tenderly, and lively turtle-doves would begin to coo and clean their feathers on the windowsill. Kissing the weary beauty, Hodja Nasreddin would say:

"It is time. Farewell, my incomparable pearl, and do not forget me."

"Wait!" she would reply, locking her lovely arms around his neck. "Are you leaving for good? But why? Listen – when it grows dark this evening, I will send the old woman to fetch you again."

"No. I have long forgotten the times when I spent two nights in a row under one roof. I must go, for I am in a great hurry."

"Go? Have you some urgent business in another city? Where do you intend to go?"

"I do not know. But dawn approaches, the city gates have opened already, and the first caravans have set out on their journey. Can you hear? The camels' bells are ringing. When this sound

1 *Chaikhana* – tea house.

reaches my ears, it is as though the djinns themselves possess my feet, and I cannot sit still!"

"Very well then, go!" the beauty would say irritably, trying in vain to hide the tears glistening on her long eyelashes. "But at least tell me your name before we part."

"You wish to know my name? Listen, then – you have spent the night with Hodja Nasreddin! I am Hodja Nasreddin, disturber of the peace and sower of discord, the same one whose name is daily trumpeted by the heralds in all the squares and bazaars along with promises of a large reward for his head. They offered three thousand tomans[2] yesterday, and I even thought: what if I were to sell my own head at so good a price? You laugh, my little star, so give me your lips quickly one last time. I would give you an emerald if I could, but I do not have an emerald – take this simple white stone instead as a keepsake!"

He would put on his ragged robe, singed in many spots by the sparks of roadside campfires, and leave quietly. A dumb, lazy eunuch, wearing a turban and soft slippers with curled toes, would snore loudly behind the door – a negligent guardian entrusted with the palace's greatest treasure. Further on, stretching out on the rugs and mats, lay the snoring guards, their heads placed on their bared Turkish swords. Hodja Nasreddin would sneak by them on tiptoes, always successfully, as if he could turn invisible during this time.

And once again, the stony white road would ring and the dust would fly under the brisk hooves of his donkey. The sun would shine over the world in the blue sky; Hodja Nasreddin could stare at it directly, without squinting. Hodja Nasreddin's song was heard by green gardens and foamy rivers, by grim mountains and green pastures, by dewy fields and barren deserts where white camel bones lie half-buried in the sand. He traveled farther and farther, never looking back, never regretting what he left behind or fearing what lay ahead.

And in the city he abandoned, his memory would live on forever.

High officials and mullahs would pale with rage when they heard his name; water-bearers, camel drivers, weavers, millers, and

2 *Toman* – Persian unit of currency.

saddle-makers would tell each other funny stories about his adventures when they gathered in the chaikhanas in the evenings – adventures where he would always emerge victorious. The sultry beauty in the harem would often gaze at the little white stone and hide it in a small pearl coffer when she heard the footsteps of her master.

"Oof!" the fat dignitary would say, panting and wheezing, as he pulled off his brocade robe. "We are completely exhausted thanks to this accursed vagrant Hodja Nasreddin: he's disturbed and agitated the entire country! I received a letter today from my old friend, the esteemed governor of the Horasan region. To think – the moment this tramp Hodja Nasreddin appeared in his city, the blacksmiths stopped paying their taxes, and the cookhouse keepers refused to feed the guards for free. What's more, this thief, this defiler of Islam and son of sin, dared to sneak into the governor's harem and dishonor his favorite wife! Truly, the world has never seen such a criminal! I regret only that this contemptible beggar did not try to penetrate my harem, or else his head would have been sticking on a post in the main square a long time ago!"

The beauty would remain silent, concealing a smile – she was both amused and saddened. And the road kept ringing and the dust flying beneath the donkey's hooves. And Hodja Nasreddin's song carried on. In ten years he had been everywhere: in Baghdad, in Istanbul and in Teheran, in Bakhchisarai, in Echmiadzin and in Tbilisi, in Damascus and in Trebizond. He knew all these cities and numerous others, and he was remembered in all of them.

Now he was returning to his hometown, to Bukhara-i-Sharif, Noble Bukhara, where he hoped to assume a false identity and rest awhile from his endless wanders.

~~ *Chapter 2* ~~

Joining a large merchant caravan, Hodja Nasreddin crossed the Bukharian border, and on the eighth day of his journey, he saw the familiar minarets of the great, famous city far away in the dusty gloom.

Tormented by thirst and heat, the caravaneers shouted hoarsely, and the camels put on speed: the sun was setting, and they had to hurry to make it to Bukhara before the city gates closed. Hodja Nasreddin was riding at the very back of the caravan, surrounded by a thick, heavy cloud of dust; it was the holy dust of his homeland, and it smelled better to him than the dust of other, distant lands. Sneezing and coughing, he spoke to his donkey:

"Well, we are home at last. By Allah, we will find happiness and good fortune here."

The caravan reached the city wall just as the guards were locking the gates. "In the name of Allah, wait!" cried the caravanbashi[1], showing them a gold coin from afar. But the gates had already closed, the bolts had clanged shut, and sentries appeared on the towers next to the cannons. A cool breeze began to blow, the rosy tinge in the sky was replaced by the clearly defined crescent of a young moon, and the high-pitched, drawn-out, mournful voices of the muezzins came from all the countless minarets in the hushed twilight, calling Muslims to their evening prayers.

The merchants and caravaneers stood on their knees, while Hodja Nasreddin walked quietly aside with his donkey.

"There merchants have plenty of reasons to thank Allah: they had dinner tonight, and now they will have supper. As for us, my faithful donkey, we have not dined tonight, nor will we sup; if Allah wishes to receive our gratitude, let him send me a bowl of pilaf and you a sheaf of clover!"

He tied his donkey to a roadside tree and lay down right on the ground nearby, placing a stone under his head. Shining webs of stars appeared before his eyes in the clear, dark sky: so frequently

---

1 *Caravan-bashi* – Leader of the caravan.

had he seen the open sky above him in ten years that he knew every constellation. And he always thought that these hours of silent, wise contemplation made him richer than the richest men – that even though a rich man can eat from golden plates, he must also spend the night under his own roof, and when, at midnight, everything grows quiet, he cannot feel the flight of the earth through the cool blue fog of stars...

Meanwhile, fires were lit under large pots in the caravanserais and chaikhanas adjoining the outside of the toothed city wall, and the rams began to bleat mournfully as they were dragged to slaughter. But the experienced Hodja Nasreddin had thoughtfully settled in to sleep on the windward side, so that the smell of the food would not mock and disturb him. Knowing Bukharian customs well, he had decided to save the last of his money in order to pay the tax at the city gates the following day.

He tossed and turned for a long time, but sleep would not come to him, and it was not at all the hunger that kept him awake. Hodja Nasreddin was plagued and tormented by bitter thoughts; even the starry sky could not console him tonight.

He loved his homeland, and there was no greater love in the world for this crafty joker with a black beard on his copper-tanned face and sly sparks in his clear eyes. The further he wandered from Bukhara in his patched robe, dirty skullcap, and torn boots, the more he loved Bukhara and pined for it. Throughout his exile he always remembered the narrow streets where the carts scrape the clay fences on either side as they pass; he remembered the tall minarets with ornate tiled caps, burning with the fiery brightness of the sun every morning and evening, and ancient, sacred elms with giant nests of storks hanging on the branches; he remembered the smoky chaikhanas built over the aryks[2] in the shade of rustling poplars, the smoke and soot of the cookhouses, the speckled commotion of the bazaars; he remembered the mountains and rivers of his homeland, its settlements, fields, pastures, and deserts; and when, in Baghdad or in Damascus, he met a fellow countryman, recognizing him by the pattern on his skullcap or the particular cut of his robe, Hodja Nasreddin's heart skipped a beat and he felt short of breath.

2 *Aryk* – Small irrigation canal typical of Central Asia.

Upon his return, he found his homeland even more miserable than when left. The old emir had been buried long ago. Over the last eight years, the new emir had managed to completely ruin Bukhara. Hodja Nasreddin saw broken bridges on the roads, meager crops of barley and wheat, dried-out aryks with the bottoms cracked from heat. The fields ran wild with tall weeds and thorny plants, the gardens were dying for lack of water, the peasants had neither bread nor cattle, and beggars sat in rows along the sides of the roads, pleading for a pittance from people just as poor as themselves. The new emir placed detachments of soldiers in every settlement and ordered the inhabitants to feed them for free, he laid the foundations of numerous new mosques and ordered the people to finish building them – he was very pious, the new emir, and twice a year he absolutely had to pay his respects to the remains of the most holy and incomparable Sheikh Bogaeddin, whose tomb towered near Bukhara. He introduced three new taxes in addition to the existing four, set fees for the crossing of every bridge, raised commercial and judicial duties, minted lots of worthless money... Tradecraft was in decline, commerce broke down, and Hodja Nasreddin found his beloved homeland in a dismal state.

...Early in the morning, the muezzins began to sing again from all the minarets; the city gates opened, and the caravan slowly entered the city to the dull jingling of bells.

The caravan stopped immediately beyond the gate: its path had been blocked by guards. There were a great many of them – some were shod and clothed; others, who had not yet managed to become rich in the emir's service, were barefoot and half-dressed. They pushed, shouted, and argued, dividing up the loot in advance. Finally, a tax collector emerged from a chaikhana – corpulent and sleepy, wearing a silk robe with dirty sleeves and slippers on his bare feet, his swollen face showing intemperance and vice. Casting a greedy glance over the merchants, he said:

"Greetings to you, merchants. I wish you good fortune in your trade. And you should know that the emir has commanded that anyone who conceals even the slightest amount of goods is to be caned to death!"

Gripped by confusion and fear, the merchants were stroking their dyed beards silently. The collector turned to the guards, who were practically dancing on the spot with impatience, and moved his fat fingers. This was the sign. The guards dashed towards the camels with hoots and howls. Crowding and hurrying, they slashed at binding ropes with their swords and ripped the sacks open noisily, tossing the goods right on the road: brocade, silk, velvet, cases of pepper, tea, and ambergris, Tibetan medicines and jugs of precious rose oil.

The merchants were speechless with horror. Two minutes later, the inspection was over. The guards lined up behind their chief. Their robes had become puffed up and swollen. The collection of duties for the goods and for entry into the city could now begin. Hodja Nasreddin had no goods, so he only owed the entry fee.

"Where have you come from, and why?" the collector asked. The scribe dipped a goose quill into his inkwell and prepared to write down Hodja Nasreddin's answer.

"I came from Isfahan, o illustrious chief. My relatives live here, in Bukhara."

"Right," the collector said. "You are here as a guest of your relatives. Therefore, you must pay the visiting tax."

"But I am not here as a guest," Hodja Nasreddin objected. "I am here on important business."

"On business!" cried the collector, and his eyes sparkled. "Therefore you are here both as a guest and on business! You must pay the visiting tax, the business tax, and donate money towards the embellishment of mosques for the glory of Allah, who has protected you from bandits on your journey."

"I'd rather he protect me now. I could deal with the bandits myself," Hodja Nasreddin thought, but remained silent: he had already determined that every new word in this conversation was costing him more than ten tanga[3]. He untied his belt and began to count off the entry tax, the visiting tax, the business tax, and the donation for the embellishment of mosques beneath the predatory, intent stares of the guards. The collector glanced at the guards menacingly, and they turned away. Tucking his face into his book, the scribe began to scribble rapidly.

Hodja Nasreddin paid up and was about to leave, but then the collector noticed that there were still a few coins left in the belt.

3 *Tanga* – Old currency in Tajikistan.

"Wait," he stopped Hodja Nasreddin. "And who is going to pay the tax for your donkey? Since you are a guest of your relatives, your donkey is a guest of your relatives as well."

"You are correct, o wise chief," Hodja Nasreddin replied humbly, untying his belt once again. "Indeed, my ass has a great many relatives in Bukhara. If he did not, our emir would long have been booted from the throne with practices like these, while you, o honorable one, would have been impaled for your greed!"

Before the collector could come to his wits, Hodja Nasreddin jumped on his donkey and set off at top speed, disappearing in the nearest alleyway. "Faster, faster!" he spoke. "Pick up the pace, my faithful donkey, pick up the pace, or else your master will have to pay one more tax – with his head!"

Hodja Nasreddin's donkey was very smart and understood everything: his long ears had picked up the din and confusion by the city gates, as well as the shouting of the guards, and he rushed along so rapidly, not heeding the road, that Hodja Nasreddin could barely manage stay in the saddle as he grasped the donkey's neck with both hands and raised his legs high in the air. An entire pack of dogs flew in his wake with hoarse barking; passers-by shrank against the fences and looked on, shaking their heads.

Meanwhile, the guards at the city gates rummaged through the entire crowd trying to find the insolent freethinker. Smirking, the merchants whispered to each other:

"Now that was a reply worthy of Hodja Nasreddin himself!"

By noon, the entire city knew of this reply; the salesmen at the bazaar whispered it to the customers, who passed it on to others, and everyone said: "Now these are words worthy of Hodja Nasreddin himself!"

And no one knew that these words belonged to Hodja Nasreddin, and that the famous and incomparable Hodja Nasreddin was now wandering the city, hungry, without a coin in his pocket, searching for any relatives or old friends who could feed and shelter him for the time being.

Chapter 3

He did not find any relatives in Bukhara, or any old friends. He did not even find his childhood home, where he was born and grew up, playing in the shaded garden; where yellow foliage rustled in the wind during clear autumn days; where ripe fruit fell on the ground with a dull, as if distant, sound; where the birds sang tenderly, and sunspots fluttered on the fragrant grass; where the busy bees hummed, collecting their last tribute from the wilting flowers; where the water babbled from its hiding place in the aryk, telling the boy its endless, incomprehensible tales... An empty plot of land remained in its place: mounds, ditches, ruts, clingy thistle, charred bricks, eroding remains of walls, pieces of decaying reed mats; Hodja Nasreddin did not see a single bird, a single bee! Only a long, oily stream poured out suddenly from under a stone he had stumbled on, flashing dimly in the sun and vanishing again under the rocks – it was a snake, a solitary and frightening inhabitant of deserted places abandoned forever by man.

His eyes downcast, Hodja Nasreddin stood in silence; grief seized his heart.

He heard a rattling cough behind him and turned around.

An old man, burdened by needs and troubles, was walking along the path leading through the empty plot. Hodja Nasreddin stopped him.

"Peace to you, old man, may Allah send you many more years of health and prosperity. Tell me, whose house was it that used to stand on this plot?"

"It was the house of the saddle-maker Shir-Mamed," the old man replied. "I knew him well, once. This Shir-Mamed was the father of the famous Hodja Nasreddin, of whom you have surely heard much, traveler."

"Yes, I have heard a few things. But tell me, what happened to this saddle-maker Shir-Mamed, father of the famous Hodja Nasreddin? What happened to his family?"

"Quiet, my son. There are thousands upon thousands of spies in Bukhara – they might hear us, and then we will have no end of trouble. You must have come from far away, and you do not know that it is strictly forbidden to mention the name of Hodja Nasreddin in our city, for it is punished by imprisonment. Lean closer to me, and I will tell you."

Concealing his excitement, Hodja Nasreddin leaned very close to him.

"It happened in the times of the old emir," the old man began. "A year and a half after Hodja Nasreddin was exiled, rumors spread in the bazaar that he had returned and was living secretly in Bukhara, composing mocking songs about the emir. The rumors reached the emir's palace, and the guards dashed off to search for Hodja Nasreddin, but they could not find him. Then the emir ordered them to seize Hodja Nasreddin's father, his two brothers, his uncle, and all his distant relatives and friends, and to torture them until they revealed where Hodja Nasreddin was hiding. Praise be to Allah that he sent them so much courage and resolve that they managed to keep quiet, and our Hodja Nasreddin escaped the emir's grasp. But his father, the saddle-maker Shir-Mamed, fell ill after the torture and soon died, while all his relatives and friends left Bukhara to escape the emir's wrath, and no one knows where they are now. And then the emir ordered their dwellings destroyed and their gardens uprooted, so as to destroy the very memory of Hodja Nasreddin in Bukhara."

"Why were they tortured?" Hodja Nasreddin exclaimed; tears were flowing down his face, but the old man was nearsighted and did not notice them. "Why were they tortured? Hodja Nasreddin was not in Bukhara at that time, I know this very well!"

"No one knows that!" the old man replied. "Hodja Nasreddin appears where he wishes and disappears when he wishes. He is everywhere and nowhere, our incomparable Hodja Nasreddin!"

With these words, the old man pressed onwards, coughing and sighing, while Hodja Nasreddin covered his face with his hands and walked to his donkey.

He hugged the donkey, pressing his face into the donkey's warm, pungent neck. "You see, my kind, faithful friend," Hodja Nasreddin spoke, "I have no close friends or relatives left, only you are my constant, unchanging companion in my travels." And, as if sensing his master's grief, the donkey stood quietly, without moving, and even stopped chewing the burr that was hanging on his lips.

But an hour later, Hodja Nasreddin steeled his heart, and the tears dried on his face. "No matter!" he cried, slapping his donkey firmly on the back. "No matter! They have not forgotten me in Bukhara, they know me and remember me, and we will manage to find friends! And then we will compose such a song about the emir that he'll burst of rage on his throne, and his foul entrails will stick to the luxurious palace walls. Onward, my faithful donkey, onward!"

Chapter 4

It was a quiet, stuffy hour in the afternoon. The dust, the rocks, and the clay fences and walls were all searing hot and exuding heat. The sweat on Hodja Nasreddin's face would dry before he could wipe it off.

Excited, Hodja Nasreddin recognized familiar streets, chaikhanas, and minarets. Nothing had changed in Bukhara in ten years – the same scruffy dogs were napping by the ponds; a slender woman was leaning down to lower a narrow, ringing pitcher into the dark water, holding her veil with her dark-skinned hand with painted fingernails. And just as tightly shut were the gates of the famous Mir-Arab madrassa, where learned ulema[1] and mudarrises[2], who had long forgotten the color of the spring leaves, the scent of the sun, and the babbling of streams, were sitting beneath heavy arches, their eyes lit with a grim fire, and laboring on thick volumes devoted to the glory of Allah and to proving the necessity of destroying to the seventh generation anyone who did not practice Islam. Hodja Nasreddin prodded his donkey with his heels as he passed this terrible place.

But where would he eat? Hodja Nasreddin tightened his belt for the third time since the previous day.

"I must think of something," he said. "Let us stop and think, my faithful donkey. And look, there is a chaikhana!"

He unbridled his donkey and sent him off to collect uneaten clover by the tethering post. Gathering the flaps of his robe, Hodja Nasreddin sat down by the aryk, where the water, thick with clay, bubbled and foamed on the turns. "This water knows not where it comes from, where it is headed, or why," Hodja Nasreddin pondered bitterly. "I, too, have not known my way, or any rest, or a home. Why have I come to Bukhara? Where will I go tomorrow? And where will I find half a tanga for dinner? Am I going to have to go hungry again? That accursed tax

1 *Ulema* – Muslim legal scholars.
2 *Mudarris* – Teacher or professor (Arabic).

collector robbed me blind and then had the gall to talk to me about bandits!"

At that moment, he saw the cause of his misfortune. The tax collector himself rode up to the chaikhana. Two guards were leading his Arabian stallion by the bridle – a handsome bay horse with a noble and passionate fire in his dark eyes. Bending his neck, the stallion shuffled his thin legs impatiently, as if disgusted at having to carry the tax collector's fat bulk on his back.

The guards unloaded their master respectfully, and he entered the chaikhana, where the keeper, trembling in servility, sat him down on silken pillows, brewed him the best tea, and handed him a fine drinking bowl of Chinese craftsmanship. "That's some reception he is getting on my money!" thought Hodja Nasreddin.

The collector drank himself full of tea and soon dozed off on the pillows, filling the chaikhana with wheezing, snoring, and smacking. All the other visitors lowered their voices to a whisper, afraid to disturb his sleep. The guards sat over him – one to the right, and one to the left – chasing off annoying flies with twigs, until they were sure that the tax collector was sound asleep. Then they winked at each other, unbridled the horse, tossed him a sheaf of clover, and retreated to the back of the chaikhana with a hookah. A minute later, the sweet smell of hashish began to drift from the darkness towards Hodja Nasreddin: the guards were using their free time to indulge in vice. "Well, time for me to go," Hodja Nasreddin decided, recalling his morning adventures at the city gates and fearing that the guards might perchance recognize him. "But still, where will I get half a tanga? O omnipotent fate that has rescued Hodja Nasreddin many times, turn your benevolent gaze towards him!" And then, someone called out to him.

"Hey you, tramp!"

He turned and saw a covered, richly decorated cart on the road. A man in a large turban and expensive robe had drawn apart the curtains and was peeking out.

And no sooner did this man – some rich merchant or official – pronounce his next word, than Hodja Nasreddin knew that his appeal to fate had not gone unanswered: as always, his good fortune had turned her gracious gaze towards him at this difficult time.

"I like this stallion," the rich man said haughtily, looking past Hodja Nasreddin and admiring the bay Arabian beauty. "Tell me, is this stallion for sale?"

"There is no horse in the world that's not for sale," Hodja Nasreddin replied evasively.

"There is probably not a lot of money in your pocket," the rich man continued. "Listen carefully. I do not know whose stallion this is, where he came from, or his previous owners. I am not even going to ask. It is enough for me to see that, judging by your dusty clothes, you have come to Bukhara from afar. It is enough for me. Do you understand?"

Full of rejoicing and delight, Hodja Nasreddin nodded his head: he understood everything right away, far beyond what the rich man was trying to communicate. He thought of only one thing: if only some foolish fly did not crawl into the tax collector's nostril or throat and wake him up. The guards worried him less: judging by the clouds of thick green smoke drifting from the shadows, they were continuing to indulge enthusiastically in vice.

"You understand yourself," the rich man continued grandly and haughtily, "that it does not befit you to ride this horse in your torn robe. It would even be dangerous for you, because everyone would ask: 'Where did that beggar get such an excellent stallion?' and you could easily end up in jail."

"You are right, o highborn one!" Hodja Nasreddin replied humbly. "The horse is indeed too good for me. I have been riding a donkey in my torn robe all my life, and I would not even dare think of mounting such a horse."

The rich man liked his reply.

"It is good that, in your state of poverty, you are not blinded with pride: a poor man must be humble and modest, for luscious flowers befit the noble almond tree, but not a wretched burr. Now tell me – do you wish to receive this purse? It contains exactly three hundred tanga in silver."

"Of course!" Hodja Nasreddin exclaimed, feeling a chill inside because the pernicious fly had crawled into the tax collector's nostril after all: he sneezed and shifted. "Of course! Who would refuse three hundred tanga in silver? It would be like finding a purse on the road!"

"Well, you seem to have found something else entirely on the road," the rich man replied with a shrewd smile. "But I am willing to trade that which you have found on the road for silver. Here are your three hundred tanga."

He handed Hodja Nasreddin the hefty wallet and signaled his servant, who was listening to the conversation silently and scratching his back with his whip. The servant headed towards the stallion. Hodja Nasreddin had time to notice that the servant, judging by his shifty eyes and the smirk on his flat, pockmarked snout, was an inveterate scoundrel, quite worthy of his master. "Three cheats on one road is too many – time for one to leave!" Hodja Nasreddin decided. Praising the rich man's piety and generosity, he hopped on his donkey and struck the beast with his heels so hard that the donkey broke straight into a gallop in spite of his laziness.

Turning, Hodja Nasreddin saw that the pockmarked servant was tying the bay Arabian stallion to the cart.

Turning once more, he saw that the rich man and the tax collector were tearing at each other's beards, and the guards were trying in vain to separate them.

Wisely choosing to avoid someone else's quarrel, Hodja Nasreddin turned and weaved through the alleys until he felt safe. Then he pulled on the reins, restraining the donkey's gallop.

"Wait, wait," he began. "We have nowhere to hurry now."

Suddenly, he heard the alarming, irregular clatter of hooves nearby.

"Hey! Onward, my faithful donkey, onward, save me!" Hodja Nasreddin shouted, but it was too late: a horseman had leapt onto the road from around a corner.

It was the pockmarked servant. He was riding the horse unharnessed from the cart. Swinging his legs, he sped by Hodja Nasreddin and reined in his horse sharply, placing it perpendicularly to the road.

"Let me by, my good man," Hodja Nasreddin said meekly. "One should ride along these narrow roads, not across."

"Aha!" the servant replied with gloating in his voice. "You will not escape the dungeon now! Are you aware that the official who is the real owner of the stallion has ripped out half my master's beard, while my master struck his nose to the point of bleeding? Tomorrow you'll be dragged before the emir to be judged. O human, your fate is truly dire!"

"You don't say!" Hodja Nasreddin exclaimed. "What could have caused such a bitter fight between those esteemed persons? But why did you stop me – I cannot be a judge in their quarrel. Let them settle it themselves, somehow!"

"Enough chatter!" the servant said. "Turn back. You'll have to answer for the stallion."

"What stallion?"

"You dare ask? The one for which my master gave you a purse of silver."

"By Allah, you are mistaken," Hodja Nasreddin replied. "The stallion had nothing to do with it. Judge for yourself – you heard the entire conversation. Your master, a generous and pious man, decided to help a poor man and asked if I wished to receive three hundred tanga in silver – and I replied that, of course, I did. And he gave me three hundred tanga, may Allah extend the days of his life! But prior to that, he decided to test my modesty and my humility so as to determine whether I deserved the reward. He said: 'I do not ask whose stallion this is, or where it came from,' wishing to make sure that I would not claim to be the owner of the stallion out of false pride. I remained silent, and the generous, pious merchant was pleased with me. He then said that such a stallion would be too good for me, and I agreed with him completely, and again he was pleased. Then he said that I had found something on the road which could be traded for silver, hinting at my passion and resolve in the practice of Islam, which I had gained through pilgrimages to holy sites. And then he rewarded me, hoping this pious deed would eventually ease his journey to heaven across the otherworldly bridge, which the holy Koran says to be lighter than a hair and thinner than the blade of a sword. In my very next prayer, I will tell Allah of the pious deed of your master, so that Allah may prepare him a railing on this bridge."

The servant pondered this and then said with a sly smirk, which immediately made Hodja Nasreddin ill at ease:

"You are correct, o wanderer! How did I not guess right away that your conversation with my master had such a virtuous meaning! But since you have decided to aid my master in his journey across the otherworldly bridge, it would be better if there were railings on both sides. That would make things stronger and more reliable. I would gladly pray for my master too, so that Allah may place a railing on the other side as well."

"So pray!" Hodja Nasreddin exclaimed. "Who's stopping you? In fact, you are required to do so. Does not the Koran prescribe for servants and slaves to pray daily for their masters, without expecting any special reward…"

"Turn the donkey around!" the servant said rudely. Moving his horse, he pressed Hodja Nasreddin to the fence. "Quickly now, don't make me waste my time!"

"Wait," Hodja Nasreddin interrupted him hastily. "I was not finished. I had intended to say a prayer of three hundred words, corresponding to the amount of tanga I received. But now I think a prayer of two hundred and fifty words might suffice. The railing on my side will be just a little thinner and shorter. Meanwhile, you will say a prayer of fifty words, and the omniscient Allah will be able to construct a railing on your side from the same wood."

"What's that?" the servant objected. "Do you mean to say that the railing on my side will be five times as short as yours?"

"But it will be in the most dangerous spot of the bridge!" Hodja Nasreddin added in a lively voice.

"No! I do not agree to such short a short railing," the servant said decisively. "This means part of the bridge will remain exposed! I grow pale, and cold sweat covers my skin at the thought of the terrible danger threatening my master! I believe we should both say prayers of one hundred and fifty words, so that the railings will be the same on either side. Let them be thinner, but on both sides. And if you do not agree, I will interpret this as malicious intent towards my master – you want him to fall off the bridge! In that case, I will call the men immediately, and you'll go straight to the dungeon!"

"Thin railings!" Hodja Nasreddin cried out in rage, almost feeling the purse shift in his belt. "According to you, it would be enough to surround the bridge with mere twigs! You must understand that it is absolutely necessary for the railing to be thicker and stronger on one side, so the merchant will have something to grab onto if he makes a false step and begins to fall!"

"It is truth itself that speaks through your lips!" the servant exclaimed happily. "Let it be thicker on my side, and I will spare no effort and say a prayer of two hundred words!"

"How about three hundred?" Hodja Nasreddin said angrily.

They argued on the road for a long time. Occasional passers-by who heard fragments of their conversation would bow respectfully, believing Hodja Nasreddin and the pockmarked servant to be pious pilgrims who had returned from worshipping at holy sites.

When they parted, Hodja Nasreddin's purse was half as heavy: they had decided that the bridge leading the merchant to heaven would be bordered on either side by identical railings, equal in length and strength.

"Farewell, wanderer," said the servant. "You and I performed a pious deed today."

"Farewell, kind, faithful, and virtuous servant, who cares so much about saving his master's soul. Let me say also that you could probably take on Hodja Nasreddin himself in an argument."

"Why did you mention him?" the servant pricked up his ears.

"No reason. Just came to mind," Hodja Nasreddin replied, thinking: "Aha!… This is no ordinary fellow!"

"Perhaps you are some distant relative of his?" asked the servant. "Or do you know any of his relatives?"

"No, I have never met him. And I don't know any of his relatives."

"Let me confide in you," the servant leaned down from saddle, "I am a relative of Hodja Nasreddin. I am his cousin. We spent our childhood together."

His suspicions confirmed, Hodja Nasreddin said nothing. The servant said into his other ear:

"His father, his two brothers, and his uncle have died. You must have heard, wanderer?"

Hodja Nasreddin remained silent.

"What savagery on the part of the emir!" the servant exclaimed in a hypocritical voice.

But Hodja Nasreddin remained silent.

"All the Bukharian viziers are fools!" the servant said suddenly, trembling with impatience and greed, for the capture of freethinkers entailed a large reward from the treasury.

But Hodja Nasreddin stubbornly said nothing.

"And our luminous emir is also a fool!" said the servant. "And, in fact, we don't even know for sure if there is an Allah in the heavens, or if he doesn't exist at all."

But Hodja Nasreddin remained silent, even though a caustic reply had been hanging on the very tip of his tongue for a while. His hopes dashed, the servant cursed and struck the horse with his whip, disappearing around the turn in two leaps. Everything grew quiet. Only the dust kicked up by the hooves whirled and sparkled in the still air, pierced by slanting rays of sunlight.

"Looks like I found myself a relative after all," Hodja Nasreddin thought derisively. "The old man was not lying: there are truly more spies than flies in Bukhara. I must be more careful, for, as the ancient proverb says, the guilty tongue is chopped off along with the head."

Thus he rode for a long time, grim one moment, as he thought of his lightened purse, and smiling the next, as he remembered the fight between the tax collector and the haughty rich man.

Chapter 5

After reaching the opposite end of the city, he stopped, entrusted his donkey to the care of a chaikhana keeper, and headed to a cookhouse without delay.

The cookhouse was cramped, smoky, and sooty, filled with noise and racket. The hot flames of the ovens illuminated the sweaty, bare-chested cooks. They hurried and shouted, pushing each other and handing out blows to the kitchen-boys, who were dashing around the cookhouse with crazed eyes, further exacerbating the congestion, the noise, and the commotion. Enormous vats covered with jittering wooden disks made bubbling noises, and a hearty steam thickened beneath the ceiling amid swarms of countless buzzing flies. Oil hissed and splashed fiercely in the gray haze, the walls of the heated braziers were aglow, and fat dripped onto the coals from the spits and burned with a stifling blue fire. They were cooking pilaf, frying kebabs, boiling offal, and baking little pies stuffed with onions, peppers, meat, and tallow; the tallow melted in the ovens and seeped through the dough, boiling with tiny bubbles. With great difficulty, Hodja Nasreddin found an unoccupied spot and squeezed in so tightly that the people he was pushing with his back and sides grunted. But no one became upset or said a word to Hodja Nasreddin, and, as for him, he did not mind at all. He had always loved the hot, crowded bazaar cookhouses, the irregular hubbub, the jokes, the laughter, the shouting, the shoving, and the friendly breathing, chewing, and champing of hundreds of people who are too busy for picky eating after a whole day of hard work: their unbreakable jaws will grind everything, be it sinew or gristle, and their cast-iron stomachs will accept anything so long as it is cheap and plentiful! Like them, Hodja Nasreddin knew how to take the edge off his hunger: without respite, he ate three bowls of noodles, three bowls of pilaf, and finally two dozen little pies, which he strained to finish, true to his rule of never leaving anything on the plate if he had already paid for it.

Then, working his elbows as hard as he could, he headed for
the exit, and by the time he reached the fresh air, he was drenched
with sweat. His limbs grew weak and languid, as if he had been in
a bathhouse, in the hands of a hefty washer-man. Feeling heavy
from the food and the heat, he headed for a chaikhana as quickly as his sluggish gait permitted. Once there, he ordered tea and
stretched out blissfully on the mats. His eyes would not stay open,
and quiet, pleasant thoughts were floating in his head. "I have a
lot of money right now. I should put it to use and open a shop –
perhaps a pottery shop or a saddle shop; I know these trades, after
all. Enough wandering, already. Am I any worse or more foolish
than other men that I cannot have a kind, beautiful wife and a
son to carry in my arms? By the prophet's beard, my loudmouth
kid will become an inveterate scoundrel, and I will certainly try to
pass all my wisdom on to him! Yes, it is decided: Hodja Nasreddin
is going to change his restless life. Firstly, I must buy a pottery or
saddle shop…"

He began to make calculations. A good shop cost at least three
hundred tanga, while he had one hundred and fifty. He recalled
the pockmarked servant with curses:

"May Allah strike that bandit blind, he took away the very half
that I needed to get started!"

And once again, fortune hurried to his rescue. "Twenty tanga!"
someone said all of a sudden, and then Hodja Nasreddin heard
the sound of dice being tossed on a copper tray.

At the edge of the platform, near the tethering post where the
donkey was tied down, several people were sitting in a tight circle,
while the chaikhana keeper was standing next to them and looking
over their heads.

"Gambling!" Hodja Nasreddin deduced, raising himself on one
elbow. "I should take a look at it, at least from a distance. I won't
play myself, of course: I'm no fool! But why can't a wise man have
a look at fools?"

He got up and approached the players.

"Foolish people!" he whispered to the chaikhana keeper.
"They are risking the last of their money hoping to acquire more.
Has Muhammad not forbidden Muslims to gamble? Thank god,
I am free of this harmful passion… I have to say, though, that

red-headed player is really lucky: he just won four times in a row… Look, look – he wins a fifth time! O madman! He is seduced by the false specter of riches, while poverty has already dug a hole on his path. What?… He's won a sixth time!… I have never seen such a streak of luck. Look, he is betting again! Truly, there is no end to human thoughtlessness; he cannot win all the time, after all! This is how people who come to believe in their false fortune are doomed! One ought to teach a lesson to that red-headed man. Well then, let him win a seventh time, and then I will bet against him myself, although deep in my soul I oppose all gambling and would have long prohibited it, were I the emir!…"

The red-headed player tossed the dice and won a seventh time.

Hodja Nasreddin stepped forward decisively, pushed the players apart, and joined the ring.

"I want to play against you," he said to the lucky man, taking the dice and inspecting them from all sides with a quick, experienced glance.

"How much?" the red-headed man asked in a hollow voice. He was shaking lightly – he was in a hurry, wishing to get as much as possible out of his fleeting burst of luck.

In response, Hodja Nasreddin took out his wallet, placed twenty-five tanga in his pocket just in case, and poured out the rest. The silver jingled and sang on the copper tray. The players met the bet with a quiet but excited din: the big game was beginning.

The red-headed man picked up the dice and shook them for a long time, hesitant to throw them. Everyone held his breath, even the donkey stretched out his muzzle and pricked up his ears. Nothing could be heard save for the clattering of the dice in the red-headed player's hands. That dry sound sent a numbing weakness creeping into Hodja Nasreddin's legs and stomach. And the redhead kept shaking and holding on to the sleeve of his robe, and could not force himself to cast the dice.

Finally, he cast them. The players leaned forward and drew back immediately with a collective sigh. The redhead grew pale and moaned through clenched teeth.

The dice numbered just three – a sure loss, for a two comes as rarely as twelve, and Hodja Nasreddin needed anything but two.

Shaking the dice in his fist, he thanked his fortune mentally, for it had been so gracious to him that day. But he forgot that fortune is wayward and fickle, and can easily betray someone who gets on her nerves. She decided to teach the self-confident Hodja Nasreddin a lesson, choosing as her weapon the donkey, or, more accurately, his tail, adorned on the end with burrs and burdocks. Turning his back to the players, the donkey flicked his tail and brushed his master's hand. The dice popped out, and at that same moment the red-headed player emitted a short, muffled yell and fell onto the tray, covering up the money.

Hodja Nasreddin had thrown a two.

He sat like a stone for a long time, moving his lips noiselessly – everything swayed and floated before his unmoving gaze, and a strange ringing resonated in his ears.

Suddenly he jumped up, grabbed a stick, and began to pummel the donkey, chasing him around the tethering post.

"Accursed donkey, o son of sin, o foul beast and shame of all living things on earth!" Hodja Nasreddin shouted. "It is not enough that you play dice with your master's money, but you have the nerve to lose! May your treacherous hide peel off, may the almighty Allah place a pit in your path so you break your legs; when will you die already, so I no longer have to gaze upon your vile snout?"

The donkey brayed, the players laughed, and the red-headed player laughed the loudest, now having complete faith in his good luck.

"Let's play again," he said, after an exhausted, panting Hodja Nasreddin had tossed aside the stick. "Let's play again: you still have twenty-five tanga."

With these words, he stretched out his left leg and wiggled it slightly as a sign of disrespect towards Hodja Nasreddin.

"Well then, let's play!" Hodja Nasreddin replied, deciding it no longer mattered: it made no sense to save the last twenty-five tanga after having lost a hundred and twenty.

He tossed the dice carelessly, without looking – and won.

"All in!" the redhead suggested, tossing his lost money onto the tray.

And Hodja Nasreddin won again.

But the redhead refused to believe that his luck had turned her back on him.

"All in!"

Thus he spoke seven times in a row, and all seven times he lost. The tray was full of money. The players froze – only their sparkling eyes testified to the fire consuming them from within.

"You cannot win so many times in a row unless the shaitan[1] himself is helping you!" the redhead cried. "You must lose sooner or later! There are one thousand six hundred tanga of your money on this tray! Will you agree to go all in one more time? Here is the money I have set aside to purchase goods for my shop on the bazaar tomorrow morning – I bet it against you!"

He took out his reserve: a small purse full of gold.

"Put your gold on the tray!" Hodja Nasreddin shouted heatedly.

The chaikhana had never seen such a high-stake game before. The chaikhana keeper forgot all about his boiling kettles, and the players were breathing heavily and haltingly. The redhead tossed the dice first and shut his eyes immediately – he was afraid to look.

"Eleven!" everyone shouted in unison. Hodja Nasreddin saw that he was doomed: only a twelve could save him.

"Eleven! Eleven!" the redheaded player kept repeating in frantic joy. "Look, I have eleven! You lost! You lost!"

Feeling a chill, Hodja Nasreddin picked up the dice and was about to throw them, but suddenly he stopped.

"Turn around!" he said to the donkey. "You managed to lose on three points, so manage to win on eleven, or else I will take you to the slaughterhouse at once!"

He took the donkey's tail in his left hand and flicked it at his right hand, which was holding the dice.

A collective yell shook the chaikhana, and the chaikhana keeper grasped his heart and sank to the floor in exhaustion.

The dice showed twelve points.

The red-headed player's eyes bulged out, and a glassy look appeared on his pale face. He got up slowly, repeating:

"O woe, o woe to me!" and left the chaikhana, swaying.

1 *Shaitan* – Devil (Arabic).

They say that no one has seen him in the city since that day: he ran away to the desert and wandered through the sands and prickly shrubs there, with a frightening appearance and overgrown hair, repeating endlessly: "O woe, o woe to me!" until he was eaten by jackals. And no one mourned him, because he was a cruel and unjust man who had done much evil by ruining gullible simpletons at dice.

As for Hodja Nasreddin, he placed his newly won riches into his saddlebags, hugged his donkey, planted a firm kiss on his warm nose, and fed him delicious, fresh bread cakes, which surprised the donkey considerably, for mere minutes ago his master had given him something else entirely.

Chapter 6

Recalling the wise rule to stay away from people who know where you keep your money, Hodja Nasreddin did not dally in the chaikhana and rode off towards the bazaar square. He glanced back from time to time to check if he was being followed, for the faces of the players, or, for that matter, the chaikhana keeper himself, did not bear the stamp of virtue.

He felt happy along the way. Now he could buy any shop, two shops, three shops. That was exactly what he decided to do. "I will buy four shops: a pottery shop, a saddle shop, a tailor shop, and a shoe shop, and hire two tradesmen for each, while I myself will only collect the profits. In two years, I will become rich and buy a house with fountains and a garden. I will hang golden cages with songbirds everywhere, and I will have two or even three wives, and each will give me three sons…"

He dove headfirst into the sweet river of fantasy. Meanwhile, the donkey stopped feeling the pull of the reins and took advantage of his master's pensiveness. Encountering a small bridge, he did not cross it, like other donkeys, but instead took a running start and jumped right over the ditch. "And when my children grow up, I will gather them and say…" Hodja Nasreddin was thinking at the time. "But why am I flying through the air? Has Allah decided to make me an angel and give me wings?"

The very next moment, Hodja Nasreddin was seeing stars, which convinced him that he did not have wings after all. Flying out of his saddle, he plopped down on the road a dozen feet in front of the donkey.

When Hodja Nasreddin got up, grunting and groaning, covered in dust, the donkey approached with a most innocent expression on his snout, flicking his ears gently, as if inviting his master to reoccupy the saddle.

"O you, who have been sent to me as punishment for my sins and for the sins of my father, grandfather, and great-grandfather, for, by the truth of Islam, it would be unjust to punish a man thus for his own sins alone!" Hodja Nasreddin began, his voice shaking with indignation. "O you, despicable cross between a spider and a hyena! O you, who…"

But then he stopped short, having noticed a group of people who were sitting nearby in the shade of a half-ruined fence.

The curses froze on Hodja Nasreddin's lips.

He understood that a man who had found himself in a funny and undignified situation in plain view of others had to, first and foremost, laugh at himself.

Hodja Nasreddin winked at the sitting group and smiled broadly, displaying all his teeth at once.

"Ha!" he said loudly and cheerfully. "That was a fine flight I took! Tell me, how many times did I flip in the air? I didn't have time to count, myself. Oh, you naughty beast!" he continued, slapping the donkey good-naturedly with the palm of his hand, even though he was of a good mind to give him a sound thrashing with the whip. "Oh, you naughty beast! That's just the way he is: look away for a second, and he will surely pull something like this!"

Hodja Nasreddin burst out in cheerful laughter, but to his surprise he noticed that no one was following his example. The people continued to sit with downcast heads and grim faces, while the women, many with infants in their arms, were weeping quietly.

"Something is not right here," Hodja Nasreddin said to himself, approaching.

"Esteemed old sage," he said to a gray-bearded old man with a haggard face. "Tell me, what happened here? Why do I not see smiles or hear laughter, why are the women crying? Why do you sit here on the road amid the heat and the dust, when it would surely be better to sit in the coolness of your homes?"

"It is better to sit at home when you have one," the old man replied mournfully. "Ah, passer-by, do not ask – our misfortune is great, and you will not be able to help us anyway. I am old and frail, and I pray to god now that he send me death as soon as possible."

"Why speak such words?" Hodja Nasreddin said with reproach. "A man must never think this way. Tell me of your misfortune, and disregard the fact that I appear poor. Perhaps I will be able to help you."

"My tale will be brief. A mere hour ago, the moneylender Jafar came down our street, accompanied by the emir's guards. I owe money to Jafar, and my debt is due tomorrow morning. So here I am, banished from my house, where I had lived all my life, and I no longer have a family or a quiet corner where I may bow my head in rest… As for all my property – my house, my livestock, and my vineyards – it will all be sold tomorrow by Jafar."

Tears appeared in the old man's eyes, and his voice trembled.

"And do you owe him a large amount?" Hodja Nasreddin asked.

"A very large amount, passer-by. I owe him two hundred and fifty tanga."

"Two hundred and fifty tanga!" Hodja Nasreddin exclaimed. "A man wishes for death because of some lousy two hundred and fifty tanga! All right now, hold still," he added to the donkey, untying his saddlebag. "Here are two hundred and fifty tanga, old sage. Give them to the moneylender, chase him from your house with kicks, and live out the rest of your days in peace and prosperity."

Everyone stirred upon hearing the jingling of the silver, while the old man could not pronounce a single word, and could only thank Hodja Nasreddin with his eyes, which glistened with tears.

"See? And you did not even want to tell me of your misfortune," Hodja Nasreddin said, counting off the final coin and thinking: "It's all right, I will hire seven tradesmen instead of eight, that will be enough for me!"

Suddenly, a woman sitting next to the man fell before Hodja Nasreddin's feet and held up her child towards him, weeping loudly.

"Look!" she said through her tears. "He is sick, his lips are dry and his face is aflame. And he will die now, my poor boy, somewhere on the road, for I have been chased from my home."

Hodja Nasreddin glanced at the child's thin, pale face, at his frail arms, and then looked over the group of sitting people. And as he peered more carefully into their faces, crisscrossed with wrinkles and wrought with grief, when he saw their eyes, which had grown dim from endless tears – it was as if a hot knife had been plunged into his heart. A quick spasm seized his throat, and a hot wave of blood colored his face. He turned away.

"I am a widow," the woman continued. "My husband, who died half a year ago, owed the moneylender two hundred tanga, and, by law, his debt was transferred to me."

"The child is indeed ill," Hodja Nasreddin said. "And he really should not be kept in the heat of the sun, for the sun's rays thicken the blood, according to Avicenna, which is surely not good for the boy. Here are two hundred tanga. Return to your home as soon as you can, and put a compress on his forehead; here are fifty more tanga so you can call a doctor and purchase medicine."

Silently, he thought: "I can manage with six tradesmen."

But then a bearded mason of enormous height tumbled before Hodja Nasreddin's feet, for his family was due to be sold into slavery tomorrow because of a four hundred tanga debt to the moneylender Jafar. "Five tradesmen is pushing it, of course," thought Hodja Nasreddin, untying his bag. But he did not have time to tie it again before two women fell on their knees before him, and their tales were so mournful that Hodja Nasreddin gave them enough money to settle with the moneylender without any hesitation. Seeing that the remaining money was barely enough to keep three tradesmen, he decided that, in this case, he should avoid shops altogether, and, with a generous hand, began to hand out money to the rest of the debtors of the moneylender Jafar.

The bag had no more than five hundred tanga left. And then Hodja Nasreddin saw one last man to the side, who had not asked for help even though grief was evident on his face.

"Hey you, listen!" Hodja Nasreddin called. "Why are you sitting there? Have you no debt to the moneylender?"

"I owe him," the man said in a hollow voice. "Tomorrow, I will go in chains to the slave market."

"Why have you been silent up till now?"

"O generous, beneficent traveler, I do not know who you are. Are you the holy Bogaeddin, emerged from his grave to help the poor, or Harun-al-Rashid himself? I did not ask you only because you have spent quite a lot already, and I owe more than anyone else – five hundred tanga – and I was afraid that, if you were to give them to me, there would not be enough left for the women and the elderly."

"You are just, noble, and conscientious," Hodja Nasreddin said, deeply moved. "But I am also just, noble, and conscientious, and I swear that you will not go in chains to the slave market tomorrow. Hold out the flap of your robe!"

He poured out everything from his saddlebag to the last tanga. Then, holding the flap of his robe with his left hand, the man hugged Hodja Nasreddin with his right and pressed against Hodja Nasreddin's chest in tears.

Hodja Nasreddin looked over all the people he saved and saw smiles, red cheeks, and sparkling eyes.

"You know something? That really was some flight you took off your donkey back there," the enormous bearded mason said suddenly, bursting out in laughter, and everyone began to laugh together – men in rough voices, and women in high-pitched voices – and the children began to smile, stretching their hands out to Hodja Nasreddin, who was laughing the loudest of all.

"O!" he said, convulsing with laughter. "You don't know the half of this donkey! He's one bastard of a donkey!…"

"No!" the woman with the sick child interrupted. "Do not speak thus of your donkey. It is the smartest, noblest, most precious donkey in the world, who has no equal and never will. I would take care of him all my life, feed him select grain, never burden him with work, clean him, and brush his tail with a comb. For if this incomparable donkey, who is not unlike a blooming rose and filled with virtue alone, had not jumped across the ditch and thrown you from your saddle, o wanderer who has come before us like the sun in darkness, you would have passed by without noticing us, and we would not have dared to stop you!"

"She is right," the old man noted thoughtfully. "In many ways, we owe our salvation to this donkey, who truly graces this world and stands out, like a diamond, among all other donkeys."

Everyone began to heap praise on the donkey and vie with each other to thrust flat bread cakes, fried corn, and dried apricots and peaches in his direction. Brushing aside annoying flies with his tail, the donkey accepted the offerings in a calm and dignified manner, although he did blink when he saw the whip that Hodja Nasreddin was shaking clandestinely in his direction.

But time went on, the shadows began to lengthen, and the red-footed storks, calling and flapping their wings, returned to their nests, where the open beaks of their chicks were stretching out greedily towards them.

Hodja Nasreddin began to say his goodbyes.

Everyone bowed and thanked him:

"Thank you. You understood our misfortune."

"How could I not understand?" he replied. "As recently as today, I lost four shops with eight most skilled tradesmen, as well as a house with a garden full of fountains and with songbirds in gold cages on all the trees. How could I not understand?"

The old man mumbled with his toothless mouth:

"I have no way to return your favor, wanderer. Here is the only thing I took when leaving my house. This is the Koran, a holy book; take it, and let it be your guiding light in the worldly ocean."

Hodja Nasreddin did not have much respect for holy books, but, because he did not wish to upset the old man, he took the Koran, placed it in his saddlebag, and jumped in the saddle.

"Your name, your name!" everyone shouted in unison. "Tell us your name, so that we know who to thank in our prayers."

"Why do you wish to know my name? True virtue has no need of glory, and, as for prayers, Allah has many angels informing him of pious deeds... And if the angels are being lazy and negligent, sleeping somewhere on the soft clouds instead of tallying up all the pious and impious deeds on earth, then your prayers would not help anyway, for Allah would be a fool to take people's word for everything instead of demanding confirmation from his subordinates."

All of a sudden, one of the women gasped quietly, then another, and then the old man gave a start and stared right at Hodja Nasreddin. But Hodja Nasreddin was in a hurry and did not notice any of this.

"Farewell. May peace and prosperity abide with you."

Accompanied by blessings, he disappeared behind a turn in the road.

The people who stayed behind were silent, a single thought flashing in everyone's eyes.

The old man broke the silence. In a heartfelt and solemn voice, he said:

"There is only one man in the world who can do something like this, and only one man in the world can speak like this, and only one man in the world can carry such a soul inside, which bathes all miserable and unfortunate people with its light and warmth, and that man is our..."

"Quiet!" another man interrupted quickly. "Or have you forgotten that fences have eyes, that rocks have ears, and that scores of hounds would dash along his tracks."

"You are right," a third man added. "We must remain silent, for it is as though he walks a tightrope now, and the smallest push can doom him."

"I would rather my tongue be cut off than pronounce his name aloud anywhere!" said the woman with the sick child.

"I will be silent," a second woman exclaimed, "for I would rather die than accidentally give him the rope!"

Everyone agreed, except for the mighty bearded mason, who was not distinguished by a particularly sharp mind and, as he listened to the conversation, could not understand why dogs would follow the tracks of the wanderer if he was not a butcher or an offal salesman, and, if the wanderer was a tightrope walker, why it was forbidden to say his name aloud, and why the woman would sooner die than give her savior a rope, so necessary in his profession. Here the mason became utterly confused; he began to breathe loudly, let out a heavy sigh, and decided to take a break from thinking, lest he lose his mind.

Meanwhile, Hodja Nasreddin was already far away, but the exhausted faces of the poor remained fresh before his eyes; he recalled the sick child with a feverish blush on his cheeks and with his lips parched from the heat, he recalled the gray hair of the old man, thrown out of his childhood home, and rage boiled up from the depths of his heart.

He could not sit still in the saddle, so he hopped off and walked next to the donkey, kicking aside the stones under his feet.

"Just you wait, moneylender, just you wait!" he whispered, and a sinister fire flared up in his black eyes. "We will meet, and your fate will be a bitter one! You too, emir," he continued, "grow pale and tremble, emir, for I, Hodja Nasreddin, am in Bukhara! O contemptible leeches that suck the blood of my poor people, o greedy hyenas and filthy jackals. You will not rejoice forever, nor will the people suffer forever! As for you, moneylender Jafar, may my name be covered in shame for all eternity if I do not get even with you for all the grief you are causing the poor!"

Chapter 7

Even for Hodja Nasreddin, who had seen a lot in his life, this day – his first day back in his homeland – was a little too restless and too rich with adventures. Hodja Nasreddin grew tired and was looking to find shelter and rest in some quiet place.

"Oh, no!" he sighed, seeing a great multitude of people gathered around a pond in the distance. "It seems I will not get any rest today! It looks like something else has happened!"

The pond was situated on the side of a large road, and Hodja Nasreddin could have passed right by, but our Hodja Nasreddin was not the kind of man who missed an opportunity to get involved in a quarrel, scandal, or brawl.

The donkey, who had learned his master's personality perfectly well over the long years, turned towards the pond without waiting for a command.

"What happened? Who's been killed? Who's been robbed?" Hodja Nasreddin shouted, steering his donkey into the thick of the crowd. "Step aside! Make way! Make way!"

When he made his way through the crowd and rode right up to the edge of the large pond, covered in greenish weeds, he saw something incredible. A man was drowning not three steps from the shore. He would emerge on the surface and sink again, sending large air bubbles from below.

Numerous people were fussing around the bank. They stretched out their arms towards the drowning man, trying to get a hold of his robe, but their grasps fell a mere foot too short.

"Give us your hand! Give it! Give it!" they shouted. It was as if the drowning man could not hear them. He would not give them his hand, but instead continued to sink and surface at regular intervals. Lazy waves were spreading across the pond and licking its edges with a soft splashing sound, marking his journeys to the bottom and back up.

"Odd!" Hodja Nasreddin said, observing. "Very odd! What could be the cause of this? Why would he not hold out his hand?

Perhaps he is a skilled diver here to settle a wager, but then why is he wearing his robe?"

Hodja Nasreddin grew pensive. While he was thinking, the drowning man surfaced four times or so, and every time he spent longer and longer at the bottom of the pond.

"Very odd!" Hodja Nasreddin repeated, dismounting. "Wait here," he said to the donkey, "and I will go take a closer look."

At this point, the drowning man sank deep down and did not appear for such a long time that some on the shore began to say funereal prayers. But suddenly, he appeared again.

"Give us your hand! Give it! Give it here!" the people shouted, stretching their hands towards him, but he glanced at them with blank eyes and sank silently and smoothly to the bottom without offering his hand.

"Oh, you people are a bit slow!" Hodja Nasreddin said. "Can you not tell by the expensive robe and the silk turban that this man is a mullah or a wealthy official? How is it that you have still not managed to learn the character of mullahs and officials, and the means of extracting them from the water?"

"Get him out quickly, if you know how!" people in the crowd shouted. "Save him, there he is again. Get him out!"

"Wait," Hodja Nasreddin replied. "I have not finished talking. Where, I ask, have you ever seen a mullah or an official who would give anything to anyone? Remember this, o know-nothings: mullahs and officials never give anything, they only take. And you must rescue them from drowning according to their character. Here, look!"

"But you are too late," people shouted from the crowd. "He will not appear again."

"You think the water spirits will accept a mullah or an official that easily? You are mistaken. The water spirits will spare no effort in trying to get rid of him."

Hodja Nasreddin squatted and began to wait patiently, watching the bubbles as they floated up from the bottom of the pond and drifted to shore, pushed along by a light breeze.

Finally, something dark began to rise from the bottom. The drowning man appeared on the surface – it would have been the last time, were it not for Hodja Nasreddin.

"Take my hand!" Hodja Nasreddin shouted, thrusting his hand towards him. "Take it!"

The drowning man clutched the extended hand feverishly. Hodja Nasreddin winced in pain.

Back on the shore, it took a while before they could get the rescued man to release his grasp.

For several minutes he lay motionlessly, plastered in weeds and covered with stinking mud, which concealed the features of his face. Then water began pouring from his mouth, his nose, and his ears.

"My bag! Where is my bag?" he groaned and would not calm down until he felt his bag on his side. Then he brushed off the seaweed and wiped the mud from his face with the flap of his robe. And Hodja Nasreddin shrank back, so hideous was this face, with a flat, broken nose, twisted nostrils, and a blind right eye. What's more, the man was hunchbacked.

"Where is my rescuer?" he asked in a screeching voice, looking over the crowded people with his only functioning eye.

"Here he is!" everyone clamored, pushing Hodja Nasreddin forward.

"Come here, I will reward you." The rescued man placed his hand into his bag, which was still sloshing with water, and took out a handful of wet silver. "Then again, there is nothing special or surprising about the fact that you pulled me out. I think I could have made it out myself," he continued in a shrewish voice.

As he spoke, his grasp loosened gradually – perhaps from weakness, or perhaps from some other cause – and the money poured back into the bag through his fingers, jingling quietly. Finally, a single coin remained in his hand – half a tanga – and he handed it to Hodja Nasreddin with a sigh:

"Here is some money. Go to the bazaar and buy yourself a bowl of pilaf."

"There is not enough here for a bowl of pilaf," Hodja Nasreddin said.

"No matter, no matter. Just buy pilaf without meat."

"Now you see," Hodja Nasreddin turned to the others, "that I was indeed rescuing him in full accordance with his character."

He headed towards his donkey.

A man stopped him midway. He was tall, thin, and sinewy, his face bearing a grim and unfriendly expression, and his hands blackened by soot and coal. Blacksmith's tongs were tucked into his belt.

"What do you want, blacksmith?" Hodja Nasreddin asked.

"Do you know," asked the blacksmith, measuring Hodja Nasreddin from head to toe with a hostile gaze, "do you know who it is you rescued in the last moment, after which no one could have rescued him? And do you know how many tears will be spilled because of what you have done, and how many people will lose their homes, fields, and vineyards and be sent to the slave market and then down the Great Khivian Road in chains?"

Hodja Nasreddin stared at him in surprise:

"I do not understand you, blacksmith! Does it befit a man and a Muslim to pass by a drowning man without offering him a helping hand?"

"So you believe that one must save all the poisonous snakes, all the hyenas and vipers from certain doom?" the blacksmith exclaimed. Then, realizing something, he added:

"Do you hail from these parts?"

"No! I have come from far away."

"Then you do not know that the man you rescued is a blood-sucking villain, and that every third man in Bukhara moans and weeps because of him?"

A horrible guess flashed in Hodja Nasreddin's head.

"Blacksmith!" he said in a shaky voice, afraid to believe his guess. "Tell me the name of the one I saved!"

"You have saved the moneylender Jafar, may he be cursed in this life and the next, and may his entire clan be stricken with festering sores to the fourteenth generation!" the blacksmith replied.

"What?" Hodja Nasreddin cried. "What did you say, blacksmith? O woe to me, o shame on my head! Did I really drag that snake out of the water with my own hands? Truly, there is no atoning for a sin like this! O woe, o shame and misery!"

His repentance touched the blacksmith, who softened a little:

"Calm down, wanderer, it is too late to do anything now. It's just your luck that you came to the pond at that exact minute. If only your donkey had misbehaved somewhere and delayed you on your way! The moneylender would have drowned in that time."

"This donkey!" Hodja Nasreddin said. "If he does delay me on my way, it is only to rid my saddlebags of money: the money is too heavy for him, you see. But if I am destined to disgrace myself by rescuing the moneylender, you can be sure this donkey will deliver me right on time!"

"Yes!" the blacksmith said. "But the deed cannot be undone. We can't throw the moneylender back into the pond, after all!"

Hodja Nasreddin perked up:

"I did an evil thing, but I myself will correct it! Listen, blacksmith! I swear that the moneylender Jafar will be drowned by me. I swear on the beard of my father that he will be drowned by me in this very pond! Remember my oath, blacksmith! I have never thrown words to the wind. The moneylender will be drowned! And when you hear it on the bazaar, know that I have redeemed myself before the people of Noble Bukhara!"

Chapter 8

Twilight was already descending upon the city when Hodja Nasreddin finally reached the bazaar square.

Bright fires lit up in the chaikhanas, and soon the entire square was girdled with lights. A great bazaar was set for tomorrow – and the camel caravans, stepping softly, followed one another and disappeared in the darkness, while the air was still filled with the even, mournful, coppery ringing of their bells; and the moment the bells of one caravan would fade in the distance, the bells of another caravan entering the square would begin to moan in their place, and this was endless, as if the darkness itself was ringing and jittering quietly above the square, full of sounds brought here from all corners of the world. Here, invisible, were bells Indian and Afghan, bells Arabian, Iranian, and Egyptian. Hodja Nasreddin kept listening and listening, and he could have listened forever. A tambourine was struck and started jingling in a chaikhana nearby, and the strings of a dutar responded. An unseen singer raised his ringing, tense voice as high as the stars themselves: he was singing of his beloved, he was complaining about her.

To the sounds of this song, Hodja Nasreddin went looking for a place to sleep.

"We have half a tanga between the donkey and me," he said to a chaikhana keeper.

"For half a tanga, you can spend the night on a mat," the keeper replied. "No blanket for you."

"And where should I tie down my donkey?"

"Look at that, as if I'm going to take care of your donkey, too."

There was no tethering post by the chaikhana. Hodja Nasreddin noticed some kind of metal bracket sticking out from under the platform of the chaikhana. He tied the donkey to the bracket without bothering to see how it was attached and then went inside the chaikhana and lay down: he was very tired.

Suddenly, he heard his own name through his slumber. He opened his eyes slightly.

Some people who had come to the bazaar were sitting in a circle nearby and drinking tea – a camel driver, a shepherd, and two craftsmen. One of them was speaking quietly:

"They also say this of Hodja Nasreddin: once he was walking through the bazaar in Baghdad, and suddenly he heard noise and shouting coming from a cookhouse. Our Hodja Nasreddin, being a curious man, as you know – he glanced inside the cookhouse. And he saw that a fat, red-faced cookhouse keeper was shaking some beggar by the collar and demanding money, while the beggar did not want to pay.

"'What's all this noise?' our Hodja Nasreddin asked. 'What is your quarrel?'

"'This beggar,' the cookhouse keeper shouted in response, 'this contemptible tramp and swindler, may his insides dry up and shrivel, walked into my cookhouse just now, took out a bread cake, and held it over the brazier for a long time, until the cake was saturated with the smell of kebab and thus became twice as delicious. Then the beggar devoured the cake, and now he does not want to pay, may his teeth fall out and his skin peel off!'

"'Is that true?' our Hodja Nasreddin asked sternly of the beggar, who was so frightened he could not speak a single word and only nodded his head in response.

"'That is not good,' Hodja Nasreddin said. 'It is not good at all to use someone's property for free.'

"'Can you hear what this respectable and worthy man is telling you, tramp?' the cookhouse keeper said contentedly.

"'Do you have money?' Hodja Nasreddin said to the beggar. The latter took out his last coppers in silence. The cookhouse keeper was already reaching for them with his fat paw.

"'Just a moment, o esteemed one!' Hodja Nasreddin stopped him. 'Let's have your ear first.'

"And he jingled the coins in his fist for a long time right over the cookhouse keeper's ear. And then, after returning the coins to the beggar, he said:

"'Go in peace, poor man!'

"'What?' the cookhouse keeper shouted. 'But I did not receive payment!'

"'He paid you in full, and you are even,' our Hodja Nasreddin replied. 'He smelled the aroma of your kebab, and you heard the jingling of his money.'"

Everyone in the chaikhana burst out in laughter. A hasty warning came from someone:

"Quiet. Or else everyone will guess right away that we are talking about Hodja Nasreddin."

"How do they even know?" Hodja Nasreddin smiled inwardly. "This was in Istanbul, not Baghdad, of course, but still – how do they know?"

A second man began to narrate quietly – he was wearing shepherd's clothes and a colorful turban, which gave him away as a resident of Badakhshan.

"They say also this. One day, Hodja Nasreddin was walking past a mullah's garden. The mullah was gathering gourds into a sack, and in his greed he loaded the sack so heavily that he could not even lift it, much less carry it. So he was standing and pondering: 'How will I ever bring this sack home?' Seeing a passerby, he rejoiced:

"'Listen, my son. Will you help me carry this sack to my house?'

"And Hodja Nasreddin just happened to be broke at the time.

"'How much will you pay me?' he asked the mullah.

"'O, my son! Why do you need money? While you are carrying my gourds, I will tell you three pieces of wisdom that will make you happy for the rest of your life.'

"'I wonder what sort of wisdom this mullah is promising to reveal to me,' our Hodja Nasreddin thought to himself.

"He was overcome with curiosity, so he heaved the sack onto his shoulders and began to carry it. The road ran steeply uphill, and passed over a precipice. When Hodja Nasreddin stopped to rest, the mullah said with a mysterious and haughty air:

"'Listen to the first piece of wisdom, for there has been no greater wisdom in the world since the times of Adam, and if you grasp its full depth, it will be equivalent to understanding the hidden meaning of the letters Alef, Lam, Ra, with which Muhammad, our prophet and teacher, opens the second surah of the Koran. Listen carefully: if any man ever tells you that walking is better than riding – do not believe that man. Remember my words and think on them incessantly night and day – and then you will grasp the wisdom contained within them. But this wisdom is nothing compared to the second piece of wisdom, which I will impart to you by that tree over there. See – riiight there, up ahead!'

"'All right!' Hodja Nasreddin thought to himself. 'Just you wait, mullah!'

"Sweating copiously, he dragged the sack to the tree.

"The mullah raised his finger:

"'Open your ears and hark, for the second piece of wisdom incorporates the entire Koran, half of Sharia, and a quarter of Tariqah[1]. One who has grasped this wisdom shall never stray from the path of virtue and never stumble on the road to truth. Try to understand this wisdom, my son, and be glad that you have received it for free. The second piece of wisdom states: if someone tells you that life is easier for a poor man than for a rich man, do not believe that man.'

"'But even this second piece of wisdom is nothing next to the third, whose brilliance can only be compared to the dazzling light of the sun, and whose depth can only be compared to the depth of the ocean. I will relate the third piece of wisdom to you by the gates of my house. Come quickly, for I have already rested.'

"'Wait, mullah!' our Hodja Nasreddin replied. 'I know your third piece of wisdom ahead of time. You wish to tell me by the gates of your house than a smart man can always make a fool carry his sack of gourds for free.'

"The astonished mullah shrank back. Hodja Nasreddin had guessed his third piece of wisdom word for word.

"'But listen now, mullah, to my single piece of wisdom which is worth more than all of yours combined,' Hodja Nasreddin continued. 'And my wisdom, I swear by Muhammad, is so dazzling and so deep that it incorporates all of Islam along with the Koran, Sharia, the book of Tariqah, and all other books, as well as the entire Buddhist faith, and the entire Judean faith, and all the Christian delusions. There is none, there has never been, and there will never be a piece of wisdom more authentic than the one I will now tell you, o mullah! But you must ready yourself so that

_____
1 *Tariqah* – An Islamic religious order.

this wisdom does not shock you too greatly, for it is so astonishing, dazzling, and immense, it can make you lose your mind. Prepare your mind, mullah, and listen: if someone tells you that these gourds are not smashed, spit in that man's face, call him a liar, and banish him from your house!'

"With these words, Hodja Nasreddin picked up the sack and tossed it off the steep precipice.

"The gourds poured from the sack, jumping and breaking loudly as they hit the stones.

"'O woe to me! O great loss and ruin!' the mullah shouted.

"And he began to shout, lament, and claw at his face, truly resembling a madman in his behavior.

"'You see?' Hodja Nasreddin spoke instructively. 'I warned you that you may well lose your mind from my wisdom!'"

The listeners burst out in cheerful laughter.

As he lay in the corner on the dusty, flea-ridden mat, Hodja Nasreddin thought:

"They found this out too! But how? There were only two of us over that precipice, and I haven't told anyone.

"The mullah probably told the story himself, having guessed afterwards who was carrying his gourds."

A third storyteller began:

"Once, Hodja Nasreddin was returning from the city to a Turkish village where he was living at the time; feeling weary, he lay down by the riverbank and, as the fragrant breath of the spring breeze washed over him, he fell asleep without noticing it. And he dreamed that he had died. 'If I am dead,' our Hodja Nasreddin decided silently, 'then I should lie still and not open my eyes.' Thus he lay without movement for a long time on the soft grass, and he found that being dead was not so bad: you can lie around all you want, free from any troubles or cares that plague us incessantly in our fleeting earthly existence.

"Some travelers were passing by and saw Hodja Nasreddin.

"'Look!' said one. 'He is a Muslim.'

"'He's dead,' added another.

"'We should carry him to the nearest village, so that he may be washed and buried in dignity,' a third suggested, naming the very village where Hodja Nasreddin had been headed.

"The travelers cut down several young trees, fashioned a pair of stretchers, and loaded Hodja Nasreddin on them.

"They carried him for a long time, while he lay still, without opening his eyes, as befits a dead man whose soul is already knocking on heaven's gate.

"Suddenly, the stretchers stopped. The travelers began to argue as to the best place to ford the river. One pointed to the right, another to the left, the third suggested crossing the river straight ahead.

"Hodja Nasreddin opened one eye ever so slightly and saw that the travelers were standing over the deepest, quickest, and most dangerous part of the river, where many a careless man had drowned. 'I need not worry for myself,' Hodja Nasreddin thought. 'I am dead anyway, and it makes no difference to me whether I lie in a grave or at the bottom of the river. But these travelers ought to be warned, or else they might lose their lives for their kindness to me, which would be quite ungrateful on my part.'

"He raised himself slightly on the stretchers, and, pointing towards the ford, said in a weak voice:

"'O travelers, when I was alive, I always crossed the river by those poplars over there.'

"And he closed his eyes again. Thanking Hodja Nasreddin for his advice, the travelers carried the stretchers onwards, pronouncing loud prayers for the salvation of his soul." While the listeners and the storyteller himself were laughing and jabbing each other with their elbows, Hodja Nasreddin muttered discontentedly:

"They garbled everything. Firstly, I never dreamed that I was dead. I'm not such a fool that I cannot tell if I am dead or alive. I can even remember clearly that a flea was biting me the entire time, and I desperately wished to scratch myself – I expect this proved quite clearly that I was really alive, for, in the opposite case, I would certainly not have felt the bites of the flea. I was simply tired and did not wish to walk further, while those travelers were hefty fellows: was it such a big deal for them to make a small detour and carry me to the village? But when they decided to cross the river where the depth was thrice the height of a man, I stopped them, worrying not so much for my family, since I do not have one, as for their families. And immediately, I tasted the bitter fruit of ingratitude: they tossed me from the stretchers and went at me with their fists – they would surely have given me quite a beating, were it not for the swiftness of my legs!… It is amazing how people can distort and garble what really happened."

In the meantime, a fourth man began his tale:

"They also say this of Hodja Nasreddin. Hodja Nasreddin lived for around half a year in a certain village and became quite popular among the villagers with the wit of his replies and the sharpness of his mind…"

Hodja Nasreddin pricked up his ears. Where had he heard that voice before – quiet but distinct, with a barely noticeable hoarseness? It was not long ago… Maybe even today… But no matter how hard he tried, he could not remember.

The storyteller continued:

"One day, the governor of the area sent one of his elephants to the village where Hodja Nasreddin lived for billeting and feeding by the villagers. The elephant was incredibly voracious. Every day, he consumed fifty measures of barley, fifty measures of jugara, fifty measures of corn, and a hundred sheaves of clover. In two weeks, the villagers had fed the elephant all their reserves, ruined themselves, and lost heart. Finally, they decided to send Hodja Nasreddin to the governor himself to ask that the elephant be removed from the village…

"And so they went to Hodja Nasreddin and began to plead with him. He agreed and mounted his donkey, whose stubbornness, depravity, and laziness, as the entire world knows, make him resemble a jackal, a spider, an asp, and a toad in one combined – and headed to the governor, remembering first to negotiate a payment for his services with the villagers, and this payment was so large that many had to sell their houses and were doomed to poverty thanks to Hodja Nasreddin."

"Ahem!" came from the corner. Hodja Nasreddin, turning and jumping on the mat, could barely conceal the rage boiling in his chest.

The storyteller continued:

"And he, Hodja Nasreddin, came to the palace, and stood for a long time in the crowd of servants and flunkies, waiting for when the luminous governor, shining with splendor and might like the sun itself, would deign to direct to Hodja Nasreddin his illustrious gaze, which dispenses joy to some and doom to others. And when the governor, who glittered among the people surrounding him like the silver moon among the stars, or the slender cypress among lowly shrubbery, deigned to gratify Hodja Nasreddin by showing his visage, which combined nobility and wisdom like a diamond and a ruby set in a single ring... when, I repeat, the governor directed his visage towards Hodja Nasreddin, the knees of the latter began to shake like a jackal's tail from fear and wonderment at such magnificence, blood froze in his veins, sweat emerged on his skin, and he became pale as chalk."

"Ahem!" came from the corner, but the storyteller paid no attention to this and continued:

"'What do you want?' asked the governor in a noble and sonorous voice, resembling the roaring of a lion.

"Hodja Nasreddin could barely control his tongue from fear, and his voice sounded shrill, like the barking of a stinking hyena.

"'O ruler!' Hodja Nasreddin replied. 'O light of our region, our sun and moon, giver of happiness and joy to all that lives in our region, hear your lowly slave, who is not even worthy to wipe the threshold of your palace with his beard. You, o luminous one, have kindly deigned to place one of your elephants in our village for billeting and feeding by the villagers. And so, we are a little displeased.'

"The governor moved his eyebrows together menacingly and began to resemble a thunderous storm cloud, while Hodja Nasreddin kneeled before him to the floor, like reeds before a tempest.

"'What displeases you?' asked the governor. 'Speak quickly! Or has your tongue become stuck to your dirty and treacherous throat?'

"'A... wa... wa...,' babbled the cowardly Hodja Nasreddin. 'We are displeased, o illustrious ruler, that the elephant is all by himself and quite lonely. The poor animal is pining away, and all the villagers have also languished and wasted away on his account. So they sent me, o noblest of the noble, who graces the earth, to ask that you deign to render unto us one more favor and send him a she-elephant for billeting and feeding.'

"The governor was quite pleased with this request and ordered it granted immediately, and he showed his favor by allowing Hodja

Nasreddin to kiss his boot, which Hodja Nasreddin instantly performed with such great zeal that the governor's boot turned reddish, while Hodja Nasreddin's lips blackened…"

But at that moment the storyteller was interrupted by the thunderous voice of Hodja Nasreddin himself.

"You lie!" Hodja Nasreddin exclaimed. "You lie, o shameless coward, who himself resembles the mixture of a jackal, a spider, an asp, and a toad! It is your lips, you filthy, mangy dog, and your tongue, and all your insides, that are black from licking the boots of rulers! But Hodja Nasreddin has never bowed before a ruler, anywhere! You slander Hodja Nasreddin! Do not listen to him, o Muslims, chase him away as a liar and soiler of purity, and let contempt be his lot forever. O Muslims, turn your eyes and hearts from him!"

He dashed forward to deal with the slanderer with his own hands, but then stopped suddenly as he recognized the flat, pockmarked face and shifty yellow eyes. It was the same servant who had quarreled with him in the street about the length of the railing on the otherworldly bridge.

"Aha!" Hodja Nasreddin exclaimed. "I have recognized you, o faithful and pious servant of your master! And I know now that you have another master, one whose name you keep secret! Tell me, how much does the emir pay you to slander Hodja Nasreddin in the chaikhanas? How much are you paid for denunciations, how much for the head of every man you betrayed, who has been executed, or thrown in the dungeon, or bound in chains, or sold into slavery? I have recognized you, emir's spy and snitch!"

The spy, who had been standing very still and looking at Hodja Nasreddin in fear, clapped his hands suddenly and shouted in a high-pitched voice:

"Guards, over here!"

Hodja Nasreddin heard the running of the guards in the darkness, the crashing of spears and ringing of shields. Wasting no time, he jumped to the side, knocking down the pockmarked spy who was blocking his path.

But here he heard the stomping of the guards running from the other side of the square.

Wherever he went, he kept bumping into the guards. And there was even a moment when he thought he would not be able to break through.

"Woe to me! I am caught!" he shouted in a loud voice. "Farewell, my faithful donkey!"

But then, something unexpected and unusual happened, and the memory of this event lives on in Bukhara even today and will never die, for great was the confusion and great was the destruction.

Hearing the woeful cries of his master, the donkey headed towards him, but then an enormous drum slid out from under the chaikhana platform. In the darkness, Hodja Nasreddin had accidentally tied the donkey to the iron bracket of the drum, which the chaikhana keeper used on major holidays to summon customers to his chaikhana. The drum got snagged on a stone and rumbled; the donkey turned around and the drum rumbled again. Then the donkey imagined that evil spirits, having already made short work of Hodja Nasreddin, were now after his own gray hide, and, braying in terror, he raised his tail and dashed across the square.

"Curses! My drum!" the chaikhana keeper wailed, giving chase.

It was no use! The donkey flew like the wind, like a storm, but the faster he flew, the more fierce, terrifying, and deafening was the crashing of the drum behind him as it bounced over rocks and bumps. The people in the chaikhanas grew alarmed and began to call to each other worriedly, asking: why is a drum sounding at this unusual hour, what has happened?

At this exact time, the last fifty camels were entering the square, loaded with crockery and sheet copper. Seeing a horribly braying, jumping, and banging round object hurtling towards them in the dark, the camels became mad with fear and scattered, spilling the crockery and the rumbling copper.

In a minute, the entire square and all adjoining streets were engulfed in great terror and unprecedented commotion: crashing, ringing, clattering, neighing, roaring, barking, howling, cracking, and rattling merged into a single infernal racket, and no one could understand a thing. Many hundreds of camels, horses, and donkeys got loose and were running around in the gloom, rumbling over the scattered copper sheets, while the drivers screamed and dashed back and forth, waving their torches. People woke up from the awful noise, jumped up, half-dressed, and ran without knowing where they were going, bumping into each other and filling the darkness with cries of desperation and sorrow, for they thought the end of the world had come. Roosters began to crow and flap their wings. The commotion grew, seizing the entire city to the very outskirts, and then the cannons on the city wall began to fire, for the city guards decided that an enemy force had burst into Bukhara; and the cannons in the palace began to fire, for the palace guards decided that a mutiny was underway. Torn, troubling voices of the muezzins came from all the countless minarets. Everything had turned head over heels, and no one knew where to go or what to do! Meanwhile, Hodja Nasreddin was running around in the very thick of it all, dodging the crazed horses and camels with great skill, and following his donkey by the banging of the drum, without success, until the rope snapped and the drum flew aside at the camels, who dashed away from it, crashing through awnings, sheds, chaikhanas, and shops.

Hodja Nasreddin would have had to chase his donkey for a long time had they not managed to bump into each other accidentally, face to face. The donkey was shaking and covered in lather.

"Come, come quickly, it's a little too noisy for us here," said Hodja Nasreddin, dragging the donkey away. "It's amazing what one little donkey can do in a big city if you tie a drum to him! Have a look at what you did! Of course, you rescued me from the guards, but I still pity the poor inhabitants of Bukhara: they'll be sorting this out till morning. Wherever could we find a quiet, secluded corner?"

Hodja Nasreddin decided to spend the night in the cemetery, judging sensibly that no matter what the commotion, the deceased would never run around, wail, shout, or brandish torches.

Thus Hodja Nasreddin, disturber of the peace and sower of discord, concluded his first day in his native city, quite worthy of his title. Tying his donkey to one of the headstones, he settled in comfortably on someone's grave and soon fell asleep. Meanwhile, the commotion carried on in the city for a long time – noise, din, shouting, ringing, and cannon fire.

Chapter 9

But as soon as dawn began to break, the stars to dim, and the hazy outlines of various objects to emerge from the darkness, many hundreds of sweepers, dustmen, carpenters, and clay workers came out onto the square. Together, they got to work: they raised the toppled awnings, repaired the bridges, fixed the holes in the fences, picked up all the chips and pieces – and the first rays of the sun did not find any trace of the nighttime commotion in Bukhara.

And the bazaar commenced.

When Hodja Nasreddin, having slept well in the shade of the headstone, arrived in the square, it was full of buzzing, excitement, and movement, flooded from end to end by a multinational, multilingual, multicolored crowd. "Make way! Make way!" shouted Hodja Nasreddin, but he could barely discern his own voice among thousands of other voices, for everyone was shouting: the merchants, the camel drivers, the water-bearers, the barbers, the wandering dervishes, the beggars, and the bazaar tooth-pullers, who were shaking the rusty and frightening tools of their trade. Multicolored robes, turbans, horsecloths, rugs, Chinese speech, Arabic, Hindu, Mongol, and many other dialects – all of it melded together, swayed, moved, and hummed, and the dust rose and darkened the sky, even as hundreds of new people came to the square in endless streams, laid out their wares, and joined the communal roar with their own voices. The potters drummed resoundingly on their pots, grabbing customers by the flaps of their robes and begging them to listen, become enchanted by the clearness of the sound, and then buy; copper blinded the eyes in the metalworking row, the air groaned with the chattering of little hammers which the artisans used to indent patterns on trays and pitchers, praising loudly their skill and denigrating the skill of their neighbors. The jewelers melted silver in tiny forges, they pulled gold and polished semi-precious Indian stones using leather disks. A light breeze sometimes brought on a thick wave of fragrance from the neighboring row, which sold perfumes, rose oil, ambergris, musk, and various spices. The endless carpet row stretched off to the side – speckled, ornate, colorful, decorated with Persian, Damascan, Tekinian rugs, Kashgarian carpets, dyed horse-cloths both expensive and cheap, for ordinary horses and for thoroughbred ones.

Then Hodja Nasreddin passed the silk row, the saddle row, the armory row, and the dye row, the slave market, the wool cleaning row – and this was just the beginning of the bazaar, while hundreds of various rows stretched out further ahead, and the more Hodja Nasreddin penetrated the crowd on his donkey, the louder was the yelling, shouting, arguing, and bargaining around him; yes, it was that very same bazaar, the famous and incomparable Bukharian bazaar, which had no equal at the time in Damascus, or Baghdad itself!

But then the rows ended, and the emir's palace appeared before Hodja Nasreddin's eyes, surrounded by a high wall with loopholes and toothed edges. The four towers at the corners were tiled skillfully with multicolored mosaics, crafted over long years by Arabian and Iranian artisans.

A speckled camp was situated before the palace gates. People languishing in the stuffy air were sitting and lying on reed mats in the shade of torn awnings, some alone and some with their families; women were rocking their infants, cooking food in pots, and sewing up torn robes and blankets; half-dressed children ran around everywhere, fighting and falling, and turning certain indecent body parts quite disrespectfully towards the palace. The men were sleeping, or engaged in various household tasks, or speaking amongst themselves as they congregated around tea kettles. "Huh! Why, these people have been here for many a day!" thought Hodja Nasreddin.

Two people attracted his attention: a bald man, and a bearded man. Their backs turned to each other, they were sitting right on the bare earth, each under his own awning, while between them was a white goat tied to a poplar peg. The goat was so thin that its ribs threatened to tear through its bare skin. Bleating pitifully, it was gnawing on the peg, which was already half-eaten.

Hodja Nasreddin was very curious and could not resist a question: "Peace to you, inhabitants of Noble Bukhara! Tell me, how long has it been since you joined the Gypsy persuasion?"

"Do not mock us, o traveler!" the bearded man replied. "We are not Gypsies, we are good Muslims like yourself."

"Then why do you not sit at home, if you are good Muslims? What are you waiting for here, in front of the palace?"

"We are waiting for the just and merciful judgment of the emir, our ruler, master, and lord, who obscures the sun itself with his brilliance."

"Right!" said Hodja Nasreddin, without concealing his derision. "And have you been waiting long for the just and merciful judgment of the emir, your ruler, master, and lord, who obscures the sun itself with his brilliance?"

"We are waiting for the sixth week now, o traveler!" the bald man interrupted. "This bearded litigious fool – may Allah punish him, may the shaitan lay his tail on his bed! – this bearded fool is my older brother. Our father died and left us a modest inheritance, and we divided up everything except this goat. Let the emir judge which of us is the rightful owner."

"But where is all the other property you have inherited?"

"We had to sell everything; after all, the scribes writing the complaints must be paid, and the clerks receiving the complaints must also be paid, and the guards must be paid, and many others."

The bald man jumped from his spot suddenly and dashed towards a dirty, barefoot dervish, who was wearing a pointed cap and had a hollow black gourd hanging at his side. "Pray for me, holy man! Pray that the judgment be in my favor!"

The dervish took the money and began to pray. And every time he pronounced the final words of the prayer, the bald man tossed a new coin into his gourd and made him say it all again.

The bearded man got up worriedly and combed the crowd with his eyes. After a brief search, he noticed a second dervish, even dirtier and more tattered, and therefore more holy, than the first. This dervish demanded an exorbitant fee, and the bearded man began to haggle, but the dervish dug under his cap and extracted a handful of large lice. Assured of his holiness, the bearded man agreed. Glancing triumphantly at his younger brother, he counted off the money. The dervish stood on his knees and began to pray loudly, his deep voice drowning out the high-pitched voice of the first dervish. Worried, the bald man gave more money to his dervish, and the bearded man to his, and then both dervishes, trying to outdo each other, began to shout and scream so loudly that Allah probably had to order his angels to shut the windows in his chambers for fear of going deaf. Gnawing at the poplar peg, the goat produced long, mournful bleats.

The bald man tossed it half a sheaf of clover, but the bearded man shouted: "Get your filthy, foul clover away from my goat!"

He threw the clover far to the side, and placed a pot of bran before the goat.

"No!" the bald brother howled angrily. "My goat will not eat your bran!"

The pot flew after the clover and broke, mixing the bran with the dirt, while the brothers were already rolling on the ground in a fierce struggle, raining blows and curses on each other.

"Two fools are fighting, two cheats are praying, and meanwhile the goat has died of hunger," Hodja Nasreddin said, shaking his head. "Hey you, virtuous and loving brothers, look over here! Allah has judged your quarrel in his own way and taken the goat for himself!"

Coming to their senses, the brothers released each other and stood with bloodied faces for a long time as they looked at the dead goat. Finally, the bald one said:

"We must skin it."

"I will skin it!" the bearded man said quickly.

"Why you?" asked the other; his bald head grew purple with rage.

"The goat is mine, and therefore the hide is mine!"

"No, mine!"

Before Hodja Nasreddin could put in a single word, the brothers were rolling on the ground once more, and it was impossible to tell anything apart in that rasping bundle. Only a dirty fist emerged for a moment, grasping a clump of black hair, leading Hodja Nasreddin to conclude that the older brother had lost a significant part of his beard.

Waving his hand hopelessly, Hodja Nasreddin rode on. He saw

a blacksmith with tongs tucked into his belt – the same one he had met the previous day by the pond.

"Greetings, blacksmith!" Hodja Nasreddin shouted happily. "We meet again, although I have not yet managed to fulfill my oath. What are you doing here, blacksmith, have you come to the emir's judgment as well?"

"Only will anything useful come of this judgment?" the blacksmith replied grimly. "I have come with a complaint from the blacksmiths' row. We were ordered to feed fifteen guards for three months, but an entire year has passed, and we keep feeding them and feeding them, and sustaining great losses."

"And I have come from the dye row," another man butted in, his hands bearing traces of dye and his face green from the noxious vapors he had to breathe from dawn till dusk. "I have come with the same complaint. We were given twenty-five guards for billeting, our trade was ruined, our profits fell. Perhaps the emir will be merciful and free us from this intolerable burden."

"And why are you ganging up on the poor guards?" Hodja Nasreddin exclaimed. "Truly, they are not the worst or the most insatiable among the inhabitants of Bukhara. You feed the emir himself without a murmur, and all his viziers and officials. You feed two thousand mullahs and six thousand dervishes – why must the poor guards go hungry? Besides, have you not heard the saying: wherever a single jackal finds a meal, ten more immediately appear? I do not understand your displeasure, o blacksmith and dyer!"

"Quiet!" said the blacksmith, glancing round. The dyer was looking at Hodja Nasreddin with reproach.

"You are a dangerous man, traveler, and your words are not virtuous. But our emir is wise and ever-merciful…"

He did not finish, because trumpets began to howl, the drums began to bang, and the entire speckled camp stirred and began to move – and then the copper-bound palace gates swung open slowly.

"The emir! The emir!" came shouts, and the people began pouring towards the palace from all directions to see their ruler.

Hodja Nasreddin occupied a very comfortable spot in the front rows.

The heralds ran out of the gates first:

"Make way for the emir! Make way for the most radiant emir! Make way for the ruler of the faithful!"

The guards jumped out after them, raining blows with their sticks left and right onto the heads and backs of the curious who had moved too close; a broad space appeared in the crowd, and then musicians emerged, bearing drums, flutes, tambourines, and karnays[1]; then came the retinue, clad in silk and gold, carrying curved swords in velvet scabbards studded with precious stones; then two elephants with tall plumes on their heads were led out; finally, a lavishly decorated sedan chair was brought out, and inside it, underneath the heavy brocade canopy, lay the great emir himself.

The crowd rumbled and buzzed as he appeared; as if a great wind had passed through the square, all the people prostrated themselves as required by the emir's edict instructing his subjects to gaze on their ruler with great servility, and always from beneath. Servants ran before the sedan chair, spreading rugs on the ground. The palace flyswatter walked on the right of the sedan chair with a large horsehair fan on his shoulder, while the emir's hookah-bearer walked haughtily and with measured steps on the left, holding a golden Turkish hookah in his hands. Guards in copper helmets brought up the rear of the procession, holding shields, spears, crossbows, and bared swords; two small cannons were towed in the very back. This was all lit up by the bright midday sun – it ignited the precious stones, it burned on the gold and silver decorations, it reflected as hot fire in the copper shields and helmets and shone on the white steel of the bared blades… But in the enormous, prostrate crowd, there were neither precious stones, nor gold, nor silver, nor even copper – nothing that could please the heart by burning and shining in the sun – only rags, poverty, and hunger. And when the emir's lavish procession moved through the sea of the dirty, uneducated, downtrodden, and tattered people, it seemed as if a thin golden thread was being threaded through a wretched rag. A tall platform, covered in rugs, where the emir was to shower his favor onto his devoted subjects, was already surrounded on all sides by guards, while the torturers

---

1 *Karnay* – Central Asian long trumpet.

and executioners were fussing around on the place of execution just beneath it, ready to perform the will of the emir: they tested the flex of their switches and the strength of their sticks, they soaked multi-tailed rawhide whips in basins, they put up gallows, sharpened their axes, and dug sharpened stakes into the ground. The head of the palace guard, Arslanbek, whose ferocity was known far beyond Bukhara, was running the show. He was red-faced, corpulent, and black-haired, his beard covered his entire chest and draped over his stomach, his voice was like the bellowing of a camel.

He was handing out punches and kicks generously, but suddenly he bent over and began to tremble with servility.

Swaying smoothly, the sedan chair was brought onto the platform, and the emir drew aside the canopy and showed his face to the people.

Chapter 10

He was not so handsome, the illustrious emir; his face, which the court poets always likened to the full silver moon in their poems, was far more reminiscent of an overripe, flabby melon. When, supported by his viziers, the emir got up from his sedan chair to sit on his gilded throne, Hodja Nasreddin ascertained that his figure, contradicting the unanimous assertion of the court poets, did not at all resemble the slender cypress; the emir's body was obese and bulky, his arms short, and his legs so crooked that even his robe could not conceal their ugliness.

The viziers took their places on his right, the mullahs and officials on his left, the scribes with their books and inkwells situated themselves below, and the court poets formed a semicircle around the back of the throne, gazing at the emir's nape with devoted eyes. The court flyswatter waved his fan. The hookah-bearer placed the golden mouthpiece in his master's mouth. The crowd around the platform held its breath. Rising in his saddle and stretching his neck, Hodja Nasreddin became all ears.

The emir nodded sleepily. The guards moved apart, clearing the way for the bald man and the bearded man, who had finally reached their turn. The brothers crawled up to the platform on their knees and touched their lips to the rug hanging down to the ground.

"Rise!" Grand Vizier Bakhtiyar commanded.

The brothers got up, not daring to brush the dust from their robes. They were tongue-tied with fear, and their words were confusing and unintelligible. But Bakhtiyar was an experienced vizier, and he was quick on the uptake.

"Where is your goat?" he interrupted the brothers impatiently.

The bald man replied:

"It has died, o noble vizier! Allah has taken our goat. But which of us shall have its hide?"

Bakhtiyar turned to the emir:

"What is your decision, o wisest of rulers?"

The emir yawned protractedly and shut his eyes with a look of utter indifference. With great respect, Bakhtiyar bowed his head, covered in a white turban.

"I have read the decision on your face, o sovereign! Hear this," he said to the brothers; they kneeled, preparing to thank the emir for his wisdom, justice, and mercy. Bakhtiyar pronounced the judgment; pens began to squeak as the scribes recorded his words in their thick books. "The ruler of the faithful and the sun of our universe, our great emir, may Allah's blessing extend over him, has deigned to judge that, since Allah has taken the goat, its hide must justly belong to Allah's deputy on earth, in other words: the great emir. It is therefore necessary to skin the goat, dry and tan the hide, bring it to the palace, and deposit it into the treasury."

The brothers looked at each other in confusion, and a light whisper ran through the crowd. Bakhtiyar continued in a loud and clear voice:

"Moreover, a court tax of two hundred tanga will be levied on the litigants, in addition to a palace tax of one hundred and fifty tanga, a scribe tax of fifty tanga, and a donation for the embellishment of mosques – this must be paid immediately in coin, or clothing, or other property."

He barely had time to finish before the guards dashed towards the brothers on Arslanbek's signal, dragged them aside, untied their belts, turned out their pockets, tore off their robes, and pulled off their boots. Then the brothers were kicked aside, barefoot and half-naked, barely able to hide their shame beneath their wretched clothing.

This took less than a minute. Immediately after the judgment was pronounced, the entire chorus of court poets stirred and began to glorify the emir in many voices:

"O wise emir, o wisest of the wise, o he who is made wise by the wisdom of the wise, o emir, wise above all the wise!..."

Thus they clamored for a long time, stretching their necks in the direction of the throne: each tried to ensure that the emir would distinguish his voice from the others. And the simple folk crowding around the platform were silent, gazing at the brothers with pity.

"Well then," Hodja Nasreddin noted in a pious voice, turning to the poor brothers, who were weeping loudly in each other's arms. "You did not sit on the square for six weeks in vain. At last you have heard a just and ever-merciful decision, for it is known to all that there is no one wiser or more merciful in this world than our emir, and if anyone should doubt that," – he looked over his neighbors in the crowd – "it would be easy enough to call the guards, and they would hand the impious wretch over to the torturers, who would easily explain to that man the full gravity of his error. Go home in peace, o brothers; if, in the future, you should quarrel over a hen, come again to the emir's judgment, but do not forget to sell your homes, vineyards, and fields, or else you will not be able to pay all the taxes."

"O, it would have been better for us to die with our goat!" the brothers exclaimed, spilling copious tears.

"You think there aren't enough fools in heaven?" Hodja Nasreddin replied. "Trustworthy men have told me that, these days, both heaven and hell are packed to the brim with fools – and neither will let in any more. Therefore, I predict you will be immortal, brothers. Now leave here quickly, because the guards are beginning to look in our direction, and, unlike you, I am not assured immortality."

The brothers left, sobbing loudly, clawing at their faces, and pouring yellow dirt on their heads.

The blacksmith then faced the emir's judgment. He relayed his complaint in a grim and hollow voice. Grand Vizier Bakhtiyar turned to the emir:

"What will be your decision, o ruler?" The emir was asleep with his mouth hanging open and snored lightly. But Bakhtiyar was not stumped in the least.

"O ruler! I can read the decision on your face!" And he announced solemnly:

"In the name of Allah, gracious and merciful: the sovereign of the faithful and our ruler, the emir, in his tireless concern for his subjects, has shown them great favor and goodwill by billeting his faithful guards, thus giving the people of Noble Bukhara an honorable opportunity to thank their emir, and thank him daily and hourly – an honor not granted to the populace of other countries bordering ours. However, the blacksmiths' row did not distinguish itself among others with its virtue. On the contrary: the blacksmith Yusuf, forgetting of the otherworldly suffering of sinners on the hair-thin bridge, has opened his mouth brazenly to express ingratitude, which he dared to bring before our sovereign and lord, the illustrious emir, who obscures the sun itself with his brilliance. Deliberating on this, our illustrious emir has deigned to judge as follows: the blacksmith Yusuf is to be granted two hundred lashes so as to inspire words of repentance in him, for otherwise he would wait in vain for the heavenly gates to open before him. As for the rest of the blacksmiths' row, the illustrious emir again shows lenience and favor, and orders twenty more guards to be billeted there, so as not to deprive the blacksmiths of the joyous opportunity to praise his wisdom and mercy every day and hour. This is the emir's judgment, may Allah extend his days for the benefit of all his faithful subjects!"

The entire chorus of court flatterers stirred once more and began to drone on in different voices, praising the emir. Meanwhile, the guards seized the blacksmith Yusuf and dragged him off to the place of execution, where the torturers were already weighing heavy whips in their hands with repugnant, bloodthirsty smiles.

The blacksmith lay face down on a mat; the whip whistled in the air and came down, decorating the blacksmith's back with blood.

The torturers beat him viciously, shredding all the skin on his back and cutting through the flesh right to the bone, but they did not manage to extract even a single moan from the blacksmith, much less a scream. When he got up, everyone noticed black foam on his mouth: he had been chewing on the dirt during the flogging to keep himself from crying out.

"This blacksmith is not of the sort that forgets easily," Hodja Nasreddin said. "Now he will remember the emir's favor until the end of his days. What are you waiting for, dyer? Go, it is your turn."

The dyer spat on the ground and walked away from the crowd without looking back.

The grand vizier quickly finished several more cases, managing to extract a benefit for the emir's treasury every time, and it was this very skill that made him famous among other dignitaries.

The torturers at the place of execution worked without respite. Cries and screams came from that direction. The grand vizier sent more and more sinners to the torturers, and they had already formed a long line – old men, women, and even a ten-year old boy who had been proven guilty of an insolent and freethinking moistening of the ground near the emir's palace. He trembled and wept, wiping his tears all over his face. Hodja Nasreddin looked at him with pity and indignation in his heart.

"Truly, he is a dangerous criminal, that boy," Hodja Nasreddin discussed loudly. "And one cannot praise enough the prudence of the emir, who defends his throne from such enemies, who are all the more dangerous since they hide their questionable state of mind beneath their young age. It was no earlier than today that I saw another criminal, even worse and more heinous than this one. That criminal – could you believe it? – he committed something even worse right by the palace wall! No punishment would have been enough for him, except perhaps to have him impaled. I only fear that the stake would have passed right through the criminal like a skewer through a chicken, for the criminal was no more than four years old. But this, of course, is no excuse, as I have already said."

Thus he spoke, trying to pass off as a mullah reading a sermon; both his voice and his words sounded well-intentioned, but people who had ears heard him, understood him, and concealed unpleasant smirks beneath their beards.

Chapter 11

Suddenly, Hodja Nasreddin saw that the crowd was thinning. Many were leaving in a hurry, even running away. "Are the guards working their way towards me, perchance?" he thought worriedly.

He understood everything as soon as he saw the moneylender approach. A decrepit old man in a clay-stained robe was walking under guard behind the moneylender, as well as a woman draped in a veil, or, more accurately, a young girl, as Hodja Nasreddin's skilled eyes determined from her gait.

"And where are Zakir, Djura, Muhammad, and Sadyk?" the moneylender asked in a squeaky voice, looking over the crowd with his only eye; the second was dim and motionless, a walleye. "They were just here, I saw them. Their debts will be due soon, they run and hide in vain. On the right day, I will find them anyway."

Limping, he dragged his hump onwards.

"Look, look, that spider has brought the potter Niyaz and his daughter to the emir's judgment!"

"He did not give the potter a single day of postponement!"

"May he be cursed, that moneylender. My debt is due in two weeks!"

"Mine – in a week."

"Look how everyone scatters before him and hides, as if he spreads leprosy or cholera!"

"He's worse than a leper, that moneylender!" Hodja Nasreddin was torn with bitter repentance. He repeated his vow: "I will drown him in that same pond!"

Arslanbek admitted the moneylender out of order. The potter and his daughter followed the moneylender to the platform, where they kneeled and kissed the fringe of the rug.

"Peace to you, honored Jafar!" the grand vizier said amicably. "What business brings you here? Relay your case to the great emir as you fall into his feet."

"O great sovereign, my lord!" Jafar began to the emir, who nodded in his slumber and began snoring and whistling yet again. "I have come to ask you for justice. This man, who is named Niyaz and who works as a potter, owes me one hundred tanga, and three hundred more in interest. Today, the debt is due, but the potter has not paid me anything. Judge us, o wise emir, the sun of our universe!"

The scribes recorded the moneylender's complaint in their books, and then the grand vizier turned to the potter:

"The great emir asks you, potter: do you admit this debt? Perhaps you dispute the day and the hour?"

"No," the potter replied in a weak voice, and hung his gray head. "No, o most wise and just vizier, I do not dispute anything – neither the debt, nor the day, nor the hour. I only ask for one month's postponement and rely on the generosity and the mercy of our emir."

"Permit me, o sovereign, to announce the decision which I have read on your face," said Bakhtiyar. "In the name of Allah most gracious and merciful: according to law, if someone cannot pay his debt on time, then he and his family will be slaves to the one he owes until such time as he pays the debt and the interest for the entire duration, including the time spent in slavery."

The potter's head sank lower and lower, and suddenly began to shake. Many in the crowd turned away, repressing heavy sighs.

The girl's shoulders trembled: she was crying under her veil.

Hodja Nasreddin repeated to himself for the hundredth time: "He will be drowned, that merciless torturer of the poor!"

"But the mercy and generosity of our ruler the emir are boundless!" Bakhtiyar continued in the meantime, raising his voice. The crowd fell silent. The old potter raised his head, and hope flashed on his face.

"Although the term of the debt has passed, the emir grants the potter Niyaz a postponement – one hour. If, after the hour has passed, the potter Niyaz continues to neglect the tenets of faith and fails to pay the entire debt with interest, then we must follow the law, as I have said. Go, potter, and may the emir's mercy continue to abide with you."

Bakhtiyar fell silent, and then the chorus of flatterers crowding behind the throne stirred and began to drone:

"O just emir, who obscures justice itself with his justice, o wise and charitable emir, o generous emir, o grace of earth and heaven's renown, our illustrious emir!"

This time, the flatterers outdid themselves and praised so loudly that they woke up the emir, who frowned unpleasantly and ordered them to be quiet. They fell silent, and all the people on the square were silent, but suddenly, the silence was interrupted by mighty, ear-rending braying.

It was Hodja Nasreddin's donkey. Perhaps he had grown bored of standing in the same spot, or maybe he noticed another one of his long-eared kin and decided to say hello, but he was braying with his tail raised, his snout stretched out, and his yellow teeth bared. His braying was deafening and unrestrained, and if he stopped for an instant, it was only to take a breath, open his mouth even wider, and bray and screech even louder.

The emir plugged his ears. The guards dashed into the crowd. But Hodja Nasreddin was already far away; he was dragging the stubborn donkey behind him and scolding him for all to hear:

"What are you so happy about, you accursed donkey? Can you not praise the emir's kindness and wisdom a little quieter? Or perhaps you wish to be appointed the chief court flatterer for your trouble?"

The crowd met him with loud laughter, making way for him and closing ranks in front of the guards, who never managed to catch Hodja Nasreddin, have him flogged for such an insolent disturbance of the peace, and confiscate the donkey for the emir's treasury.

Chapter 12

"Well, the judgment is over, and now my power over you is boundless," the moneylender Jafar spoke to the potter Niyaz and his daughter Guljan after they had all left the place of judgment following the pronouncement of the sentence. "My beauty, since I saw you by chance, I have been deprived of sleep and peace. Show me you face. Today, in exactly one hour, you will enter my house. And if you are kind to me, I will give your father an easy job and good food, but if you are stubborn, then I swear by the light of my own eyes that I will feed him raw beans, make him carry heavy stones, and sell him to the Khivians, whose cruelty to their slaves is known to all. Do not be stubborn and show me your face, o beautiful Guljan!"

He raised her veil with his voluptuous, crooked fingers. She shoved his hand away with an angry motion. Guljan's face was open for only an instant, but even that was enough for Hodja Nasreddin, who was riding by on his donkey, to sneak a peek. And the beauty of the girl was so wondrous and incredible, that Hodja Nasreddin almost lost consciousness: the world went dark before his eyes, and his heart stopped beating. He grew pale, swayed in his saddle, and covered his eyes with his hand, shaken. Love struck him instantly, like lightning. It took some time for him to recover.

"And this limping, hunchbacked, blind ape would encroach upon this fantastic beauty!" he exclaimed. "Why, why did I drag him from the water yesterday? Already my deed has turned against me! But we'll see, we'll see yet, dirty moneylender! You are not yet the master of the potter and his daughter, they have a whole hour's postponement, and Hodja Nasreddin can do in one hour what would take another man a whole year!"

Meanwhile, the moneylender took a wooden sundial from his bag, and marked the time.

"Wait for me here, potter, beneath this tree. I will return in one hour, and do not attempt to escape, for I will find you even at the bottom of the sea and treat you like any other escaped slave. And as for you, beautiful Guljan, think on my words: your father's fate now depends on your kindness."

And, with a triumphant smile on his filthy snout, he headed for the jewelers' row to buy decorations for his new concubine.

The potter, doubled over in grief, remained with his daughter in the shade of the roadside tree. Hodja Nasreddin approached:

"Potter, I have heard the sentence. You are in trouble, but perhaps I can help?"

"No, kind man," the potter replied with desperation in his voice. "I see by the patches in your clothing that you are not rich. I would need four hundred tanga! I have no friends that wealthy, all my friends are poor, ruined by requisitions and taxes."

"I also have no rich friends in Bukhara, but nevertheless I will attempt to get the money," Hodja Nasreddin interrupted.

"Get four hundred tanga in one hour!" The old man shook his gray head with a bitter smirk. "You must be mocking me, passerby! Only Hodja Nasreddin himself could possibly succeed in such an endeavor!"

"O passerby, save us, save us!" Guljan exclaimed, hugging her father. Hodja Nasreddin glanced at her and saw that her hands were perfect; she met his glance with a prolonged look, and he saw the glistening of her eyes, full of pleading and hope, through the veil. His blood began to boil and ran down his veins with searing fire; his love increased many fold. He said to the potter:

"Sit here, old man, and wait for me. May I be the lowest and most contemptible of all men if I do not obtain four hundred tanga before the moneylender arrives!"

Jumping on his donkey, he vanished in the bazaar crowd...

Chapter 13

The square was a lot less noisy and crowded than in the morning, during the peak hours of trading, when everyone was running, shouting, and hurrying, afraid to miss out on a lucky deal. Noon was approaching, and people had left for the chaikhanas to escape the heat and find a quiet moment to tally their profits and losses. The sun flooded the square with a hot glow, and the shadows were short and well-defined, as if they had been carved out in the firm ground. Beggars huddled in shaded spots, and sparrows hopped beside them, picking at crumbs and chirping happily.

"Spare some money, kind man, in the name of Allah!" the beggars twanged, showing Hodja Nasreddin their deformities and ulcers.

He replied crossly:

"Get your hands away. I am no richer than you, I need four hundred tanga myself."

The beggars took his words for mockery and showered Hodja Nasreddin with curses. Deep in thought, he did not reply.

He found the biggest and most crowded chaikhana, one that did not have any expensive rugs or silken pillows. He entered, dragging the donkey along instead of leaving him down at the tethering post.

Hodja Nasreddin was met by a surprised silence, but he was not the tiniest bit embarrassed. He reached into his saddlebag, pulled out the Koran that the old man had given him the previous day, and placed it, open, before the donkey.

He did all this calmly and unhurriedly, without a hint of smile on his face, as if it was perfectly normal.

The people in the chaikhana began to exchange glances. The donkey tapped his hoof on the hollow wooden flooring.

"Already?" Hodja Nasreddin asked, turning the page. "You are showing noticeable improvement."

Then the paunchy, good-natured chaikhana keeper got up from his spot and approached Hodja Nasreddin.

"Listen, my good man, is this really the place for your donkey? And why have you placed a holy book in front of him?"

"I am teaching this donkey theology," Hodja Nasreddin said calmly. "We have almost finished the Koran and will soon move on to Sharia."

The buzz of voices and whispers filled the chaikhana. Many got up so they could see better.

The chaikhana keeper's eyes became round and his mouth opened slightly. He had never seen such wonders before in his life. Just then, the donkey tapped his hoof again.

"Good," Hodja Nasreddin praised him, turning the page. "Very good! A bit more effort, and you could become the chief theologian in the Mir-Arab madrassa." Turning to the chaikhana keeper, Hodja Nasreddin added: "Only he cannot turn the pages himself, so I have to help him… Allah gave him a sharp mind and a phenomenal memory, but forgot to provide him with fingers."

The people in the chaikhana abandoned their kettles and came closer; in less than a minute, a crowd had formed around Hodja Nasreddin.

"This donkey is no ordinary donkey!" Nasreddin announced. "He belongs to the emir himself. One day, the emir summoned me and asked: 'Can you teach theology to my favorite donkey, so that he knows as much as I do?' I was shown the donkey, I tested his abilities, and I said: 'O illustrious emir! In terms of the sharpness of his mind, this phenomenal ass yields to none of your ministers, nor to you. I will undertake to teach him theology, and he will know all that you know and more, but this will take me twenty years.' The emir gave me five thousand tanga in gold from his treasury and said: 'Take this donkey and teach him, but, by Allah, if in twenty years he does not know theology and cannot recite the Koran from memory, I will have you beheaded!'"

"Well, that means you can kiss your head goodbye!" the chaikhana keeper exclaimed. "Who has ever heard of donkeys studying theology and reciting the Koran from memory?"

"There are many such donkeys in Bukhara alone," Hodja Nasreddin replied. "Let me say, also, that it's not every day that a man can get five thousand tanga in gold and a good donkey. As for my head, do not cry for it, because in twenty years, one of us will surely die – either myself, or the emir, or this donkey. And after that, good luck finding out which of us three knew more theology!"

The chaikhana nearly collapsed from the explosion of thunderous laughter, while the chaikhana keeper himself tumbled on a mat in convulsions, laughing so hard that his face became drenched with tears. He was a very cheerful and easily amused man, that chaikhana keeper!

"Did you hear?" he shouted, hoarse and gasping for breath. "Good luck finding out which of them knew more theology!" He probably would have burst from laughter, if something had not dawned on him.

"Wait! Wait!" He waved his hands, calling for everyone's attention. "Who are you and where do you come from, o one who teaches theology to his donkey? Are you, perchance, Hodja Nasreddin himself?"

"And why are you so surprised? You have guessed correctly, chaikhana keeper! I am Hodja Nasreddin. Greetings to you, people of Noble Bukhara!"

Everyone froze on the spot for a long time, and then someone's joyous voice broke the silence:

"Hodja Nasreddin!"

"Hodja Nasreddin!" another took up, and then a third and a fourth; and so it went through the chaikhana, through other chaikhanas, and through the entire bazaar – repeating and reverberating everywhere:

"Hodja Nasreddin! Hodja Nasreddin!"

People ran towards the chaikhana from every corner – Uzbeks, Tajiks, Iranians, Turkmens, Arabs, Turks, Georgians, Armenians, Tatars – and when they reached it, they shouted loud greetings to their favorite, the famous trickster and joker Hodja Nasreddin.

The crowd grew.

A bag of oats appeared out of nowhere before the donkey, as well as a sheaf of clover and a bucket of clean, cold water.

"Greetings to you, Hodja Nasreddin!" people kept shouting. "Where have you traveled? Say something, Hodja Nasreddin!"

He walked up to the very edge of the platform and gave a low bow to the people:

"Greetings to you, people of Bukhara! For ten years I have been parted with you, and now my heart rejoices at our meeting. You asked me to say something – let me sing instead!"

He grabbed a large clay pot, poured out the water, and, striking it with his fist like a tambourine, began to sing loudly:

Ring, pot, sing and shout,
Give praise to one we hold so dear!
And tell the world, my pot, about
The favors of our kind emir!

The earthen pot, it hums and rings
And in an angry voice it sings!
And in a hoarse voice it repeats,
It calls to folk on all the streets!

Come hear a tale that came to pass:
"There lived a potter, old Niyaz,
He worked the clay and pots he made
But very poor was his trade.
With all his savings, he could not
E'en hope to fill a tiny pot.

"Jafar the hunchback never sleeps,
Enormous pots of wealth he keeps,
The palace treasury as well
With gold and plundering does swell.
The palace guardsmen never sleep
Enormous pots of wealth they keep.

"But now to old Niyaz comes grief,
His home invading like a thief.
And he is seized and swiftly brought
To judgment at the emir's court,
Behind him walks the cruel Jafar
His hump displaying from afar."

How long shall we injustice bear
Tell me, o pot, so all may hear.
Your tongue of clay will never lie,
Where did the potter go awry?
The pot will sing, the pot will ring,
The pot will say the truthful thing:

"The old man is damned because
A spider has him in its claws.
The spider's web in which he fell
Has seized him with an evil spell.

"The old Niyaz in court appears,
To the emir he bows in tears.
He says: 'Tis' known to all mankind
That the emir is good and kind.
Let his great mercy now console
My modest heart and pleading soul.'

"Said the emir: 'Weep not, I say,
I give you time – an hour's stay!
For it is known to all mankind
That the emir is good and kind!'"

How long shall we injustice bear?
Tell me, o pot, so all may hear.
The pot will sing, the pot will ring,
The pot will say the truthful thing:

"Only a madman would demand,
True justice from the emir's hand.
The price of favors he'll bestow
Is always low, is always low!
What's an emir? A sack of dung,
Where a head should be, a pot is hung."

Tell me, o pot, so all may hear,
How long shall the emir we bear?
When will my troubled people find
Some happiness and peace of mind?
The pot will sing, the pot will ring,
The pot will say the truthful thing:

"Now the emir has you in thrall,
But even he one day will fall.
Your days of woe will end and cease.
The years will pass. And fear you not,

In time, he'll shatter into pieces,
Just like a brittle earthen pot!"

Hodja Nasreddin raised the pot high above his head and hurled it to the ground. The pot burst with a ringing noise and shattered into hundreds of tiny fragments. Straining, Hodja Nasreddin shouted over the noise in the crowd:

"So let us, together, save Niyaz the potter from the money-lender and from the emir's favors. You know Hodja Nasreddin, his debts do not go unpaid! Who will lend me four hundred tanga for a short duration?"

A barefoot water-bearer stepped forward.

"Hodja Nasreddin, where would we get the money? Our taxes are so high. But I have this belt, it's nearly new; perhaps you can sell it."

He tossed the belt on the platform at Hodja Nasreddin's feet; the din and the movement in the crowd increased, and a multitude of skullcaps, slippers, belts, kerchiefs, and even robes began to land near Hodja Nasreddin. Everyone considered it an honor to help Hodja Nasreddin. The fat chaikhana keeper brought two of his best kettles and a copper tray, and looked at the others proudly, for he had given generously. The pile of things kept growing and growing. Straining his voice, Hodja Nasreddin shouted:

"Enough, enough, o generous people of Bukhara! Enough, do you hear? Saddle-maker, take back your saddle – enough, I say! Have you decided to turn Hodja Nasreddin into a junk dealer? I am starting the sale! Here is a water-bearer's belt – whoever buys it will never experience thirst. Step right up, it's cheap! Here is a pair of old, patched slippers – they must have been to Mecca at least twice, whoever puts them on will have practically completed the pilgrimage! I have knives, skullcaps, robes, shoes! Buy them; I am selling them cheaply and without haggling, for time is much more precious to me right now!"

But the great Bakhtiyar, in his tireless efforts to care for his faithful subjects, had managed to establish such an order in Bukhara that not a single coin lingered in the pockets of the people and instead passed immediately into the emir's treasury, lest the people be overburdened with full pockets. Hodja Nasreddin shouted in vain as he praised his goods – there were no buyers.

Chapter 14

Meanwhile, the moneylender Jafar was passing by, his bag weighed down by gold and silver jewelry he had bought in the jewelers' row for Guljan.

Although the hour had almost elapsed, and the moneylender was hurrying along in a state of voluptuous impatience, his greed surpassed all other emotions when he heard the voice of Hodja Nasreddin announcing a cheap sale.

The moneylender drew nearer and the crowd quickly began to thin, for every third man owed him money.

The moneylender recognized Hodja Nasreddin:

"It seems the man who pulled me from the water yesterday is trading here. But how did you get so many goods?"

"You yourself gave me half a tanga yesterday, o esteemed Jafar," Hodja Nasreddin replied. "I put this money to use and was blessed with good fortune in my trade."

"You've managed to trade this entire pile of merchandise in one morning?" the moneylender exclaimed in surprise. "My money has been good for you. How much do you want for this pile?"

"Six hundred tanga."

"You have gone mad! Have you no shame, trying to rip off your benefactor like that? Do you not owe your good fortune to me? Two hundred tanga – that is my price."

"Five hundred," Hodja Nasreddin replied. "In view of my respect for you, esteemed Jafar – five hundred tanga!"

"Ingrate! I repeat, do you not owe your good fortune to me?"

"And do you not owe your life to me, moneylender?" Hodja Nasreddin replied, losing his patience. "Of course, you gave me only half a tanga for saving your life, but since your life is not worth any more, I bear no grudge! If you wish to buy, then name a fair price!"

"Three hundred!"

Hodja Nasreddin remained silent.

The moneylender dawdled for a long time, pricing the goods with his trained eye, and when he determined that all the robes, shoes, and skullcaps could be sold for seven hundred tanga at the very least, decided to raise the price.

"Three hundred fifty."

"Four hundred."

"Three hundred seventy five."

"Four hundred."

Hodja Nasreddin stood firm. The moneylender left and came back again, raising the price one tanga at a time, and finally he agreed. They shook hands, and the moneylender began to count off the money with loud lamentations.

"By Allah, I paid twice what this merchandise is worth. But such is my character that I always bear a loss because of my kindness."

"Fake," Hodja Nasreddin interrupted, returning a coin. "And there are not four hundred tanga here. There are three hundred and eighty, you must have poor eyesight, esteemed Jafar."

The moneylender had to add twenty tanga and replace the fake coin. Then he hired a carrier for a quarter tanga, loaded him up, and commanded him to follow. The poor carrier doubled over and nearly collapsed under the heavy load.

"We are headed in the same direction," Hodja Nasreddin said. He could not wait to see Guljan again, and he kept putting on speed. The moneylender, with his lame leg, kept falling behind.

"Where are you going in such a hurry?" the moneylender asked, wiping off sweat with his sleeve.

"The same place as you," Hodja Nasreddin, and a sly spark flashed in his dark eyes. "You and I are going to the same place on the same business, esteemed Jafar."

"But you do not know my business," the moneylender replied. "If you knew, you would envy me."

Hodja Nasreddin understood the hidden meaning of these words, and he replied with a hearty laugh:

"But if you knew my business, moneylender, you would envy me ten times more."

The moneylender frowned: he had caught the insolence in Hodja Nasreddin's reply.

"You have an intemperate tongue; one of your stature should tremble when speaking to me. There are not many people in

Bukhara I would envy. I am rich, and there are no barriers to my desires. I have come to desire the most beautiful girl in Bukhara, and today she will be mine."

Just then, they bumped into a cherry salesman carrying a flat basket on his head. As he passed by, Hodja Nasreddin took a single cherry with a long stalk from the basket and showed it to the moneylender:

"Hear me, esteemed Jafar. They tell of a certain jackal who once saw a cherry high up on a tree. And he said to himself: 'I must eat that cherry at any cost.' And he spent the next two hours trying to climb the tree and tearing his hide on the boughs. But as soon as he flung his maw wide open to enjoy the cherry, a falcon swooped from somewhere, grabbed the cherry, and carried it away. It took the jackal another two hours to descend from the tree, and he injured himself even more. Spilling bitter tears, he said: 'Why did I climb to get the cherry? It has long been known to all that cherries do not grow on trees for jackals to eat.'"

"You are a fool," the moneylender said haughtily. "I see no meaning in your tale."

"Deep meanings are not grasped right away," Hodja Nasreddin replied.

The cherry was hanging behind his ear, the stalk tucked under his skullcap. The road turned a corner. The potter and his daughter were sitting on the rocks just past the turn.

The potter got up; his eyes, which had still held the glimmer of hope, faded. He decided that the stranger did not manage to get the money. Guljan turned away with a brief moan.

"Father, we are doomed!" she said, and her voice was so full of suffering that it could have made a stone shed tears, but the moneylender's heart was harder than any stone. As he spoke, the only emotions expressed on his face were spiteful triumph and voluptuousness.

"The time is up, potter. From now on, you are my slave, and your daughter is my slave and concubine."

He wanted to wound and demean Hodja Nasreddin, and so he exposed the girl's face with an authoritative, masterly hand:

"Look at her, is she not beautiful? Tonight I will sleep with her. Tell me now who should envy whom."

"She truly is beautiful!" Hodja Nasreddin said. "But do you have the potter's receipt?"

"Of course. How can one deal in money without receipts? All men are cheats and thieves. Here is the receipt: it indicates both the amount of the debt and the term. The potter's fingerprint is right below."

He handed the receipt to Hodja Nasreddin.

"The receipt is valid," Hodja Nasreddin confirmed. "So take the money you are owed on this receipt. Stop for a moment, esteemed folk! Be our witnesses," he added to the people passing by on the road.

He tore the receipt in half, and then four more times in half, and tossed the pieces into the wind. Then he untied his belt and returned all of the moneylender's coins that he had just received.

The potter and his daughter froze in surprise and joy, and the moneylender in anger. The witnesses winked at each other, happy to see the hated moneylender disgraced.

Hodja Nasreddin took the cherry, put it in his mouth, and, winking at the moneylender, smacked his lips loudly.

The moneylender's ugly body shook slowly, his hands twisted, his only eye spun angrily in its socket, his hump shuddered.

The potter and Guljan asked Hodja Nasreddin:

"O passerby, tell us your name so that we know who to mention in our prayers!"

"Yes!" the moneylender echoed, spraying spittle. "Tell me your name, so that I know who to curse!"

Hodja Nasreddin's face was glowing, and he replied in a firm and ringing voice:

"In Baghdad and in Teheran, in Istanbul and in Bukhara, I am known by one name – Hodja Nasreddin!"

The moneylender shrank away and turned pale:

"Hodja Nasreddin!"

And he dashed away in horror, prodding his carrier in the back.

Everyone else shouted in welcoming voices:

"Hodja Nasreddin! Hodja Nasreddin!" Guljan's eyes shone under the veil, while the potter could not even come to his senses and understand that he had been saved – he only muttered incoherently, spreading his hands in confusion.

Chapter 15

The emir's judgment continued. The torturers and executioners had been changed several times. The line of people awaiting
lashings kept growing. Two condemned men were squirming on
stakes, one lay decapitated on the ground, which was dark with
blood. But the moans and cries did not reach the hearing of the
dozing emir, drowned out by the chorus of the court flatterers,
who were hoarse with effort. They did not forget the grand vizier and the other ministers in their praises, or Arslanbek, or the
flyswatter, or the hookah-bearer, judging correctly that they needed to please everyone: some to obtain benefit, others to prevent
harm.

Arslanbek had been listening worriedly for a while to the strange
hum coming from afar.

He sent two of his most skillful and experienced spies.

"Go and find out why the people are agitated. Return here immediately."

The spies departed, one dressed in the rags of a beggar and the
other in the garb of a wandering dervish.

But before the spies could return, the pale moneylender came
running, stumbling and tripping on the flaps of his robe.

"What happened, honorable Jafar?" asked Arslanbek, his face
changing.

"Trouble!" the money-lender replied with trembling lips. "O
honorable Arslanbek, a great misfortune has occurred. Hodja
Nasreddin has appeared in our city. I just saw him and spoke with
him."

Arslanbek's eyes bulged out and froze. The stairs bending under
his hulk, he ran up on the platform and leaned down to the dozing
emir's ear.

The emir jumped so high on his throne as if someone had
jabbed him with an awl just below the back.

"You lie!" he shouted, and his face became distorted with fear
and rage. "This cannot be! The caliph of Baghdad wrote to me

recently that he had cut off his head! The Turkish sultan wrote that he had him impaled! The shah of Iran wrote to me personally that he hanged him! The Khivian khan announced publicly last year that he had him skinned alive! He could not have escaped unharmed from the hands of four sovereigns, that accursed Hodja Nasreddin!"

The viziers and dignitaries grew pale upon hearing the name of Hodja Nasreddin. The flyswatter trembled and dropped his fan, the hookah-bearer choked on the smoke and began to cough, the poets' groveling tongues froze to their teeth in fear.

"He is here!" Arslanbek repeated.

"You lie!" the emir exclaimed, and gave him a hefty slap on the face with his regal palm. "You lie! And if he is really here, then how could he have snuck into Bukhara, and what good are all your guards? So it was him, then, who caused all the commotion on the bazaar last night! He wanted to stir up the people to rebel against me, and you were asleep and heard nothing!" And the emir dealt Arslanbek another slap. Arslanbek gave a low bow and kissed the emir's hand in midair.

"O ruler, he is here, in Bukhara. Can you not hear?"

The distant hum grew stronger and louder, like an approaching earthquake, and soon the crowd around the place of judgment also began to hum, quietly and indistinctly at first, and then louder, stronger, until the emir felt the platform and his gilded throne swaying unsteadily. Just then, something floated out of the slurred communal hum, which had begun to turn into a powerful roar, and it was repeated again and again, reverberating in all ends of the crowd:

"Hodja Nasreddin! Hodja Nasreddin!" The guards dashed towards the cannons with lit fuses in their hands. The emir's face twisted in alarm.

"Enough!" he shouted. "To the palace!" Picking up the flaps of his brocade robe, he dashed towards the palace; after him, stumbling, ran the servants, carrying the empty sedan chair on their shoulders. Seized with confusion, the viziers, the executioners, the musicians, the guards, the flyswatter, and the hookah-bearer ran, shoving and overtaking each other, losing their slippers and not bothering to pick them up. Only the elephants proceeded with their previous dignity and slow pace, for, even though they belonged to the emir's retinue, they had no reason to fear the people.

The heavy, copper-bound palace gates closed after letting in the emir and his retinue.

And the bazaar square, filled with people, hummed and fussed in agitation as it repeated again and again the name of Hodja Nasreddin.

Part 2

"Here is a tale of some curious events;
part of them happened in my presence,
and other parts were related to me
by trustworthy people."

Usama ibn-Munkyz, *The Book of Edification*

Chapter 16

Since time untold, the potters of Bukhara had settled by the eastern city gates near a large mound of clay, and they could not have picked a better spot: the clay was right nearby, and the aryk flowing along the city wall supplied them with plenty of water. The grandfathers, great-grandfathers, and great-great-grandfathers of the potters had already used up half the mound: they built their homes from clay, they made their pots from clay, and it was into clay they were placed to the mournful cries of their relatives. It had probably happened more than once that some potter would make a pot many years after, dry it in the sun, treat it with flames, and then marvel at its incredibly strong and pure sound without even suspecting that some distant ancestor, looking after his descendant's welfare and success in trade, had ennobled the clay with a tiny part of his remains and made it ring like pure silver.

Here, too, stood the house of the potter Niyaz – right over the aryk, in the shade of mighty, ancient elms. The leaves rustled in the wind, the water babbled, and the songs of the beautiful Guljan could be heard in the little garden from dawn till dusk.

Hodja Nasreddin refused to settle in Niyaz's house:

"They may capture me in your house, Niyaz. I will spend the nights not far from here, I have found a safe spot. And in the daytime I will come here and help you in your work."

That was exactly what he did: every morning, before the sun would rise, he would come to Niyaz and sit at a pottery wheel next to the old man. There was no trade in the world that Hodja Nasreddin did not know; he knew pottery very well, and his pots turned out smooth, with a clear ring and the ability to keep water ice-cold even in the strongest heat. Before this, the old man, whose eyes had begun to let him down more and more over the past few years, could barely manage to make five or six pots a day, but now, long rows of them were drying in the sun along the fence – thirty, forty, and often fifty pots and jugs. On bazaar days, the old man came home with a full purse, and the scent of meat pilaf spread through the entire street from his house in the evening.

The neighbors were happy for the old man, saying:

"At last Niyaz happened on some good fortune and left his poverty behind, hopefully forever!"

"They say he has hired a worker to help him. And they say also that this worker is extremely skilled in the trade of pottery. Once, I deliberately stopped by Niyaz's house to see his helper. But as soon as I closed the gate behind me, the helper got up, walked away, and did not show his face again."

"The old man is hiding his helper. He is probably afraid that one of us will try to hire away such a skilled worker. Silly man! Are we, potters, so devoid of conscience that we would dare encroach on the well-being of an old man who has at last found his fortune?"

This is what the neighbors concluded, and of course no one even entertained the thought that old Niyaz's helper was Hodja Nasreddin himself. Everyone was quite sure that Hodja Nasreddin had long since left Bukhara, for he had spread those rumors himself to deceive the spies and reduce their zeal in searching for him. And he achieved his goal: ten days later, the supplementary pickets were removed from all the city gates, and the night patrols stopped bothering the inhabitants of Bukhara with the light of their torches and the clanging of their weapons.

One day, Niyaz looked at Hodja Nasreddin, and, after grunting and hesitating for a long time, finally said:

"You have saved me from slavery, Hodja Nasreddin, and my daughter from dishonor. You work alongside me and do ten times more than I do. Here are three hundred and fifty tanga, the net profit from selling the pots since you have started helping me. Take this money, it is rightfully yours."

Hodja Nasreddin stopped his wheel and stared at the old man in surprise.

"You must be ill, esteemed Niyaz! You are speaking nonsense. You are the master here, and I am your worker, so if you give me one tenth of the profit – thirty-five tanga – I will be most glad."

He took Niyaz's worn purse, counted off thirty-five tanga,

placed them in his pocket, and returned the rest to the old man. But the old man was stubborn and would not accept it.

"This is not right, Hodja Nasreddin! This money belongs to you! If you do not wish to take it all, take at least half."

Hodja Nasreddin became annoyed:

"Hide your purse, esteemed Niyaz, and please do not break the earthly customs. What would happen in the world if all the masters begin sharing their profits equally with their workers? Then there would not be any more masters on earth, or any workers, or any rich or poor, or any guards, or any emirs. Think: would Allah tolerate such a disruption of order? Take your purse and hide it somewhere far away, lest you bring down the wrath of Allah onto men and thus doom the entire human race!"

With these words, Hodja Nasreddin resumed spinning the pottery wheel with his foot.

"This will be an excellent pot!" he spoke, slapping the wet clay with his hands. "With a nice ring, just like our emir's head! We'll have to take it to the palace: let them keep it there in case the emir loses his head."

"Watch it, Hodja Nasreddin, you will lose your head yourself one day for this sort of talk."

"Huh! You think it is easy to remove Hodja Nasreddin's head?

"I, Hodja Nasreddin, always free have I been,
And I say – 'tis no lie – that I never shall die!
Let the emir decree a sharp axe just for me
And announce with spite that I steal and incite.
But I, Hodja Nasreddin, always free have I been,
And I say – 'tis no lie – that I never shall die!
I will live, sing, and praise, at the sun I will gaze,
And declare instead: let the emir drop dead!
Yes, the sultan already has an axe at the ready,
There's a noose in Tehran, and a stake with the khan.
But I, Hodja Nasreddin, always free have I been,
And I say – 'tis no lie – that I never shall die!
Poor, tattered, and bare, I have never a care,
I will live, sing, and praise, at the sun I will gaze,
By the people respected, and by fortune protected,

At the khan, the emir, and the sultan I sneer!
I, Hodja Nasreddin, always free have I been,
And I say – 'tis no lie – that I never shall die!"

Guljan's laughing face appeared in the green of the grapevines behind Niyaz. Hodja Nasreddin interrupted his song and began to exchange happy, mysterious signs with Guljan.

"What are you looking at? What do you see there?" Niyaz asked.

"I see a bird of paradise the like of which the world has never seen!"

The old man turned around, grunting, but Guljan had already disappeared in the greenery, and only her silvery laugh could be heard from afar. Shielding his face from the sun, the old man squinted with his nearsighted eyes for a long time, but did not see anything except for a sparrow hopping on the poles.

"Come to your senses, Hodja Nasreddin! Where did you see a bird of paradise? This is an ordinary sparrow!"

Hodja Nasreddin laughed, while Niyaz could only shake his head, ignorant of the reason for this mirth.

After dinner, the old man saw Hodja Nasreddin to the door, climbed up on the roof, and fell asleep there, fanned by a warm, gentle breeze. Soon he began snoring and wheezing, and then a light cough came from behind the low fence: Hodja Nasreddin had returned. "He is asleep," Guljan replied in a whisper. He leaped over the fence in a single bound.

They sat down by the pond in the shade of the poplars, which were dozing quietly, wrapped in their long green robes. The moon floated high in the clear sky, casting a bluish tint on everything; the water in the aryk babbled very softly, sparkling and flashing one moment, and vanishing in the shadows the next.

Guljan was standing before Hodja Nasreddin, lit up by the full moon and herself resembling the full moon, slender and lithe, girdled by her long hair. He spoke to her quietly:

"I love you, o queen of my soul, my first and only love. I am your slave, and I will perform whatever you wish! My entire life was spent waiting to meet you, and now I have seen you and will never forget you, and I will not be able to live without you!"

"This is probably not the first time you are saying this," she said with jealousy.

"Me?" he exclaimed with indignation in his voice. "How could you even think that?"

And his voice sounded so sincere that she believed it, softened, and sat down beside him on the earthen bench. He pressed his lips to hers and would not release for so long that she felt short of breath.

"Listen," she said afterwards. "Girls are supposed to receive gifts in exchange for kisses, whereas you have been kissing me every night for over a week, and I have yet to receive even a pin from you!"

"I simply did not have any money," he replied. "But today I received payment from your father, and tomorrow, Guljan, I will bring you a luxurious gift. What would you like – a necklace, or a shawl, or perhaps a ring with an amethyst stone?"

"It doesn't matter," she whispered. "It doesn't matter, my dear Hodja Nasreddin, so long as I receive this gift from your hands."

The blue water babbled in the aryk, and the stars trembled with bright and pure light in the transparent sky; Hodja Nasreddin drew closer to the girl, reached for her breast – and his hand became full. He froze, but then his cheek was scalded with such a heavy slap that he saw stars. He shrank back, shielding himself with his elbow just in case. Guljan got up, her breath heavy with anger.

"I seem to have heard the sound of a slap," Hodja Nasreddin said meekly. "Why hit, when it is possible to express oneself with words?"

"Words!" Guljan interrupted. "It is not enough that I have abandoned all modesty and revealed my face to you, but you also had to stick your long arms where you shouldn't."

"But who decides where one should stick his arms, and where one shouldn't?" Hodja Nasreddin objected in utter embarrassment and confusion. "If you had read the books of the most wise Ibn-Tufeil…"

"Thank god," she interrupted heatedly, "thank god that I have not read these dissolute books, and that I protect my honor like a decent girl should!"

She turned and left; the ladder creaked under her light steps, and soon light appeared in the slits of the walls surrounding the balcony.

"I upset her," Hodja Nasreddin pondered. "How did I mess up like that? No fear: now I know her personality. If she slapped me, then she will slap another as well and make a faithful wife. I would be happy to receive ten more slaps from her before the wedding, so long as she dispenses slaps just as generously to others after the wedding!"

He approached the balcony on tiptoes and called in a quiet voice:

"Guljan!" She did not reply.

"Guljan!"

The fragrant darkness remained silent. Hodja Nasreddin grew sad. Quietly, so as not to wake up the old man, he began to sing:

"You have stolen my heart with your eyelashes.

"You judge me, yet you use your eyelashes to steal. And then you demand payment for having stolen my heart! O, wonders! O, miracles! Who has ever heard of anything like this?

"Who has ever heard of paying a thief? Give me two or three kisses for free.

"No, that's not enough for me. Some kisses are like bitter water – the more you drink, the more thirsty you become. You have closed your doors before me.

"O, let my blood pour out on the ground! Where will I find peace?

"Perhaps you can tell me? This is my lament for your eyes that cast arrows, this is my lament for your curls, fragrant as musk!"

He kept singing, and although Guljan did not appear and did not reply, he knew that she was listening closely, and he knew also that not a single woman could resist such words. And he was not mistaken: the shutter opened slightly.

"Come!" Guljan whispered from above. "Only be quiet, so that my father does not wake up."

He climbed up the ladder, sat next to her again, and the wick floating in the saucer of melted tallow crackled and burned until dawn; they talked and could not get their fill of talking. In other words, everything was as it should have been, and as it is described by the most wise Abu-Muhammad Ali-ibn-Hazm in the book known as *The Dove's Necklace*, in the chapter entitled: "A word on the nature of love."

"Love – may Allah glorify it – is at first a joke, but in the end a very important thing. Its qualities are too subtle and elevated to describe, and its true nature cannot be divined except with great effort. As for the cause of the fact that love, in the majority of cases, arises from a beautiful appearance, it is quite understandable that the soul is beautiful, and it is attracted to all beautiful things and perfect images. And, having seen one of these, the soul begins to study it, and if it discerns something similar to itself beneath this appearance, the soul will enter a union with it, and true love will arise... It is truly wondrous how appearance connects the distant parts of the soul!"

Chapter 17

The old man began to toss and turn on the roof. He croaked, coughed, and called Guljan in a hoarse, sleepy voice to bring him some cold water. She pushed Hodja Nasreddin towards the door; he flew down the stairs, barely touching the steps, leaped over the fence, and, a short time later, after washing up in an aryk and wiping himself with the flap of his robe, he was already knocking on the gate from the outside.

"Good morning, Hodja Nasreddin," the old man greeted him from the roof. "How early you have been getting up these days. When do you have time to sleep? Let us have some tea and, with a blessing, begin our work."

At midday, Hodja Nasreddin left the old man and went to the bazaar to buy Guljan a gift. As usual, he put on a colorful Badakhshan turban and a false beard out of caution. In this outfit he was unrecognizable and could prowl the trading rows and the chaikhanas without fearing spies.

He picked out a coral necklace whose color reminded him of the lips of his beloved. The jeweler turned out to be an agreeable man, and after only an hour or so of noise, shouting, and arguing, Hodja Nasreddin took possession of the necklace for thirty tanga.

On the way back, Hodja Nasreddin saw a large crowd near the bazaar mosque. The people were crowding and clambering on each other's shoulders. Drawing closer, Hodja Nasreddin heard a sharp, piercing voice:

"See with your own eyes, o faithful: he is paralyzed and has been lying without movement for ten years now! His limbs are cold and lifeless. Look, he does not even open his eyes. He has come to our city from afar; good relatives and friends brought him here to try the final cure. In a week, on the day of the memorial of the most holy and incomparable Sheikh Bogaeddin, he will be placed on the steps of the tomb. The blind, the lame, and the paralyzed have been cured many times by this means: let us pray, o faithful, that the holy sheikh take pity on this poor man and cure him!"

The crowd said a prayer; then the sharp voice came again:

"See with your own eyes, o faithful: he is paralyzed and has been lying without movement for ten years now!…"

Hodja Nasreddin squeezed into the crowd, got up on his toes, and saw a tall, bony mullah with mean little eyes and a thin beard. Pointing his finger at his feet, where the paralyzed man was lying on a stretcher, he was shouting:

"Look, look, Muslims, how pathetic and pitiful he is, but in a week the holy Bogaeddin will send him a cure, and this man will return to life!"

The paralyzed man lay with his eyes closed, maintaining a mournful and pitiful expression on his face. Hodja Nasreddin gasped quietly in surprise: without a doubt, he would have recognized this pockmarked face with a flat nose among a thousand other faces! Apparently the servant had become paralyzed some time ago, for his face had grown considerably fatter from lying still and from general idleness.

From that day, no matter when Hodja Nasreddin would pass by the mosque, he would always see the mullah and the paralyzed man, the latter lying prone with a pitiful expression his face, which grew fatter and plumper day by day.

Then came the memorial day of the most holy sheikh. According to legend, the holy man had died in May, on a clear noon, and even though there had not been a single cloud in the sky, the sun darkened in the hour of his death, the earth shook, and the houses of many sinners were destroyed, while the sinners themselves perished in the ruins. Thus spoke the mullahs in the mosques, calling on Muslims to visit the tomb of the sheikh and worship his remains, so as not to appear impious and share the fate of the aforementioned sinners.

The pilgrims set off to worship while it was still dark, and when the sun rose, the entire enormous square surrounding the tomb was already filled with people from corner to corner. The streams of people on the roads did not thin out; everyone was walking barefoot, as required by ancient custom. There were people who had come from far away – the particularly pious, or, conversely, those who had committed great sins and had come here hoping to receive absolution. Husbands brought their barren wives, mothers carried their sick children, old men were hobbling along on crooked crutches, lepers had gathered in the distance and were staring hopefully at the white dome of the tomb.

The service did not start for a long time: they were waiting for the emir. The people were standing under the burning sun in the dense crowd, pressing against one another firmly and not daring to sit. The eyes of the people burned with a greedy, insatiable fire: having lost their faith in earthly happiness, the people were hoping for a miracle and shuddering with every loud noise. The waiting became unbearable, two dervishes collapsed on the ground in convulsions and, yelling loudly, began to chew the dirt, producing copious gray foam. The crowd stirred in agitation, women began crying and screaming everywhere, and then a thousand-voiced rumble carried through the square:

"The emir! The emir!"

Working their sticks diligently, the palace guards cleared a path in the crowd, and the emir walked down this broad path, which was covered with carpets, to pay his respects to the holy remains. He was barefoot, his head lowered, immersed in virtuous thoughts and impenetrable to earthly sounds. His retinue followed silently in his footsteps, and the servants fussed as they rolled up the carpets behind them and laid them out in front.

Tears of tenderness appeared on many of the faces in the crowd.

The emir ascended an earthen dais adjoining the wall of the tomb. He was handed a prayer rug and, supported on both sides by his viziers, got down on his knees. Mullahs in white garments gathered in a semicircle and began to sing, raising their arms to the sky, which was hazy with heat. The service had begun.

It went on endlessly, interspersed with sermons. Hodja Nasreddin stepped out of the crowd covertly and headed towards a small shed on the side, where the blind, lame, and paralyzed men waiting for their turn to be healed, as promised.

The doors of the shed were wide open. The curious were peeking inside and exchanging their impressions. The mullahs who were supervising the area were holding large copper trays to gather donations. The senior mullah narrated:

"…and since that day, the blessing of the most holy Sheikh Bogaeddin stands firmly and eternally over sacred Bukhara and her sun-like emirs. And every year on this day, the holy Bogaeddin gives us, humble servants of god, the power to perform miracles. These blind, lame, mad, and paralyzed men are waiting to be healed, and we hope to rid them of their suffering with the aid of the holy Bogaeddin."

As if responding to him, the men in the shed began to weep, howl, moan, and gnash their teeth. Raising his voice, the mullah continued:

"Make a donation for the embellishment of mosques, o faithful, and your gift will be remembered by Allah!"

Hodja Nasreddin peeked into the shed. The pockmarked, fat-faced servant was lying on his stretcher right by the entrance; many more people could be seen behind him in the shadows, holding crutches, lying on stretchers, and wearing bandages. And then the voice of the head ishan[1] came from the tomb, where he had just finished his sermon:

"A blind man! Bring me a blind man!" Pushing Hodja Nasreddin aside, the mullahs dove into the stuffy darkness of the shed and, a minute later, brought out a blind man wearing pitiful beggar's rags. He stumbled on rocks as he walked along, feeling the air with his hands.

Approaching the head ishan, the blind man fell before him and kissed the steps of the tomb; the ishan laid his hands on the blind man, who was healed instantly.

"I can see! I can see!" he shouted in a trembling, high-pitched voice. "O most holy Bogaeddin, I can see, I can see! O incredible healing, o great miracle!"

A crowd of worshippers gathered around him, buzzing; many approached and asked him: "Tell me which hand I just raised – right or left?" and he replied without mistake, and everyone ascertained that he was in fact cured.

And then an entire squad of mullahs with copper trays headed into the crowd, calling out:

"O faithful, you have seen the miracle with your own eyes, make a donation for the embellishment of mosques!"

1 *Ishan* – A spiritual leader belonging to one of the mystical orders of Islam.

The emir was the first to throw a handful of gold coins onto the tray, then all his viziers and officials tossed a single gold coin each, and then the people began to heap silver and copper on the trays generously; the trays filled up, and the mullahs had to change them three times.

When the stream of donations began to thin, a lame man was led out of the shed. Touching the steps of the tomb, he was cured just as instantly, and, tossing aside his crutches, he began to dance, throwing his feet high in the air. And the mullahs moved into the crowd with fresh trays, calling out:

"Donate, o faithful!"

A gray-bearded mullah approached Hodja Nasreddin, who was pondering something in deep concentration as he looked at the walls of the shed.

"O faithful man! You have seen a great miracle. Make a donation, and your gift will be remembered by Allah."

Loudly, so that everyone around him could hear, Hodja Nasreddin replied:

"You call this a miracle and ask me for money. Firstly, I have no money, and secondly, mullah, are you aware that I am a holy man myself, and can perform a far greater miracle?"

"You are a blasphemer!" the mullah shouted angrily. "Do not listen to him, Muslims, it is the shaitan himself speaking through his lips!"

Hodja Nasreddin turned to the crowd:

"The mullah does not believe that I can perform miracles! Very well, I will prove it! There are blind, lame, feeble, and paralyzed men gathered in this shed, and I will heal them all at once, without even touching them. I will say but two words – and they will be healed and run away so quickly that even the fastest Arabian stallion will not be able to catch them."

The walls of the shed were thin, and the clay had deep cracks in several places. Hodja Nasreddin picked out a spot that was completely surrounded by cracks and pressed on it firmly with his shoulder. The clay gave way with a dry, sinister crackle. He pushed again, and a huge part of the wall tumbled inside the shed with a hollow noise; clouds of dust appeared from the gaping black hole.

"Earthquake! Run!" Hodja Nasreddin shouted in a savage voice and knocked over a second piece of clay.

The shed was quiet for a moment, and then a commotion ensued: the paralyzed pockmarked servant was the first to dash to the exit, but his stretchers became stuck, and he barred the way for the rest of the lame, blind, and feeble men who were crowding behind him, yelling and howling. And when Hodja Nasreddin knocked over a third slab of clay into the shed, they pressed mightily on the pockmarked servant and pushed him out, along with the door and the doorposts, and dashed in all directions, forgetting their ailments.

The crowd shouted, whistled, laughed, and hooted. Hodja Nasreddin's loud voice sounded over the general noise:

"You see, Muslims, I was right when I said they could all be healed with a single word!"

No longer listening to the sermons, the curious ran from all directions, fell to the ground laughing when they heard what happened, and then passed the story of the miraculous healing on to others. Soon, all who had gathered had learned about what happened, and when the head ishan called for quiet by raising his hand, the crowd replied with curses, shouts, and whistles.

And again, as in the square before, the name appeared, hummed, and reverberated in the crowd:

"Hodja Nasreddin! He has returned! He is here, our Hodja Nasreddin!"

Cursed and mocked, the mullahs grabbed their trays and ran from the crowd in fear.

Hodja Nasreddin was far away already. He hid his colorful turban and false beard in his robe, for he had no reason at that moment to fear spies, who had their hands full around the tomb.

He did not notice, however, that the lame moneylender Jafar was following in his footsteps, hiding behind the corners of houses and roadside trees.

Hodja Nasreddin approached a fence in an empty, deserted alley, and pulling himself up with his arms, he coughed lightly. Light steps sounded and a female voice replied:

"It is you, my beloved!"

Hiding behind a tree, the moneylender easily recognized the voice of the beautiful Guljan. Then he heard whispers, restrained laughter, and the sound of kisses. "You have taken her from me to enjoy for yourself," the moneylender thought, consumed by bitter jealousy.

Bidding goodbye to Guljan, Hodja Nasreddin walked on so quickly that the moneylender could not keep up and soon lost him in the maze of narrow streets. "That means I will not receive a reward for his capture," Jafar thought with regret. "But instead... beware, Hodja Nasreddin, I have prepared you a terrible revenge!"

Chapter 18

The emir's treasury bore a heavy loss. The collections from the tomb of the holy Bogaeddin totaled less than one tenth of the profits of previous years. Moreover, the seeds of insolent free-thinking had been sown once more among the people. Spies reported that the rumors of the events near the tomb had reached the most distant corners of the country and had already elicited a response: in three kishlaks[1], the inhabitants refused to finish building their mosques, while in a fourth, they expelled their mullah in disgrace.

The emir ordered Grand Vizier Bakhtiyar to assemble the divan – the state council. The divan assembled in the palace garden. It was an excellent garden, one of the most beautiful in the world. Exotic fruit ripened here on luxurious, branchy trees – apricots of the camphor, almond, and Horasan varieties, plums, figs, wild oranges, and many other fruits, too many to list. Clumps of roses, violets, gillyflowers, anemones, and lavender grew in the garden, filling the air with heavenly fragrance. The chamomiles laughed under the loving gazes of the narcissuses, the fountains babbled, schools of goldfish swam in marble pools, and silver cages were hanging everywhere, filled with the ringing, whistling, and twittering of exotic birds. But the viziers, officials, sages, and poets passed by with indifference, untouched by the magical beauty, without hearing or seeing anything, for all their thoughts were preoccupied with concerns about further elevating themselves, about fending off the attacks of their enemies and, in turn, carrying out similar attacks against them. There was no room for anything else in their callous, withered hearts, and if all the flowers in the world were to wilt and all the birds to fall silent, they would not have noticed it, consumed by ambitious and greedy designs. Their eyes devoid of spark and their lips pursed and bloodless, they walked, shuffling, along the sandy paths, entered the pavilion, which was braided with dark, luxurious basilica leaves, and,

1 *Kishlak* – A rural settlement in Central Asia.

leaning their turquoise-encrusted staffs against the wall, occupied their spots on the silken pillows. Bowing their heads, burdened with enormous white turbans, they waited in silence for their sovereign. When he entered in a heavy gait, looking at no one, grim pensiveness stamped on his face, everyone rose and bowed almost to the ground. Thus they stood without rising until he gave them a brief signal with his hand. Then they got down on their knees, as required by palace custom, and leaned all the way back on their feet, touching the rugs with the fingers of their lowered hands. Everyone was trying to guess on whose head the emir's wrath would fall today, and what gain could be obtained from this.

The court poets gathered behind the emir's back in a semicircle, as usual, clearing their throats with quiet coughs. The most skillful among them, titled King of the Poets, recalled the verses he had composed earlier in the day and prepared to recite them before the emir, as if in a burst of supernatural inspiration.

The palace flyswatter and hookah-bearer took their assigned spots.

"Who is the ruler of Bukhara?" the emir began in a quiet voice, which made everyone shudder. "Who is the ruler of Bukhara, we ask you, us or him – that accursed blasphemer Hodja Nasreddin?!"

He choked for a moment and then, taking control of his rage, concluded menacingly:

"The emir is listening! Speak."

A horsehair fan was swaying over his head; the retinue was silent, gripped with fear. The viziers prodded each other with their elbows imperceptibly.

"He has stirred up the entire country!" the emir began once more. "Thrice already he has managed to disturb the peace in our capital! He has robbed us of peace and quiet, and our treasury of lawful profits! He openly calls the people to insurrection and mutiny! What should be done with such a criminal? We await answers."

The viziers, officials, and sages answered in a single voice:

"He undoubtedly deserves the most brutal execution, o focus of the universe and sanctuary of the world!"

"Then why is he still alive?" asked the emir. "Or perhaps we, your sovereign, whose very name you must pronounce with trepidation and awe, prostrated on the ground – which, by the way, you fail to do because of your laziness, insolence, and negligence – perhaps we should go to the bazaar and catch him ourselves, while you indulge in idle gluttony and perversion in your harems and recall your duties only on the day you receive your wages? What will you say to us, Bakhtiyar?"

Hearing Bakhtiyar's name, everyone else sighed in relief. A gloating smile appeared on the lips of Arslanbek, who had a long-running feud with Bakhtiyar. Folding his arms on his stomach, Bakhtiyar bowed down low before the emir.

"May Allah guard the great emir from all manner of troubles and misfortunes!" he began. "The loyalty and the merits of this lowly slave, who is but a speck of dust in the emir's rays of glory, are known to the emir. Until my appointment as grand vizier, the treasury was always empty. But I instituted many duties, introduced fees for appointments and offices, I taxed everything in Bukhara, and now a man may not so much as sneeze without paying something to the treasury. Moreover, I have cut in half the salaries of all minor officials, soldiers, and guards, leaving their care to the inhabitants of Bukhara, which has saved a substantial amount for the treasury, o sovereign. But I have more to say about my merits: through my efforts, I arranged for miracles to be performed once again near the tomb of the most holy Sheikh Bogaeddin, which has attracted many thousands of pilgrims to the tomb, while the treasury of our ruler, who makes all the other sovereigns of the world look like mere dust, was filled with donations every year, and the profits increased many fold…"

"Where are these profits?" the emir interrupted. "Hodja Nasreddin took them away from us. And we did not ask you about your merits – we have heard about them many times. Tell us instead: how do we catch Hodja Nasreddin?"

"O sovereign!" Bakhtiyar replied. "The capture of criminals is not one of the duties of the grand vizier. In our state, such matters are entrusted to the esteemed Arslanbek, head of the palace guard and the troops."

With these words he bowed low once more before the emir, glancing at Arslanbek with gloating triumph.

"Speak!" the emir commanded.

Arslanbek rose and cast a malicious glance at Bakhtiyar. He sighed deeply, and his black beard shifted on his belly.

"May Allah keep our sun-like ruler from troubles and woes, from illness and sadness! My merits are known to the emir. When the Khivian khan waged war on Bukhara, the emir, who is the focus of the universe and Allah's shadow on earth, deigned to place me in command of Bukharian troops. I arranged it so that we repelled the enemy victoriously and without bloodshed, and the entire affair ended to our benefit. Namely: by my order, all the towns and villages starting at the Khivian border and stretching deep into our land, over many days of travel, were reduced to ruins; the crops and gardens were wiped out, and the roads and bridges were destroyed. And when the Khivians entered our land and saw only desert, devoid of gardens or any life, they said to themselves: 'Let us not go to Bukhara, for there is nothing to eat there and nothing to plunder.' They turned around and left, ridiculed and profaned! And our ruler the emir deigned to acknowledge that the destruction of a country by its own troops is such a wise and useful deed that he ordered not to fix anything and leave the towns, settlements, fields, and roads in the same ruined state, so that foreign tribes would not dare enter our land in the future. This is how I defeated the Khivians. Moreover, I introduced many thousands of spies in Bukhara…"

"Silence, braggart!" the emir exclaimed. "So why have your spies still not caught Hodja Nasreddin?"

Arslanbek held an embarrassed silence for a long time and finally admitted:

"O sovereign, I used all sorts of techniques, but my mind is helpless before this villain and blasphemer. I believe, sovereign, that we should seek the counsel of the sages."

"By our ancestors, you should all be hanged on the city wall!" the emir exploded, and dealt an irritable, casual blow to his hookah-bearer, who happened to be near the regal hand at the moment. "Speak!" he commanded to the oldest sage, famous for his beard, which he could wrap twice around his waist like a belt.

The sage got up and, after pronouncing a prayer, ran his fingers along his famous beard. This he could not accomplish all at once, but only gradually, threading it through the fingers of his left hand with his right.

"May Allah extend the shining days of our sovereign eternally, for the benefit and joy of his people!" he began. "Since the afore-mentioned villain and rabble-rouser Hodja Nasreddin is neverthe-less a man, we can conclude that his body is arranged in the same way as all other men; in other words, it consists of two hundred forty bones and three hundred sixty veins which control the lungs, the liver, the heart, the spleen, and the bile. The sages instruct us that the most important of these is the heart vein, which serves as the source of all others, and this is an unimpeachable and holy truth, contrary to the heretical teachings of the impious Abu-Iz-khak, who dared make the false claim that the true foundation of a man's life is the lung vein. According to the books of the most wise Avicenna, the pious Muhammad-al-Rasul, the Greek healer Hippocrates, and also Averroes from Cordoba, for we use the fruit of their meditations to this day, and also according to the teachings of al-Kendi, al-Farabi, and Abubazer-ibn-Tufeil, I will say and dare affirm that Allah created Adam from four elements – water, earth, fire, and air – and made it such that the yellow bile have the quality of fire, which we see in actuality, for it is hot and dry, the black bile the quality of earth, for it is cold and dry, saliva the quality of water, for it is cold and wet, and blood the quality of air, for it is hot and wet. And if one were to deprive a man of any of these fluids contained within him, then the aforementioned man would inevitably die, leading me to conclude, o luminous sovereign, that the aforementioned blasphemer and rabble-rous-er Hodja Nasreddin should be deprived of blood, which is best done through the removal of his head from his body, for when the blood pours out of a man's body, life vanishes and does not return. This is my advice, o luminous ruler and sanctuary of the world!"

The emir listened to all this carefully, and, without a word, sig-naled the second sage with a barely noticeable movement of his eyebrows. Although the second sage could not match the first in the length of his beard, he exceeded the long-bearded sage immeasurably in the size and splendor of his turban, whose im-mense weight had caused his neck to become crooked over the long years, giving him the appearance of a man who was always peeking sideways through a crack in the door. Bowing to the emir, he said:

"O great ruler, whose brilliance rivals the sun itself! I cannot agree with this method of ridding us of Hodja Nasreddin, for it is known that not only blood is necessary to sustain a man's life, but also air, and if one were to squeeze a man's throat with a rope and thus block the passage of air to his lungs, the man would inevitably die and could never be resurrected…"

"Right!" the emir said in a quiet voice. "You are quite correct, o wisest of the wise, and your advice is undoubtedly precious to us! Indeed, how would we rid ourselves of Hodja Nasreddin if you did not give us such precious advice?"

He stopped, unable to control his anger and rage; his cheeks trembled, his nostrils flared, and thunderbolts flashed in his eyes. But the court flatterers – the philosophers and poets who were standing in a semicircle behind the emir's back – did not see the menacing face of their ruler and, taking these words to be sincere, decided that the sages really did distinguish themselves before the emir and would be elevated and lavished with favors. As a result, it was necessary to secure their goodwill at once, so as to derive benefit from it in the future.

"O wise sages, o pearls in the crown of our illustrious ruler, o wise sages whose wisdom exceeds wisdom itself, o those who are made wise by the wisdom of the wisest!"

Thus they praised, each trying to outdo the other in refinement and zeal, without noticing that the emir had turned, trembling with rage, and directed a piercing stare at them, while a sinister silence fell all around.

"O luminaries of knowledge and vessels of wisdom!" they continued, closing their eyes rapturously and shuddering in servile delight. But suddenly, the King of the Poets noticed the emir's stare and almost swallowed his flattering tongue – he stumbled backwards in terror, and the others fell silent in his wake and began to tremble, having understood their error, which originated from an excessive desire to praise.

"O cheats, o loafers!" the emir exclaimed in indignation. "As if we do not know that if we chop off a man's head or strangle him with a rope, he cannot be resurrected! But in order to do this, it is necessary to catch the man first, whereas you lazy cheats, loafers, and fools did not say a single word about how to catch him. All the viziers, officials, sages, and poets present here are to be deprived of wages until Hodja Nasreddin is caught. And we announce a reward of three thousand tanga to the one who catches him! And we also warn you that, having been assured of your laziness, denseness, and negligence, we have sent for a new sage from Baghdad to serve us, named Hussein Huslia, who had until now been serving my friend, the caliph of Baghdad. He is already on his way and will soon be here, and then woe betide you, o kneaders of mattresses, swallowers of food, and stuffers of your bottomless pockets!" he continued, growing more and more furious. "Away with them!" he shouted to the guards. "Kick them all out of here! Kick them out!"

The guards dashed towards the stunned courtiers, snatched them without any regard or respect, dragged them to the door, and tossed them down the stairs, where they were caught by other guards and helped along with smacks, punches, shoves, and kicks. The courtiers ran, overtaking each other; the white-haired sage got tangled in his own beard and fell, while the second sage stumbled on him and came crashing down headfirst into a thorny rose bush, where, shocked by the fall, he lay for a long time with his crooked neck, as if peeking through a crack in the door.

Chapter 19

The emir was grim and menacing all through the evening. The night passed, and the next morning, the fearful courtiers once again noticed the dark stamp of anger on his face.

All the efforts to distract and amuse him were in vain. The dancers who twisted before him in the smoke of fragrant incense, swaying their full hips, flashing their pearl teeth, and baring, as if by accident, their dark breasts, brought no result. Wasted were the gimmicks of the jesters, the acrobats, the magicians, and the Indian fakirs who could charm snakes with the song of their reed pipes.

The courtiers whispered among themselves:

"O accursed Hodja Nasreddin, o son of sin! What unpleasantness we have to suffer on his account!" They all directed hopeful gazes at Arslanbek. He gathered his most skillful spies in the guards' quarters, including the pockmarked spy who was so miraculously cured of paralysis by Hodja Nasreddin.

"Know this," said Arslanbek. "By the order of our illustrious emir, you are deprived of wages until the villainous Hodja Nasreddin is captured! And if you fail to track him down, then you will lose not only your wages but also your heads, this I promise. But, conversely, the one who spares no effort and captures Hodja Nasreddin will receive a reward of three thousand tanga and, on top of that, a promotion: he will be appointed head spy."

The spies immediately set off to work, dressed up as dervishes, beggars, water-bearers, and traders, while the pockmarked spy, whose cunning exceeded all the others, took a rug, beans, prayer beads, and ancient books, and headed to the section of the bazaar where the jewelry and the musk rows intersected, intending to pass off as a fortune teller and interrogate the women.

An hour later, hundreds of heralds appeared on the bazaar square, calling all Muslims to attention with their shouts. They pronounced the emir's firman[1]. Hodja Nasreddin was declared an

---

1 *Firman* – Royal decree (Persian).

enemy of the emir and a defiler of the faith. The people were forbidden to interact with him in any way, much less shelter him, which was punishable immediately by death. However, the one who delivered him into the hands of the emir's guards was promised a reward of three thousand tanga and other favors.

The chaikhana keepers, coppersmiths, blacksmiths, weavers, water-bearers, and camel drivers whispered to each other:

"The emir is going to have to wait a long time!"

"Our Hodja Nasreddin is not the sort that gets caught!"

"And the inhabitants of Noble Bukhara are not the sort to be enticed by money and betray their own Hodja Nasreddin!"

But the moneylender Jafar, who was conducting his usual rounds on the bazaar and tormenting his debtors, thought otherwise. "Three thousand tanga!" he lamented. "Yesterday, that money was almost in my pocket! Hodja Nasreddin will come to see the girl again, but I will not be able to capture him myself, and if I tell anyone, they will steal my reward! No, I will do otherwise!"

He headed to the palace.

He knocked for a long time. No one opened. The guards did not hear him: they were talking spiritedly, thinking of plans to capture Hodja Nasreddin.

"O brave warriors, have you fallen asleep?" the moneylender kept calling in a desperate voice as he knocked with the iron ring, but a lot of time passed before he heard footsteps and the clanging of the bolts – and then the gate opened.

After listening to the moneylender, Arslanbek shook his head:

"Esteemed Jafar, I would advise you not to see the emir today. He is grim and wrathful."

"I have just the means to cheer him up," the moneylender replied. "O esteemed Arslanbek, pillar of the throne and tamer of its enemies, this matter cannot be delayed. Tell the emir that I have come to lift his sorrow."

The emir met the moneylender gloomily:

"Speak, Jafar. But if your news does not cheer us up, you will receive two hundred cane blows on the spot."

"O great ruler, who obscures all the past, present, and future kings with his light," the moneylender said. "Your worthless slave has become aware that there is a girl living in our city that I can confidently say is the most beautiful of all beautiful girls."

The emir livened up and raised his head.

"O ruler!" the emboldened moneylender continued. "I have no words worthy of praising her beauty. She is tall, lovely, slender, and proportionate, with a glowing brow and rosy cheeks, with eyes reminiscent of the eyes of a gazelle, with eyebrows that are like the thin crescent of the moon! Her cheeks are like anemones, and her mouth like the seal of Solomon, and her lips like coral, and her teeth like pearl, and her breast like marble decorated with two cherries, and her shoulders…"

The emir interrupted his outburst of eloquence:

"If the girl is indeed as you describe, then she deserves to take a place in our harem. Who is she?"

"She is from a common and ignoble family, o ruler. This is the daughter of a potter, whose worthless name I dare not pronounce lest it insult the ruler's ears. I can point out her house, but will the faithful slave of the emir be rewarded for this?"

The emir nodded to Bakhtiyar, a purse fell to the moneylender's feet. The moneylender snatched it, his face altered by greed.

"If she turns out to be worthy of your praise, then you will receive another like this," said the emir.

"Our ruler's generosity be praised!" exclaimed the moneylender. "But let the ruler hurry, for I have discovered that this gazelle is being hunted!"

The emir's eyebrows moved together and a deep frown crossed the bridge of his nose:

"By who?"

"Hodja Nasreddin!" the moneylender replied.

"Again Hodja Nasreddin! Here, too, Hodja Nasreddin! He has time for everything, this Hodja Nasreddin, while you," – tipping the throne, the emir turned sharply to the viziers – "you are always late, you do nothing and inflict shame on our majesty. Hey, Arslanbek! Let this girl be delivered here, to the palace, immediately, and if you do not bring her, the executioner will be waiting for you as you return!"

No more than five minutes later, a large detachment of guards left the palace, their weapons clanging and their shields glinting in the sun. It was led by Arslanbek himself, who had attached a gold badge to his brocade robe to signify his power and authority.

On the side, limping and hobbling nefariously, walked the moneylender; he kept falling behind the guards and catching up to them in a jumping gait. The people stepped aside, following the moneylender with unkind gazes, trying to guess what new evil he had concocted.

Chapter 20

Hodja Nasreddin had just finished his ninth pot and, placing it in the sun, he picked up a large lump of clay from the tub to begin his next one, the tenth.

Suddenly, there was a loud and authoritative knock at the gate. The neighbors, who frequently stopped by Niyaz's house to borrow an onion or a pinch of spices, did not knock like this. Hodja Nasreddin and Niyaz exchanged worried glances, while the gate rang out again under a hail of heavy blows. This time, Hodja Nasreddin's ear caught the jingling of copper and iron. "Guards," he whispered to Niyaz. "Run," Niyaz replied. Hodja Nasreddin leaped over the fence, while Niyaz fussed with the gate for a long time to give Hodja Nasreddin a chance to escape. Finally, he undid the latch. Immediately, starlings dashed in all directions from the vineyard. But the old Niyaz had no wings, and he could not fly away. He grew pale and bent over in a bow before Arslanbek.

"Your house is blessed with a great honor," said Arslanbek. "The ruler of the faithful and Allah's deputy on earth, our master and lord – may his blessed years be extended – the great emir himself, has deigned to remember your unworthy name! He has learned that a beautiful rose grows in your garden, and he wishes to grace his palace with this rose. Where is your daughter?"

The potter's gray head began to shake, and his vision went dark. He could barely hear the brief, as if deathly, moan of his daughter as the guards dragged her from the house into the yard. The old man's legs buckled at the knees; he fell on the ground face down and no longer saw or heard anything.

"He has fainted from such great joy," Arslanbek explained to his guards. "Leave him alone, let him come to, and then he may come to the palace to pour out his boundless gratitude before the emir. Come."

Hodja Nasreddin had already managed to run around in a circle and emerge on the opposite side of the same street. He hid in the bushes. From there, he could see the gate of Niyaz's house, two guards by the gate, and a third man, who he soon recognized to be the moneylender Jafar. "Aha, you lame dog! So it was you who brought the guards to seize me!" he thought, still not guessing the truth. "Very well, look for me! You'll have to leave with empty hands!"

No! They did not leave with empty hands! Chilled with horror, Hodja Nasreddin watched them lead his beloved out of the gate. She tried to free herself and shouted in a broken voice, but the guards held her firmly, surrounding her with a double ring of shields.

It was noon in July – it was very hot, but Hodja Nasreddin was shivering, and meanwhile the guards were approaching, and the road led right past the bushes where Hodja Nasreddin was hiding. His mind clouded. He pulled a curved knife from its sheath and dropped to the ground. Arslanbek was walking in front, his gilded badge shining, and the knife would have first plunged right into his fat neck, under the beard. But then someone's heavy arm landed on Hodja Nasreddin's shoulder and pressed him to the ground. He shuddered, shrank back and raised the arm with the knife – and then lowered it when he saw the familiar, sooty face of Yusuf the blacksmith.

"Stay down!" the blacksmith whispered. "Stay down and do not move. You are mad: they are twenty men, all armed, and you are alone and unarmed; you will die yourself and not save her; stay down, I say!"

He kept pressing Hodja Nasreddin to the ground until the detachment of guards escorting Guljan had vanished around the turn.

"Why, why did you stop me?" Hodja Nasreddin exclaimed. "Would it not have been better for me to lie here dead?"

"The hand against the lion and the fist against the sword are not the province of sensible men," the blacksmith replied sternly. "I followed these guards all the way from the bazaar and got here in time to prevent your reckless deed. You must not die for her, but fight and save her, which is more honorable, though far more difficult. Do not waste time on grief, go forth and act. They have swords, shields, and spears, but Allah has furnished you with powerful weapons – a sharp mind and cunning that no one else can match."

Thus he spoke; his words were courageous and firm, like the iron that he had forged all his life. These words strengthened Hodja Nasreddin's trembling heart, just like the iron.

"Thank you, blacksmith!" he said. "I have not yet endured moments more difficult than these, but it does not befit me to despair. I am leaving, blacksmith, and I promise you that I will use my weapons valiantly!"

He stepped from the bushes onto the road. At the same moment, the gate of the nearest house opened to reveal the moneylender, who had stayed behind to remind one of the potters about his debt.

They met face to face. Growing pale, the moneylender whisked back in, shut the door, and closed the bolt.

"Woe betide you, Jafar, o viper's spawn!" said Hodja Nasreddin. "I saw everything, I heard everything, I know everything!"

There was a moment of silence, and then the moneylender's voice replied:

"The jackal did not get the cherry. But neither did the falcon. The lion got the cherry!"

"We'll see about that!" said Hodja Nasreddin. "But you, Jafar, mark my words: I pulled you out of the water, but I swear that I will drown you in that very same pond: the mud will envelop your filthy body, the weeds will choke you!"

Without waiting for a response, he pressed on. He walked past Niyaz's house, fearing that the moneylender would see him and snitch on the old man; turning a corner and making sure that no one was watching, Hodja Nasreddin ran quickly through an empty lot overgrown with weeds and returned to Niyaz's house by jumping a fence.

The old man was lying face down on the ground. The small pile of silver left by Arslanbek was sparkling dimly nearby. The old man raised his face, covered in tears and dust, towards Hodja Nasreddin; his lips twisted, and he wanted to say something but could not get it out, and when his gaze landed on a handkerchief dropped by his daughter, he began to beat his gray head against the hard ground and tear his beard.

Hodja Nasreddin had to fuss with him for quite some time. Finally, he managed to sit him down on a bench.

"Listen, old man!" he said. "You are not alone in your grief. Do you know that I loved her, and that she loved me also? And do you know that we had decided to get married, and that I was only waiting for an opportunity to obtain a large sum of money and pay you a rich dowry?"

"Why would I need a dowry?" the old man replied, weeping. "Would I ever dare contradict my little dove in anything? But it's too late to talk about it, everything is lost, she is in the harem and tonight the emir will have her!... O woe, o shame!" he cried. "I will go to the palace and fall to his feet, I will beg, wail, and scream, and if only the heart in his chest is not made of stone..."

Swaying, he walked towards the gate on unsteady feet.

"Stop!" said Hodja Nasreddin. "You forgot that emirs are built very differently from other people: they don't have hearts at all, and it is useless to plead with them. You can only take something away from them by force, and I, Hodja Nasreddin – can you hear me, old man? – I will take Guljan from him!"

"He is strong, he has thousands of soldiers, thousands of guards, and thousands of spies! What can you do against him?"

"I do not yet know what I will do. But I do know one thing: he will not visit her tonight! And he will not visit her tomorrow. And he will not visit her the next day! He will never visit her, he will never have her, and this is as true as the fact that everyone from Bukhara to Baghdad calls me Hodja Nasreddin! Restrain your tears, old man, stop wailing right over my ear, and let me think!"

Hodja Nasreddin did not think for long:

"Old man, where do you keep the clothing of your deceased wife?"

"It is in that chest over there." Hodja Nasreddin took the key, entered the house, and soon emerged dressed as a woman. His face was concealed by a veil made of a dense weave of black horsehair:

"Wait for me, old man, and do not try anything yourself."

He led his donkey from the shed, saddled him up, and left Niyaz's house for a long time.

Chapter 21

Before taking Guljan to the palace garden to see the emir, Arslanbek called the old hags from the harem and commanded them to prepare Guljan so that the emir's gaze would be pleased to contemplate her perfection. The hags immediately set about their customary work: they washed Guljan's tear-stained face with warm water, dressed her in light silk, put surma on her eyebrows and rouge on her cheeks, poured rose oil on her hair, and painted her nails red. Then they summoned His Great Chasteness, the head eunuch, from the harem – a man once known to all of Bukhara for his debauchery, he had been called into the emir's service as a result of his knowledge and experience, castrated by the palace physician, and placed on one of the highest posts in the country. He was responsible for tirelessly watching the emir's one hundred and sixty concubines, so that they would always have an enticing look and be able to arouse passion in the emir. This post became more difficult every year, because the emir became more and more satiated, while his strength diminished. And in the mornings, the head eunuch would not infrequently receive ten lashes from his ruler instead of a reward, which, however, was not that great a punishment for the eunuch. As he prepared the beautiful concubines for their meetings with the emir, he experienced torments far more horrible and quite comparable to those awaiting hell-bound sinners, who are condemned to be surrounded by nude houri while bound to posts with iron chains.

When the head eunuch saw Guljan, he took a step back, stunned by her beauty.

"She is truly magnificent!" he exclaimed in a high-pitched voice. "Lead her to the emir, get her out of my sight!" He hurried away, bashing his head against the walls, grinding his teeth, and exclaiming:

"O, how hard is my life, how bitter!"

"This is a good sign," said the hags. "It means our sovereign will be pleased."

The poor, silent Guljan was led to the palace garden.

The emir got up, approached her, and lifted her veil.

All the viziers, officials, and sages covered their eyes with the sleeves of their robes.

The emir could not take his eyes off her beautiful face for a long time.

"The moneylender did not lie to us!" he said loudly. "Triple the reward he was promised." Guljan was led away. The emir cheered up considerably.

"He is pleased, he has cheered up! The nightingale of his heart has taken to the roses of her face!" the courtiers whispered. "Tomorrow morning, he will be happier still! Allah be praised, the storm has passed over our heads without striking us with either thunder or lightning."

The court poets, gaining courage, stepped forward and began to praise the emir, comparing his face, in verse, to the full moon, his body to the slender cypress, and his reign to the moonlight. The King of the Poets finally found an opportunity to recite, as if in a burst of inspiration, the verses that had been hanging on the tip of his tongue since the previous morning.

The emir tossed him a handful of small coins. And the King of the Poets went crawling on the rugs to gather them, remembering first to press his lips to the emir's slipper.

Laughing graciously, the emir said:

"We have also thought of some verses just now: When we walked into the garden in the evening, The moon, ashamed of its wretchedness, hid in the clouds, And the birds fell silent, and the wind grew quiet, While we stood there – great, glorious, invincible, sun-like, and mighty…"

All the poets fell to their knees, shouting: "O greatness! He has eclipsed Rudaki himself!" while some fell face down on the rugs, as if they had fainted.

The dancers entered the room, followed by the jesters, the magicians, and the fakirs, and the emir rewarded them all generously.

"I only regret," he said, "that I cannot give orders to the sun, or else I would have commanded it to set more quickly today."

The courtiers responded with subservient laughter.

Chapter 22

The bazaar hummed and buzzed, it was the peak hour of trade, and people were selling, buying, and bartering as the sun rose higher and higher, chasing everyone into the thick, pungent shade of the covered rows. The sheer rays of the midday sun fell through the round windows in the reed roofs, appearing as smoky, dusty pillars, their brilliance causing the brocade to shine, the silk to glimmer, and the velvet to light up with a soft, mysterious flame. Turbans, robes, and dyed beards flickered everywhere. Polished copper blinded the eyes, only to be challenged and defeated by the purest glitter of noble gold strewn on leather mats in front of the moneychangers.

Hodja Nasreddin stopped his donkey by the same chaikhana where he had addressed the people of Bukhara a month ago with a request to save Niyaz the potter from the emir's favors. Not a lot of time had passed since then, but Hodja Nasreddin had already managed to become good friends with the round-bellied chaikhana keeper Ali, a straightforward and honest man who could be trusted.

After waiting for a quiet moment, Hodja Nasreddin called out: "Ali!"

The chaikhana keeper turned around, his face expressing confusion: the voice calling him belonged to a man, while in front of him he saw a woman.

"It's me, Ali!" Hodja Nasreddin said, without raising his veil. "Do you recognize me? For Allah's sake, do not stare – have you forgotten about the spies?"

Glancing round, Ali led him to a dark back room, where he kept his firewood and spare kettles. It was cool and damp here, the noise of the bazaar was muffled.

"Take my donkey, Ali," Hodja Nasreddin said. "Feed him and keep him ready always! I may need him at any minute. And do not speak a word about me to anyone."

"But why are you dressed up as a woman, Hodja Nasreddin?"

the chaikhana keeper asked, shutting the door tightly. "Where are you headed?"

"I am going to the palace."

"You have gone mad!" the chaikhana keeper exclaimed. "You wish to put your head right into the tiger's mouth!"

"I have to, Ali. You will soon find out why. Let us say goodbye just in case – I am going on dangerous business."

They hugged firmly, and tears appeared on the kind chaikhana keeper's face and began to roll down his round, red cheeks. He saw Hodja Nasreddin out and, suppressing the heavy sighs that perturbed his belly, went to attend to his guests.

Worry clawed at the chaikhana keeper's heart; he was sad and absentminded; guests had to jingle the lids of their kettles two or three times, reminding him of their unsatiated thirst. In his heart, the chaikhana keeper was by the palace, next to his tireless friend.

The guards did not let Hodja Nasreddin inside.

"I have brought incomparable ambergris, musk, rose oil!" Hodja Nasreddin spoke, altering his voice skillfully to sound like a woman. "Let me through to the harem, valiant warriors, I will sell my wares and share the profit with you."

"Get out of here woman, sell them somewhere on the bazaar," the guards replied rudely.

After his efforts met with failure, Hodja Nasreddin grew pensive and grim. He was running out of time, the sun had already crossed the midday point… Hodja Nasreddin walked around the palace wall. The stones lay firmly, welded together by a special Chinese slurry, and Hodja Nasreddin could not find a single hole or crack in the wall, while the exit points of the aryks were protected with closely spaced cast iron bars.

"I must get into the palace," Hodja Nasreddin said to himself. "Such is my unyielding purpose, and I will achieve it! If the emir has stolen my bride by some divine predestination, why can't there be some predestination for me to get into the palace and get her back? I can even feel somewhere deep in my soul that such a predestination exists!"

He went to the bazaar. He believed that if a man's will is unyielding and his courage inexhaustible, destiny will always come to his aid. Among thousands of meetings, conversations, and encounters, there will always be one meeting, one encounter that will inevitably conspire to create a favorable opportunity a skillful man can use to overturn all the obstacles between him and his goal, thus fulfilling the predestination. Such an opportunity awaited Hodja Nasreddin somewhere in the bazaar. He believed this adamantly and went to look for it.

Nothing escaped Hodja Nasreddin's attention: not a single word, not a single face in the noisy crowd of many thousands. His mind, hearing, and eyesight had sharpened and reached the sort of state where a man can easily transcend the boundaries imposed on him by nature and thus achieve victory, since his opponents meanwhile remain bound by their regular human limitations.

At the intersection of the jewelry and perfume rows, Hodja Nasreddin heard someone's sneaky voice through the hum and din of the crowd:

"You say your husband no longer loves you and refuses to share his bed with you. Your problem can be solved. But for this, I must consult Hodja Nasreddin. You have heard, of course, that he is in our city; find out where he is hiding, tell me, and then we will bring back your husband."

Approaching, Hodja Nasreddin saw the pockmarked spy telling fortunes. A woman was standing before him, holding a silver coin. Having strewn beans onto his rug, the fortune teller was leafing through an ancient book.

"If you do not find Hodja Nasreddin," he was saying, "then woe betide you, o woman, for your husband will leave you forever!"

Hodja Nasreddin decided to teach the fortune teller a lesson – he squatted in front of his rug:

"Tell my fortune, o wise foreseer of other people's fates." The fortune teller tossed his beans.

"O woman!" he exclaimed, as if struck by horror. "Woe betide you, woman! Death has already raised its black hand over your head."

Several curious onlookers had already gathered round.

"I could have helped you to ward off its blow, but I am helpless to do this alone," the fortune teller continued. "I must consult

Hodja Nasreddin. If you could find out where he is hiding and tell me, your life would be saved."

"Very well. I will bring Hodja Nasreddin to you."

"You will bring him!" The fortune teller gave a happy start. "But when?"

"I can bring him right now if you want. He is very close."

"Where is he?"

"Here. Two steps away."

The fortune teller's eyes lit up with a greedy fire.

"I do not see him."

"But you are a fortune teller. Surely you could have guessed? Here he is!"

The woman opened her veil with a brisk motion, and the fortune teller jumped back in amazement when he saw Hodja Nasreddin's face.

"Here he is!" Hodja Nasreddin repeated. "What did you wish to ask him? You are lying, you are no fortune teller, you are a spy of the emir! Do not believe him, Muslims, he is cheating you! He is here to find Hodja Nasreddin!"

The fortune teller looked around, his eyes darting, but did not see a single guard nearby. With tears in his eyes and his teeth gnashing, he let Hodja Nasreddin escape. The crowd around him rumbled menacingly.

"Emir's spy! Filthy dog!" came from all directions.

The fortune teller rolled up his rug with trembling hands and dashed to the palace as fast as he could.

Chapter 23

The guards' quarters were dirty, dusty, smelly, and smoky. The guards were sitting on a worn mat, which was a breeding ground for fleas, and fantasizing about catching Hodja Nasreddin as they scratched themselves.

"Three thousand tanga!" they said. "Just imagine: three thousand tanga and the post of head spy!"

"And to think that someone is going to collect this fortune!"

"Ah, if only it were me!" sighed a lazy, fat guard, who was dumber than everyone else and remained in the emir's service only because he had learned to swallow raw eggs whole without breaking the shell, which he sometimes used to entertain the luminous emir and obtain small handouts, although this later caused him horrible pain.

The pockmarked spy burst into the guards' quarters like a whirlwind:

"He is here! Hodja Nasreddin is in the bazaar! He is dressed as a woman!"

Grabbing their weapons as they ran, the guards dashed to the gate.

The pockmarked spy ran after them, screaming:

"The reward is mine! Do you hear? I saw him first! The reward is mine!"

Seeing the guards, the people scattered. A jam ensued. Panic seized the bazaar. The guards plunged into the crowd at full speed, and the most zealous of them, who ran in front, grabbed some woman and tore off her veil, revealing her face to all.

The woman screamed piercingly, and an equally piercing woman's scream responded from afar. Then a third woman began to scream, trying to free herself from the hands of the guards, a fourth, a fifth… In a minute, the entire bazaar was filled with women's screams, wails, shouts, and weeping.

The crowd froze, dumbfounded and stunned. Never before had such sacrilege taken place in Bukhara. Many grew pale, others grew purple: not a single heart was calm at that moment. The guards continued to run wild, seizing women, shoving, throwing, beating, tearing off clothes.

"Save us! Save us!" cried the women.

The voice of Yusuf the blacksmith rose menacingly above the crowd:

"Muslims! What are you staring at? It is not enough that they rob us blind, but now they also dishonor our wives in broad daylight!"

"Save us!" cried the women. "Save us!"

The crowd began to hum and stir. Some water-bearer heard the voice of his wife and dashed towards her. The guards pushed him away, but two weavers and three coppersmiths came to his aid and pushed the guards back. A fight broke out.

It grew rapidly. The guards brandished their swords as they were showered from all sides with pots, trays, pitchers, kettles, horseshoes, and firewood, and they could not dodge it all. The fight spread through the entire bazaar.

Meanwhile, the emir was enjoying a peaceful nap in his palace.

Suddenly, he jumped up, ran to the window, opened it, and shut it again in horror.

Bakhtiyar came running, pale and with trembling lips.

"What's this?" the emir muttered. "What's going on in the square? Where are the cannons? Where is Arslanbek?" Arslanbek ran in and fell face down on the floor:

"Have me beheaded, my ruler!"

"What is this?! What's going on in the square?!" Arslanbek responded without rising:

"O ruler, sun-like and eclipsing…"

"Enough!" the emir stomped his foot in rage. "Save that for later! What's going on in the square?"

"Hodja Nasreddin!… He dressed up as a woman. It's all because of him, because of Hodja Nasreddin! Order my head to be cut off, my ruler!"

But the emir had other things to worry about!

Chapter 24

That day, Hodja Nasreddin valued every minute of his time. As a result, he did not dally and, after breaking the jaw of one guard, crushing the teeth of another, and flattening the nose of a third, he returned safely to the chaikhana of his friend Ali. Here he took off his woman's dress in the back room, placed a colorful Badakhshan turban on his head, put on a fake beard, and sat in the highest spot of the chaikhana, where it was easiest to see everything.

Pressed by people on all sides, the guards fought back fiercely. A tussle ensued right near the chaikhana, by Hodja Nasreddin's feet. He could not resist and poured out the contents of his kettle onto a guard, accomplishing this so deftly that the scalding water went right down the neck of the lazy and fat swallower of raw eggs. The guard howled and fell on his back, flailing his arms and legs. Without even glancing at him, Hodja Nasreddin immersed himself back in thought.

He heard a cracking, elderly voice:

"Let me through! Let me through! In the name of Allah, what's going on here?"

Not far from the chaikhana, right in the thick of the fighting, a hook-nosed, white-bearded old man was towering atop his camel. His look and dress showed him to be an Arab, while the end of his turban was rolled up, signifying his learnedness. Scared out of his wits, he was clinging to the hump of his camel as the battle boiled around him. Someone grabbed hold of the old man's leg and would not let go, even though the old man was jerking it fiercely and trying to free himself. Shouts, hoarse cries, and savage howls came from all around.

In search of a safe place, the old man somehow made it to the chaikhana. Looking round and shuddering, he tied his camel by the leg next to Hodja Nasreddin's donkey and stepped onto the platform.

"For Allah's sake, what is going on here in Bukhara?"

"The bazaar," Hodja Nasreddin replied curtly.

"Is the bazaar always like this in Bukhara? How will I make it to the palace through all this fighting?"

As soon as he said the word 'palace,' Hodja Nasreddin realized immediately that his meeting with the old man was that very encounter, that very chance that could enable him to carry out his plan: penetrate the emir's harem and free Guljan.

But haste, as it is known, stems from the devil, and moreover anyone can recall the verses of the most wise Sheikh Saadi of Shiraz: "Only the patient man will complete his task, the hasty one will fall." Hodja Nasreddin rolled up the carpet of impatience and placed it in the coffer of waiting.

"O almighty Allah, o shelter of the faithful," the old man sighed and moaned. "How will I get to the palace now?"

"Wait here until tomorrow," Hodja Nasreddin replied.

"I cannot!" the old man exclaimed. "I am expected in the palace!"

Hodja Nasreddin laughed:

"O esteemed and white-haired old sage, I do not know your rank or your business, but why do you think that they cannot live without you in the palace, even for a day? Many respectable people in Bukhara wait for weeks to get into the palace; why do you think you deserve an exception?"

"Let it be known to you," the old man said with dignity, somewhat wounded by Hodja Nasreddin's words, "that I am a famous sage, astrologer, and healer who has come here from none other than Baghdad, at the emir's request, in order to serve him and aid him in governing the country."

"O!" Hodja Nasreddin replied, bowing respectfully. "Greetings to you, wise old sage. I have been to Baghdad before, and I know the sages there. Tell me your name."

"If you have been to Baghdad, then you have surely heard of me and of my services to the caliph, whose favorite son I saved from death, which was announced throughout the land. Hussein Huslia is my name."

"Hussein Huslia!" Hodja Nasreddin exclaimed. "Are you really Hussein Huslia himself?"

The old man could not conceal a smile, quite pleased by the fact that his fame had spread so far beyond his native Baghdad.

"Why are you surprised?" the old man continued. "Yes, I am the famous Hussein Huslia himself, a great sage that no one can match in wisdom, or the art of reading the stars, or the art of curing illnesses. But I am completely free of pride and smugness – look how easily I can speak to someone as lowly as you."

The old man took a pillow and leaned on it, preparing to extend his condescension to his companion even further and speak in detail about his great wisdom – hoping that the companion, driven by vanity, would start telling on every corner how he met the famous sage Hussein Huslia, extolling the sage's wisdom and even exaggerating it in order to inspire more respect for the sage, and consequently for himself, among his listeners – for this is exactly how people act when they have garnered the attention of highly placed persons. "And this will serve to increase and strengthen my fame among the common folk," Hussein Huslia thought, "which cannot hurt; the talk among the people will reach the emir himself through spies and eavesdroppers, and confirm my wisdom to him, for confirmation from a third party is, undoubtedly, the best kind of confirmation, and through all this I will obtain benefit for myself."

In order to completely convince his companion in his incredible learnedness, the sage began to tell him about constellations and their locations, referring at every opportunity to great sages of antiquity.

Hodja Nasreddin listened carefully, trying to remember every word.

"No," he said at last. "I still cannot believe it! Are you really that same Hussein Huslia?"

"Of course!" the old man exclaimed. "What is so surprising about it?"

Hodja Nasreddin moved away warily. Then he exclaimed with alarm and compassion in his voice:

"O wretch! Your head is lost!" The old man choked and dropped his cup. It was like a game of chess, where, incidentally, few could rival Hodja Nasreddin.

All the pomp and haughtiness evaporated from the old man in an instant.

"How? What? Why?" he asked fearfully. Hodja Nasreddin pointed at the square, where the battle had not yet quieted down:

"Don't you know that all this confusion is because of you?! The illustrious emir has heard that, upon leaving Baghdad, you swore publicly to penetrate the emir's harem – o, woe betide you, Hussein Huslia! – and dishonor the emir's wives!"

The sage's mouth fell open, his eyes turned white, and he began to hiccup repeatedly in fear…

"Me?" he muttered. "Me – the harem?"

"You swore this by the foundation of Allah's throne. The heralds announced it today. And our emir ordered to seize you as soon as you entered the city, and immediately have you beheaded."

The sage moaned in exhaustion. He could not understand which of his enemies had managed to deal him this blow; the rest he did not doubt, for, during courtly skirmishes, he frequently crushed his enemies in similar ways and then admired their heads contentedly as they hung on posts.

"And so, today," Hodja Nasreddin continued, "spies informed the emir that you had arrived, and he ordered the guards to seize you. The guards dashed to the bazaar and began to search for you everywhere, rummaging through shops, and trade was disrupted, and the peace was disturbed. By mistake, the guards seized a man who looked like you, and hastily removed his head, while he turned out to be a mullah well known for his piety and virtue. The worshippers from his mosque were incensed – and now look what is going on in Bukhara thanks to you!"

"O woe to me!" the sage exclaimed in horror and despair.

He began to clamor, moan, and complain bitterly, leading Hodja Nasreddin to conclude that the ploy had been a complete success.

In the meantime, the fight moved on towards the palace gates, where the beaten and mangled guards were retreating, having lost their weapons. The bazaar continued to rumble in agitation, but less loudly than before.

"To Baghdad!" the sage exclaimed, moaning. "Back to Baghdad!"

"But you will be seized at the city gates!" Hodja Nasreddin objected.

"O woe! O great misfortune! Allah knows that I am innocent; I have never given such a bold, such an impious oath to anyone! My enemies have slandered me to the emir! Help me, good Muslim!"

This was exactly what Hodja Nasreddin wanted, for he did not wish to arouse suspicion by offering his aid first.

"Help?" he asked. "How can I help you, even if we forget that I, as a faithful and devoted slave of my ruler, should hand you over to the guards without delay?"

Hiccuping and trembling, the sage directed a pleading gaze at Hodja Nasreddin.

"But you say that you were slandered unjustly," Hodja Nasreddin hastened to calm him down. "I believe you, for your age is so great that you have no business being in a harem."

"True!" the old man exclaimed. "But is there a way to save me?"

"There is," Hodja Nasreddin replied and then led the old man to the dark back room of the chaikhana, where he handed him a bundle of women's clothing. "I happened to buy this today for my wife, and, if you like, I can trade these clothes for your robe and turban. Under a woman's veil, you will be able to escape the spies and the guards."

The old man grabbed the women's clothing with declarations of delight and gratitude, and put it on. Hodja Nasreddin dressed himself in the sage's white robe and put on the turban with the rolled-up end, as well as the sage's broad belt with images of stars. The old man offered to trade his camel for the donkey as well, but Hodja Nasreddin did not wish to part with his faithful friend.

Hodja Nasreddin helped the old man climb onto the camel.

"May Allah protect you, o sage! Just don't forget that you will have to speak in a high voice to everyone, like a woman."

The old man set off on the camel at a brisk trot. Hodja Nasreddin's eyes were shining. The road to the palace was open!

Chapter 25

After making sure that the fight in the square was quieting down, the luminous emir decided to go to the courtiers in the grand hall. He composed a sorrowful but calm expression on his face, so that none of the courtiers would dare think that fear can penetrate the regal heart of the emir.

He walked out, and the courtiers froze, trembling at the thought that the emir might guess from their eyes and faces that they knew his true feelings.

The emir was silent, and the courtiers were silent; a menacing silence loomed.

Finally, the emir broke it:

"What will you say to us and how will you advise us? It is not the first time that we have asked you this!"

No one raised his head, no one replied. A fleeting thunderbolt flashed in the emir's face. And no one knows how many heads, crowned with turbans and framed by gray beards, would have lain on the block that day, and how many flattering tongues, bitten all the way through in deathly throes, would have fallen silent forever, sticking out between blue lips, as if taunting the living and reminding them of the utter fragility of their well-being, of the futility and vanity of all their endeavors, troubles, and hopes!

But all the heads remained on their shoulders, and all the tongues remained ready to perform the deed of flattery, because the palace overseer entered the hall and announced:

"Praise to the center of the universe! An unknown man has arrived at the gates, calling himself Hussein Huslia, a sage from Baghdad. He declared that he is here on important business and must immediately appear before the radiant gaze of the sovereign."

"Hussein Huslia!" the emir exclaimed, livening up. "Let him in! Summon him here!"

The sage did not walk, but ran inside, without even taking off his dusty shoes, and prostrated himself before the throne.

"Greetings to the great and glorious emir, the sun and the moon of the universe, its menace and its blessing! I rushed here night and day to warn the emir of a terrible danger. Let the emir say whether he visited a woman today. Let the emir answer his most worthless slave, I implore the sovereign!…"

"A woman?" the emir asked, confused. "Today? No… We were going to, but we did not yet do so."

The sage rose. His face was pale. He had been waiting for this response in great agitation. A long, deep sigh unburdened his chest, and color began to return slowly to his cheeks.

"Praise the almighty Allah!" he exclaimed. "Allah did not permit the light of wisdom and mercy to be extinguished! Be it known to the great emir that, last night, the planets and the stars had arranged themselves quite unfavorably for him. And I, unworthy and deserving only to kiss the dust in the emir's footsteps, studied and calculated the arrangement of the planets and found out that, until they enter a favorable and auspicious arrangement, the emir must not touch a woman, or else his doom is inevitable! Praise Allah that I got here in time!"

"Wait, Hussein Huslia," the emir interrupted. "You are not making any sense…"

"Praise Allah that I got here in time!" the sage kept exclaiming (it was, of course, Hodja Nasreddin). "Now I will take pride until the end of my days that I prevented the emir from touching a woman and did not permit the universe to be orphaned."

He spoke with such happiness and passion that the emir could not help but believe him:

"When I, a lowly gnat, was bathed in the rays of greatness emanating from the emir, who deigned to remember my unworthy name and commanded me to enter his service in Bukhara, I was immersed in a sweet sea of unprecedented joy. And, of course, I carried out this order without delay and departed immediately, spending only a few days to compile the emir's horoscope, so that, during my journey, I could already serve him by tracking the motion of the planets and stars that can influence his fate. And then, last night, as I glanced at the sky, I saw that the stars were arranged in a most terrible and sinister fashion for the emir, namely: the star Al-Kalb, signifying a stinger, was standing opposite the star

Al-Shual, which signifies the heart; moreover, I saw the three stars Al-Gafr, which signify the veil of a woman, two stars Al-Iklil, signifying the crown, and two stars Al-Sharatan, signifying horns. This was on Tuesday, the day of the planet Mars, and this day, contrary to Thursday, indicates the deaths of great men and is quite unfavorable for emirs. Juxtaposing all these signs, I, a lowly astrologer, understood that the stinger of death would threaten the heart of the one who wears the crown should he touch the veil of a woman, and in order to warn the wearer of the crown, I hurried night and day, drove two camels to death, and entered Bukhara on foot."

"O almighty Allah!" spoke the shocked emir. "Were we really in such terrible danger? Perhaps you are simply mistaken, Hussein Huslia?"

"Mistaken?" the sage exclaimed. "Let it be known to the emir that I have no equal anywhere from Baghdad to Bukhara in wisdom, or in the ability to read stars or cure illnesses! I could not be mistaken. Let the master and the heart of the universe, the great emir, ask his sages whether I named the stars accurately and whether I interpreted their arrangement in the horoscope correctly."

Obeying the emir's sign, the sage with the crooked neck stepped forward:

"My incomparable partner in wisdom, Hussein Huslia, has named the stars correctly, proving his knowledge, which none may dare doubt. But," the sage continued, and Hodja Nasreddin sensed guile in his voice, "why did the most wise Hussein Huslia not name to the great emir the sixteenth position of the moon and the constellations which correspond to this position? For without these designations, it would be baseless to claim that Tuesday – the day of the planet Mars – indicates the deaths of great men, including those who wear the crown, for the planet Mars has its house in one constellation, its ascendant in another, its descendant in a third, and its waning in a fourth, and as a result the planet Mars has four different indications rather than just one, as stated by the most esteemed and wise Hussein Huslia."

The sage fell silent, a snakelike smile playing on his lips; the courtiers whispered approvingly, happy to see the newcomer disgraced. Protecting their income and high posts, they tried not to let any outsider into the palace and saw a dangerous opponent in any new man.

But when Hodja Nasreddin started something, he never gave up. Moreover, he could see right through the sage, and the courtiers, and the emir himself. Without a hint of embarrassment, he replied condescendingly:

"Perhaps my esteemed and wise partner exceeds me incomparably in some other sphere of knowledge, but when it comes to stars, his words reveal a complete lack of familiarity with the teachings of the wisest of all wise sages, Ibn-Badjj, who states that the planet Mars, which has its house in the constellations of Ram and Scorpio, its ascendant in the constellation of Capricorn, its descendant in the constellation of Cancer, and its waning in the constellation of Libra, nevertheless corresponds only to the day of Tuesday, where it exerts its influence, so harmful to those who wear the crown."

As he replied, Hodja Nasreddin did not have the slightest fear that his ignorance would be exposed, for he knew that such arguments were always won by the one whose tongue was hung best, and, in this area, few compared to Hodja Nasreddin.

He stood waiting for the sage's objections and preparing a worthy reply. But the sage did not accept his challenge. He remained silent. Although he strongly suspected Hodja Nasreddin of fraud and ignorance, suspicion is not the same as certainty, and mistakes can be made, whereas the sage knew of his own extreme ignorance with utter certainty and did not dare argue. As a result, his attempt to disgrace the newcomer caused the reverse. The courtiers hissed at the sage, and he signaled with his eyes that the opponent was too dangerous to challenge in the open.

None of this escaped Hodja Nasreddin's attention, of course. "Just you wait!" he thought. "I'll show all of you!"

The emir sank into deep thought. No one moved a muscle, afraid to disturb him.

"If you have named and designated all the stars correctly, Hussein Huslia," the emir said, "then your interpretation is indeed valid. We only cannot understand why the two stars Al-Sharatan, signifying horns, ended up in our horoscope. You have truly arrived in time, Hussein Huslia! Just this morning, a girl was brought into our harem, and we were going to…"

Hodja Nasreddin threw up his arms in mock terror.

"Banish her from your thoughts, luminous emir, banish her!" he cried, as if forgetting that the emir could not be addressed directly, but only indirectly, in third person. He decided that this breach of rules, which was seemingly caused by extreme emotional upheaval stemming from devotion to the emir and fear for the emir's life, would not only be overlooked, but, on the contrary, it would convey the sincerity of his feelings and elevate him further in the eyes of the emir.

He was so passionate as he begged and pleaded with the emir not to touch the girl, so that he, Hussein Huslia, would not have to spill rivers of tears and put on the black robes of mourning, that the emir was touched.

"Calm down, calm down, Hussein Huslia. We are not our people's enemy, to leave them orphaned and drowning in sorrow. We promise you that, out of concern for our precious life, we will not go to this girl or even into the harem until the stars change their arrangement, which you will then relate to us. Come closer."

With these words, he signaled his hookah-bearer, and then personally handed the golden mouthpiece to the new sage, which was a great honor and favor. Bending his knees and lowering his eyes, the sage accepted the emir's favor, and his entire body shuddered ("From delight!" thought the courtiers, consumed by malicious envy).

"We declare our favor and grace to the sage Hussein Huslia," said the emir, "and appoint him the head sage of our country, because his learnedness, wisdom, and also his great devotion to us are worthy of all manner of imitation."

The court chronicler, whose responsibility consisted of describing, in expressions of praise, all the deeds and words of the emir, so that his greatness would not wane in coming centuries (which was a source of great concern for the emir), began to scribble with his reed pen.

"But to you," the emir continued, turning to the courtiers, "we, on the contrary, declare our displeasure, for your ruler, in addition to all the troubles caused by Hodja Nasreddin, was also in danger of death, and yet you did not lift a finger! Look at them, Hussein Huslia, look at these dunces, look at their snouts, which quite resemble those of asses! Truly, no other sovereign has ever had to deal with such stupid and negligent viziers!"

"The illustrious emir is completely right," Hodja Nasreddin said, looking over the silent courtiers, as if taking aim for his first blow. "I can see that the faces of these people do not bear the stamp of wisdom!"

"Exactly, exactly!" the emir approved. "That's exactly right – do not bear the stamp of wisdom!"

"I will also say," Hodja Nasreddin continued, "that I, likewise, do not see any faces bearing the stamp of honesty and virtue."

"Thieves!" the emir said confidently. "All of them, thieves! Every last one! Would you believe it, Hussein Huslia, they rob us by night and by day! We must personally look after every little thing in the palace, and every time we inspect palace property, we find something missing. Only this morning, we forgot our new silk belt in the garden, and, half an hour later, it was no longer there!… One of them managed… you see, Hussein Huslia?"

At these words, the eyes of the sage with the twisted neck drooped in a particularly meek and meager fashion. At any other time, this would have gone unnoticed, but today all of Hodja Nasreddin's senses were sharpened: he noticed everything and guessed everything at once.

He walked up to the sage confidently, thrust a hand into the bosom of his robe, and extracted a richly decorated silk belt.

"Was this, perchance, the belt the emir regretted losing?" The courtiers froze in amazement and horror. The new sage turned out to be a truly dangerous opponent, and the very first man to challenge him had already been crushed and reduced to dust. The hearts of many sages, poets, officials, and viziers skipped a beat in that moment.

"By Allah, it is the very same belt!" the emir cried. "Hussein Huslia, you are truly an incomparable sage! Aha!" the emir said triumphantly to the courtiers, his face expressing a most sincere, lively happiness. "We have got you at last! Now you won't be able to steal a single thread from us; we have suffered enough from your thievery! As for this contemptible thief who has stolen our belt, pluck out every hair on his head, chin, and body, give him one hundred cane blows to the soles of his feet, sit him naked on a donkey, facing the tail, and parade him around the city, announcing everywhere that he is a thief!"

At Arslanbek's signal, torturers seized the sage and pushed him outside; they set to work right there on the doorstep. Two minutes later, the torturers pushed the sage back into the hall — naked, devoid even of hair, indecent to the extreme. Now everyone saw at once that, up until now, only his beard and enormous turban concealed the wretchedness of his mind and the mark of vice stamped on his face; that a man with such a crooked face could never have been anything but the most inveterate scoundrel and thief.

The emir wrinkled his face:

"Take him away!"

The torturers dragged the sage away, and soon his screams came from the outside, accompanied by the juicy sounds of a cane hitting his feet.

Then he was placed naked on a donkey, facing the tail, and taken to the bazaar square, accompanied by the terrifying roar of trumpets and the banging of drums.

The emir conversed with the newly arrived sage for a long time. The courtiers stood motionlessly, which was quite painful for them: the heat was increasing, and their sweaty backs were itching unbearably beneath their robes. Grand Vizier Bakhtiyar, who feared the new sage more than anyone else, was preoccupied with thoughts on how he could draw the courtiers to his side in order to crush his opponent with their help; the courtiers, who could already guess the outcome of such a battle, were thinking of the most profitable ways to renounce Bakhtiyar at the crucial moment, betray him, and thus earn the trust and favor of the new sage.

Meanwhile, the emir kept asking about the caliph's health, about news from Baghdad, and about the journey. Hodja Nasreddin had to invent answers on the spot. Everything was coming off well, and the emir, tired from the conversation, ordered a bed to be prepared so he could rest, but then voices came from the open windows, followed by someone's scream.

The palace overseer walked quickly into the hall. His face was shining with joy. He announced:

"Let it be known to the great ruler that the blasphemer and disturber of the peace Hodja Nasreddin has been caught and brought to the palace!"

Immediately following these words, the carved walnut doors swung wide open. Clanging their weapons triumphantly, the guards brought in a hook-nosed, white-bearded old man in women's clothing and flung him on the floor before the throne.

Hodja Nasreddin felt a chill. The palace walls seemed to sway before his eyes, and a greenish fog engulfed the faces of the courtiers...

Chapter 26

The Baghdad sage, the real Hussein Huslia, had been caught right by the city gates, where, through his veil, he could already see fields and roads stretching in all directions, each promising him salvation from a horrible execution.

But the guards who were watching the gate at that hour called out:

"Where are you going, woman?"

The sage replied in a voice resembling a hoarse young rooster:

"I am hurrying home to my husband. Let me by, valiant warriors."

The guards exchanged glances – the voice sounded suspicious. One of them took the camel by the bridle.

"Where do you live?"

"Not far from here," the sage replied in an even higher voice. But then he held the air in his throat a bit too long and emitted a very hoarse and wheezing cough.

The guards tore off his veil. Their jubilation was boundless.

"It's him! It's him!" they shouted. "Tie him up! Grab him!"

They led the old man to the palace, discussing along the entire way the horrible execution that awaited him and the three thousand tanga of reward for his head. Every word from the guards was like a hot coal placed on his heart.

He lay before the throne, weeping bitterly and pleading for mercy.

"Lift him up!" the emir commanded. The guards lifted the old man. Arslanbek stepped out from the crowd of courtiers.

"Let the emir hear the words of his faithful servant. This is not Hodja Nasreddin, this is a completely different man. Hodja Nasreddin is not even forty, while this man is very old."

The guards grew anxious: the reward was slipping from their fingers. Everyone else remained in confused silence.

"Why were you hiding in women's clothing?" the emir asked menacingly.

"I was headed to the palace to see the great and all-merciful emir," the old man replied, trembling. "But then I met a man I did not know, who told me that the emir had ordered my head cut off before I even arrived in Bukhara, and I, gripped with fear, decided to flee in women's clothing."

The emir smirked knowingly.

"You met a man… who you did not know. And you believed him at once? A fascinating story! And why did we wish to cut off your head?"

"For the fact that I had allegedly given a public vow to infiltrate the great emir's harem… But, as Allah is my witness, I never thought of it! I am old and frail, and have long since abandoned my own harem…"

"Infiltrate our harem?" the emir asked, pursing his lips. His face showed that he found this old man more and more suspicious. "Who are you, and where are you from?"

"I am Hussein Huslia, a sage, astrologer, and healer from Baghdad, and I have come to Bukhara at the command and desire of the great emir!"

"So your name is Hussein Huslia? You lie in our face, contemptible old man!" the emir thundered with such force that the King of the Poets fell to his knees quite inappropriately. "You lie! Here is Hussein Huslia!"

Obeying the emir's gesture, Hodja Nasreddin stepped forward intrepidly and stood before the old man, looking him in the face openly and boldly.

The old man stepped back in amazement. But then, coming to his senses, he shouted:

"Aha! This is the very man who I met on the bazaar and who said the emir wanted to cut off my head!"

"What is he saying, Hussein Huslia?" the emir exclaimed in utter confusion.

"He's no Hussein Huslia!" the old man screamed. "I am Hussein Huslia, and he is simply a cheat! He stole my name!"

Hodja Nasreddin bowed low before the emir.

"May the great ruler forgive my bold words, but this old man's shamelessness knows no bounds! He says I stole his name. Perhaps he will also say that I stole this robe?"

"Of course!" the old man shouted. "This is my robe!"

"Perhaps this turban is yours as well?" Hodja Nasreddin asked mockingly.

"Yes! It is my turban! You traded my robe and turban for women's clothing!"

"Right!" Hodja Nasreddin said, even more mockingly. "And is this belt yours, perchance?"

"Mine!" the old man replied testily. Hodja Nasreddin turned to the throne.

"Our illustrious ruler, the emir, can see for himself who stands before him. Today, this contemptible, deceitful old man says that I took his name, that this robe is his robe, as well as the turban and the belt, and tomorrow he will say that this palace is his palace, and the country is his country, and that the real emir of Bukhara is not our great and sun-like ruler, but him – this deceitful, contemptible old man! He is capable of anything! After all, he already arrived in Bukhara with the intention of entering the emir's harem as if it were his own!"

"You are right, Hussein Huslia," said the emir. "We have determined that this is a suspicious and dangerous man, and that his head is full of black thoughts. And we believe that we should immediately separate his head from his body."

The old man fell to his knees with a moan, covering his face.

But Hodja Nasreddin could not allow a man to be sent to the block for crimes he did not commit, even if it was a court sage, who had undoubtedly doomed many others with his guile.

Hodja Nasreddin bowed before the emir.

"Let the great emir graciously hear my words. It is never too late to chop off his head. But we should first find out his true name and his true business in Bukhara, so as to learn whether he has any accomplices, or if he is a foul dark magician who decided to take advantage of the unfavorable position of the stars to obtain dust from the great emir's footprints, mix it with the brains of a bat, and then place it in the emir's hookah in order to cause harm. Let the great emir allow him to live for now and hand him over to me, for he may be able to place evil spells on ordinary prison guards, while before my wisdom he will be powerless, for I know all the tricks of magicians and all the methods of counteracting their sorcery. I will lock up this old man, pronounce over the locks some pious prayers known only to me – so that he will not be able to undo the locks without a key through sorcery – and then, using brutal torture, I will force him to reveal all!"

"Well, then," the emir replied. "Your words are quite sensible, Hussein Huslia. Take him and do what you want with him, just make sure he does not escape his prison."

"I will answer to the great emir with my head."

Half an hour later, Hodja Nasreddin – now the emir's head sage and astrologer – proceeded to his new dwelling, prepared for him in one of the towers of the palace wall; after him, accompanied by guards, walked the dejected criminal – the genuine Hussein Huslia.

Above Hodja Nasreddin's dwelling, the tower had a small round chamber with cast iron bars on the window. Hodja Nasreddin unlocked the tarnished copper lock with an enormous key and opened the chamber door. The guards shoved the old man inside and tossed him a wispy bundle of hay. Hodja Nasreddin closed the door and muttered something over the lock for a long time, although he did it so quickly and unintelligibly that the guards could not understand anything except for frequent appeals to Allah…

Hodja Nasreddin was quite pleased with his quarters. The emir had sent him twelve blankets, eight pillows, a number of various utensils, a basket of fresh white bread cakes, a ewer of honey, and many other delicacies from his table. Hodja Nasreddin was very tired and hungry, but, before sitting down to eat, he took six blankets and four pillows, and carried all this upstairs to his prisoner.

The old man was sitting on the hay in the corner, his eyes flashing in the darkness, resembling a furious cat.

"Well, now, Hussein Huslia," Hodja Nasreddin said calmly. "You and I will settle in quite well in this tower – me below, and you above, as befitting your years and wisdom. How much dust there is here! I will sweep it up."

Hodja Nasreddin went downstairs and brought a pitcher of water and a broom. He swept the stone floor clean, laid down the blankets and pillows, and then went down once again and brought bread cakes, honey, halva, pistachios, and split it all evenly right before his prisoner's eyes.

"You will not die of hunger, Hussein Huslia," he spoke. "We will manage to get food. Here is a hookah, and I have placed some tobacco here."

After setting up the small chamber like this, so that it almost looked better than the room below, Hodja Nasreddin left and locked the door.

The old man was left alone. He was completely confused. He thought for a long time, pondering and weighing, but still could not understand what was going on. The blankets were soft, and the pillows were comfortable, and neither the bread cakes, nor the honey, nor the tobacco contained poison… Worn out by the day's misadventures, the old man went to sleep, entrusting his subsequent fate to Allah.

Meanwhile, the cause of his misfortunes, Hodja Nasreddin, was sitting by the window in the lower chamber and watching the slow transition of twilight into darkness as he thought about his amazingly turbulent life and about his beloved, who was now nearby, although she did not yet know anything. A fresh coolness drifted in through the window, and the ringing, sad voices of the muezzins weaved over the city like silver threads. Stars appeared in the dark sky, shining, burning, and fluttering with clean, cold, distant flames, and there was the star Al-Shual, signifying the heart, and the three stars Al-Gafr, signifying the veil of a woman, and the two stars Al-Sharatan, signifying horns, and only the sinister star Al-Kalb, signifying the stinger of death, was absent in the blue heavens…

Part 3

"Praise be to him who lives and does not die!"

One Thousand and One Nights

Chapter 27

Hodja Nasreddin earned the emir's trust and favor, and became his closest advisor in all affairs. Hodja Nasreddin made the decisions, the emir signed, and Grand Vizier Bakhtiyar only applied the carved copper seal. "O great Allah, what is going on in our country?" the vizier exclaimed in his head as he read the emir's decrees to cancel taxes, allow free use of roads and bridges, and reduce collections on the bazaar. "At this rate, the treasury will be empty before long! This new sage, may his insides rot all the way through, has destroyed my labor of over ten years in a week!"

Once, he dared express his doubts to the emir. The sovereign replied:

"What do you know, wretch, and what do you understand? We are just as saddened by all these decrees that are emptying our treasury, but what can we do if the stars are commanding this? Calm yourself, Bakhtiyar – this is only for a short time, until the stars enter a favorable alignment. Explain it to him, Hussein Huslia."

Hodja Nasreddin took the grand vizier aside, sat him down on the pillows, and explained to him for a long time why the additional tax on the blacksmiths, the coppersmiths, and the armory workers had to be repealed immediately.

"The stars Al-Abba in the constellation of Virgo and Al-Balda in the constellation of Sagittarius stand in opposition to the stars Sad-Bula in the constellation of Aquarius," Hodja Nasreddin spoke. "You must understand, o esteemed and luminous vizier, they stand in opposition and are far from union."

"So what if they stand in opposition?" Bakhtiyar objected. "They were in opposition before, and it did not prevent us from collecting taxes in the least."

"But you forgot about the star Ak-Dabaran in the constellation of Taurus!" Hodja Nasreddin exclaimed. "O vizier, look at the sky and you will see for yourself!"

"Why should I look at the sky?" the stubborn vizier replied. "My business is the protection and enlargement of the treasury. I can see that, since the day you appeared in the palace, the treasury's profits have diminished, and the flow of taxes has lessened. The time has come to collect taxes from the city tradesmen, so explain to me why we cannot collect them!"

"What do you mean, why?" Hodja Nasreddin exclaimed. "I've been explaining this to you for a whole hour now! How can you still fail to understand that each of the twelve signs of the Zodiac is associated with two and one third positions of the moon?"

"But I must collect the taxes!" the vizier interrupted again. "The taxes, do you understand?"

"Wait," Hodja Nasreddin stopped him. "I have not yet explained to you that the constellation of Al-Sureya and the eight stars An-Naimi…"

Here Hodja Nasreddin launched into such vague and lengthy explanations that the grand vizier's head begin to ring and his eyes clouded. He got up and left the room, swaying, while Hodja Nasreddin returned to the emir:

"O sovereign! Although old age has covered his head with silver, it has enriched him on the outside only, without turning into gold that which lies within the head. He could not absorb my wisdom. He did not understand anything, sovereign. O, if only he possessed but one thousandth of the great emir's mind, which eclipses Lukman himself!"

The emir smiled a gracious and self-satisfied smile. Every day, Hodja Nasreddin took great pains to make the emir fancy himself incomparably wise, with much success. And now, when he explained something to the emir, the latter listened with a pensive look and never objected, afraid to reveal the true depth of his mind.

The next day, Bakhtiyar spoke among the courtiers:

"The new sage, this Hussein Huslia, will ruin us all! We only grow rich on the days of tax collection, when we can scoop from the wide and deep river flowing into the emir's treasury. And now it has come time for us to scoop, but this Hussein Huslia is standing in our way. He refers to the arrangement of the stars, but who has ever heard of stars, which are controlled by Allah, arranging themselves to the detriment of distinguished and noble people, while benefiting contemptible tradesmen, who – I am sure – are even now eating shamelessly through their earnings instead of giving them to us! Who has ever heard of such an arrangement of stars? There is not a single book that describes this, for even if such a book had been written, it would have been burned immediately, while the man who wrote it would have been cursed and subjected to execution as a great blasphemer, heretic, and villain!"

The courtiers remained silent, not yet knowing whether it would be more profitable for them to take the side of Bakhtiyar or the new sage.

"Already, the inflow of taxes is decreasing every day," Bakhtiyar continued. "And the time is not far off when the treasury will become depleted, and we, the emir's closest servants, will be ruined. Instead of brocade robes, we will put on plain, rough ones, and instead of twenty wives we will have to make do with two, and instead of silver platters we will be served on clay ones, and instead of tender young lamb, we will be forced to garnish our pilaf with stringy beef, suitable only for dogs and tradesmen! This is what the new sage Hussein Huslia has in store for us, and he who does not see this is blind, and woe betide him!"

Thus he spoke, trying to incite the courtiers against the new sage.

His efforts were in vain.

Hussein Huslia achieved greater and greater successes in his rise to power.

He distinguished himself especially well during the 'day of praise.' According to ancient custom, all the viziers, officials, sages, and poets would compete every month before the emir in praising him. The winner was rewarded.

Everyone expressed his praise, but the emir remained unsatisfied.

"You said the same things last time," he said. "And we find that you are insufficiently diligent in your praising. You do not wish to burden your head, but today we will make you work. We will ask you questions, and you will answer, combining praise with truthfulness."

The emir asked:

"If we, the great emir of Bukhara, are mighty and unconquerable, as you state, then why have the rulers of neighboring Muslim countries not yet sent us envoys bearing rich gifts and expressions of their complete submission to our unconquerable dominion? We await your answers to this question."

The courtiers were seized by utter confusion. They mumbled something unintelligibly, trying to avoid a direct answer as best they could. Only Hodja Nasreddin maintained a state of confident calm. When his turn came, he said:

"May the great emir deign to hear my lowly words. Our sovereign's question is easy to answer. All the rulers in neighboring countries are in a state of constant fear and trepidation before the almightiness of our ruler. And they reason thusly: 'If we send the great, glorious, and mighty emir of Bukhara rich gifts, then he will think that our land is very wealthy and this will entice him to come with his army and take our land. And if, on the contrary, we send him poor gifts, he will take offense and send his army anyway. The emir of Bukhara, is great, glorious, and mighty, and it is best not to remind him of our existence.' This is what the other rulers are thinking, and the reason they are not sending their envoys with rich gifts to Bukhara should be sought in their constant trepidation before the almightiness of our sovereign."

"Yes!" the emir shouted, completely delighted by Hodja Nasreddin's answer. "This is how you should answer the emir's questions! Did you hear? Learn, o dunces and blockheads! Truly, Hussein Huslia exceeds you all tenfold in his wisdom! We proclaim our goodwill to him."

The palace chef ran up to Hodja Nasreddin and filled his mouth with halva and candy. Hodja Nasreddin's cheeks puffed up; he was suffocating, and thick, sweet spittle ran down his chin.

The emir posed several more equally crafty questions. Hodja Nasreddin's responses were the best every time.

"What is the paramount duty of a courtier?" asked the emir.

Hodja Nasreddin replied thus:

"O great and luminous sovereign! The paramount duty of a courtier consists of exercising his spine every day, so as to make it sufficiently flexible; otherwise, the courtier cannot properly express his devotion and his reverence. The spine of the courtier must be able to bend, and even undulate, in every possible direction, unlike the hardened spine of some commoner, who cannot even bow properly."

"Precisely!" cried the delighted emir. "Precisely, of exercising his spine every day! We proclaim our goodwill to the sage Hussein Huslia a second time!"

For the second time, Hodja Nasreddin's mouth was stuffed with halva and candy.

That day, many of the courtiers crossed over from Bakhtiyar's side to the side of Hodja Nasreddin.

In the evening, Bakhtiyar invited Arslanbek over. The new sage posed an equal threat to them both, and they forgot their ancient enmity for a time in order to destroy him.

"It would be nice to mix a little something into his pilaf," said Arslanbek, who was an expert in such matters.

"And then the emir will remove our heads!" Bakhtiyar objected. "No, esteemed Arslanbek, we must do otherwise. We must praise and exalt Hussein Huslia's wisdom in every way, so as to make the emir suspect that, in the eyes of the courtiers, Hussein Huslia's wisdom exceeds his own. Meanwhile, we will continue to tirelessly praise and exalt Hussein Huslia, and there will come a day when the emir will become jealous. And that day will be the last day of Hussein Huslia's rise and the first day of his downfall!"

But fate took good care of Hodja Nasreddin and turned even his blunders to his benefit.

When the combined efforts of Bakhtiyar and Arslanbek – who had been praising the new sage every day and beyond measure – had almost achieved their goal, and the emir was already becoming jealous, albeit secretly, it so happened that Hodja Nasreddin made a blunder.

He was walking in the garden with the emir, breathing in the fragrance of the flowers and enjoying the singing of the birds. The emir was silent. Hodja Nasreddin detected a hidden animosity in this silence, but could not understand its cause.

"And how is your prisoner, that old man?" asked the emir. "Have you discovered his true name and his reasons for coming to Bukhara, Hussein Huslia?"

Hodja Nasreddin was thinking of Guljan at the time, and replied absentmindedly:

"May the great sovereign forgive his lowly slave. I could not get a single word out of the old man. He is silent as a fish."

"But have you tried to torture him?"

"Of course, o great sovereign! Two days ago, I was dislocating his joints, while yesterday I loosened his teeth all day with iron tongs."

"That is a good method of torture, loosening the teeth," said the emir. "It is odd that he remains silent. Perhaps I should send a skilled and experienced torturer to assist you?"

"O no, the great sovereign need not burden himself! Tomorrow I will attempt a new method of torture – I will pierce the tongue and gums of this old man with a red hot awl."

"Wait, wait!" the emir exclaimed, and his face lit up. "But how will he be able to tell you his name after you have pierced his tongue with a hot awl? You did not think it through, Hussein Huslia, and you did not anticipate the problem, but we, the great emir, have considered, foreseen, and prevented your mistake. This shows that, although you are an incomparable sage, our own wisdom exceeds yours many fold, as you have just seen."

The joyous, glowing emir had the courtiers summoned at once, and when they had assembled, he announced to them that he had just exceeded the wisdom of Hussein Huslia by preventing a mistake that the sage was about to commit.

The court chronicler wrote down the emir's every word with diligence, so as to spread the fame of the emir's wisdom in the coming centuries.

Since that day, jealousy left the heart of the emir.

Thus, thanks to an accidental blunder, Hodja Nasreddin destroyed the cunning schemes of his enemies.

But he was also afflicted more and more frequently by unbearable anguish during the solitary hours of the night. The full moon floated high above Bukhara; the tiled caps of countless minarets glimmered with a faint glow, while their massive stone foundations disappeared in the thick gloom. A light breeze wafted through the air, cool on the roofs and stuffy below, where the walls and the ground, which had absorbed a lot of heat in the daytime, had not yet cooled. Everything around him was asleep – the palace, the mosques, the huts – and only the owls disturbed the hot sleep of the sacred city with their piercing cries. Hodja Nasreddin would sit by an open window. His heart knew that Guljan was awake, thinking of him, and perhaps they were both now looking at the same minaret, but without seeing each other, separated by walls, bars, guards, eunuchs, and hags. Hodja Nasreddin had managed to unlock the gates of the palace, but the harem was still shut firmly to him, and only some chance occurrence could open it. He sought that chance tirelessly, but in vain! He could not even manage to send Guljan a message.

He sat by the window, kissing the wind, and speaking to it: "Would it really be that hard for you? Fly through her window for an instant, touch her lips. Give Guljan my kiss and my whisper, tell her that I have not forgotten her, that I will save her!" The wind flew on. Hodja Nasreddin remained alone with his anguish.

Daylight would come, and with it the usual worries and troubles. He would have to go to the grand hall again, wait for the emir's entrance, hear the obsequious words of the courtiers, guess at Bakhtiyar's cunning schemes and catch his glances, full of hidden venom. Then he had to prostrate himself before the emir, praise him, spend long hours alone with him, staring at his puffy, wrinkled face with concealed disgust, pay close attention to his foolish words, explain the position of the stars to him. Hodja Nasreddin was so tired and disgusted with it all that he even stopped inventing new excuses for the emir, explaining everything – the emir's headache, the drought in the fields, the rising costs of grain – with the same words, referring to the same stars.

"The stars Sad-ad-Zabikh," he spoke in a bored voice, "stand in opposition to the constellation of Aquarius, while the planet Mercury is positioned to the left of the constellation of Scorpio. This explains the sovereign's insomnia last night."

"The stars Sad-ad-Zabikh stand in opposition to the planet Mercury, while… I will have to remember this. Say it again, Hussein Huslia."

The emir had absolutely no memory. The next day, the conversation began anew:

"The plague of cattle in the mountainous regions can be explained, o great emir, by the fact that the stars Sad-ad-Zabikh stand in union with the constellation of Aquarius, while the planet Mercury stands in opposition to the constellation of Scorpio."

"I see, the stars Sad-ad-Zabikh," the emir spoke. "I will have to remember this."

"Almighty Allah, how dumb he is!" Hodja Nasreddin thought wearily. "He is even dumber than the caliph of Baghdad! How tired I am of him! How long until I can escape from this place?"

And the emir would speak again:

"There is complete peace and calm in our country right now, Hussein Huslia. And there are no news about that miscreant, Hodja Nasreddin. Where could he have gone, and why does he remain silent? Explain it to us, Hussein Huslia."

"O almighty ruler, center of the universe! The stars Sad-ad-Zabikh…" Hodja Nasreddin began in a bored, drawling voice, and repeated everything he had already said many times before. "And moreover, o great emir, this miscreant Hodja Nasreddin has been to Baghdad and has certainly heard of my wisdom. When he learned that I had come to Bukhara, he hid in fear and trepidation, for he knows that I could easily capture him."

"Capture! That would be very good! But how do you intend to capture him?"

"I will wait for a favorable arrangement of the stars Sad-ad-Zabikh with the planet Jupiter."

"The planet Jupiter," the emir repeated. "I will have to remember that. Do you know, Hussein Huslia, of the wise thought that visited us last night? We thought that we should expel Bakhtiyar from his post and make you the grand vizier."

And Hodja Nasreddin had to prostrate himself before the emir, praise and thank him, and then explain that the vizier could not be changed at this time, for the stars Sad-ad-Zabikh did not favor it. "Escape, escape this place as soon as possible!" Hodja Nasreddin exclaimed mentally.

Thus Hodja Nasreddin led a joyless, anguished existence in the palace as he waited for an opportune moment. He was drawn to the bazaar, to the crowds, to the chaikhanas, into the smoky cookhouses. He would have given up all the emir's delicacies for a single bowl of spicy mutton stew with onions, for the sinew and gristle in a cheap bazaar pilaf. He would have traded his brocade robe for rags if he could only hear simple, artless words and sincere laughter from the heart instead of praises and exaltations.

But fate continued to test Hodja Nasreddin and did not send him a favorable opportunity. Meanwhile the emir kept asking more and more frequently when the stars would at last permit his regal hand to lift the veil of his new concubine.

Chapter 28

One day, the emir summoned the Baghdad sage at an unusual hour. It was very early, and the entire palace was asleep and quiet save for the splashing of the fountains, the cooing of doves, and the rustling of their wings. "Why does he need me?" Hodja Nasreddin wondered as he ascended the jasper staircase leading to the emir's bedroom.

Bakhtiyar slinked out of the bedroom to meet him, silent as a shadow. They exchanged greetings. Hodja Nasreddin pricked up his ears, sensing a trap.

Inside the bedroom, Hodja Nasreddin found the head eunuch. His Great Chasteness was moaning pitifully as he lay prostrate before the emir's bed, while the pieces of a palm tree cane, embellished with gold, were scattered nearby on the carpet.

Heavy velvet curtains separated the bedroom from the fresh morning breeze, from the rays of the sun and the twittering of the birds. The room was lit by the dull flame of a lamp, which, though it was made of solid gold, stank and fumed not a whit less than an ordinary clay one. An ornate censer gave off smoke in the corner, exuding spicy, sweet fragrance, which was nevertheless powerless to drown out the sooty smell of sheep tallow. The air in the bedroom was so thick that Hodja Nasreddin felt a tickling sensation in his nose and throat.

The emir was sitting on the bed, his hairy legs sticking out from under his silk blanket. Hodja Nasreddin noticed that the soles of the ruler's feet were dark yellow, as if he smoked them every now and again over his Indian censer.

"Hussein Huslia, we are extremely upset," said the emir. "Our head eunuch, who you see before you, is to blame for this."

"O great sovereign!" Hodja Nasreddin exclaimed, feeling a chill. "Surely he did not dare?…"

"Oh, no!" the emir waved his hand and wrinkled his face. "How can he dare anything of the sort when we, in our due wisdom, had foreseen everything and taken care of it before appointing him head eunuch? A different matter entirely. We found out today that this scoundrel has criminally neglected his duties and forgotten the great favor we bestowed upon him by placing him on one of the highest posts in the country. Taking advantage of the fact that we have not been visiting our concubines lately, he dared to leave the harem for three days in order to indulge in a destructive vice; namely – the smoking of hashish. And peace was disturbed in the harem, and the calm was disrupted, and our concubines, deprived of supervision, fought amongst each other, scratching faces and tearing out hair, which has caused us, the great emir, a significant loss, for women with scratched faces and torn hair cannot be considered perfect in our eyes. Moreover, another thing transpired which has cast us into sadness and sorrow: our new concubine has fallen ill and has not taken any food for the third day now."

Hodja Nasreddin perked up. The emir stopped him with a motion of his hand:

"Wait, we have not finished speaking. She is ill and may lose her life. If we had visited her even once, her illness and even her death would not have wounded our heart so much, but now, as you can understand, Hussein Huslia, we are quite, quite upset. This is why we have decided," the emir continued, raising his voice, "so as not to subject ourselves in the future to sadness and distress, to banish this scoundrel and debaucher from his post, deprive him of all our favors, and give him two hundred lashes. Conversely, o Hussein Huslia, we have decided to extend you a great favor and appoint you to the newly freed post, in other words, the head eunuch of our harem!"

Hodja Nasreddin's knees buckled, his breath halted, and his insides grew cold. Moving his eyebrows together, the emir queried menacingly:

"It seems you intend to object to us, Hussein Huslia? Perhaps you prefer vain and transient pleasures to the great joy of serving our regal person? Say if this is so!"

Hodja Nasreddin had already regained control of himself. He bowed to the emir:

"May Allah protect our great sovereign. The emir's kindness to me, a worthless slave, is boundless. The great ruler possesses a magical quality of guessing the most secret and sacred wishes of those around him, which gives him the ability to constantly shower them with his goodwill. How many times have I, a worthless slave, dreamed of taking the place of this lazy and stupid man, who is now lying on the carpet and moaning in a high-pitched voice after receiving just punishment with a cane. How many times have I dreamed of this, but never dared tell the sovereign of my wish. But now, the great sovereign himself…"

"So what is the problem?" the emir interrupted amicably and happily. "We will summon the surgeon presently, he will take his knives, and you will retire with him to some secluded spot. Meanwhile, we will command Bakhtiyar to write a decree appointing you the head eunuch. Hey!" the emir shouted and clapped his hands.

"May the sovereign lend his ears to my lowly words," Hodja Nasreddin said hastily, glancing at the door with apprehension. "I would accompany the surgeon with great joy and readiness to a secluded spot even now, and it is only my concern for the sovereign's welfare that stops me. After the procedure, I will have to lie in bed for a long time, and in the meantime the sovereign's new concubine may die, and the emir's heart will be enshrouded in the black fog of sorrow. The very thought of this is unbearable and intolerable for me. This is why I believe that we must first banish the illness from the concubine's body, and then I will go to the surgeon and prepare myself for the post of head eunuch."

"Hmm!" said the emir, glancing at Hodja Nasreddin with great doubt.

"O sovereign! After all, she refuses to take food for the third day now."

"Hmm!…" the emir repeated and then asked the eunuch lying before him:

"Tell us, you lowly spawn of a spider: is our new concubine truly ill, and should we really worry for her life?"

Hodja Nasreddin felt streamlets of cold sweat crawling down his neck. He awaited the response with immense anxiousness.

The eunuch said:

"O great ruler, she has become thin and pale like the young moon; her face is as though made of wax, and her fingers are cold. The hags say that these are very unfavorable signs…"

The emir contemplated this. Hodja Nasreddin stepped back into the shadows and mentally thanked the smoky gloom of the bedroom for hiding the paleness of his face.

"Well!" said the emir. "If this is so, then she may well die, which will upset us greatly. The main thing is that we have not visited her even once. But are you sure, Hussein Huslia, that you will be able to heal her?"

"The great sovereign knows well that there is no healer more skilled than I anywhere from Bukhara to Baghdad."

"Go, Hussein Huslia, and prepare her medicine."

"Great ruler, I must first determine her illness. And to do that, I must look at her."

"Look?" the emir smirked. "When you are head eunuch, Hussein Huslia, you can look all you want."

"O sovereign!" Hodja Nasreddin bowed to the ground. "I must…"

"Worthless slave!" the emir shouted. "Do you not know that no mortal can, under penalty of horrible execution, see the faces of our concubines? Do you not know this?"

"I know this, o sovereign!" Hodja Nasreddin replied. "But I am not talking about her face. I would never dare glance at her face. I need only to look at her hand, for a healer as skilled as I can identify any illness by the color of the fingernails."

"Her hand?" the emir asked. "Why did you not say so right away, Hussein Huslia, and instead made us irate for no reason? The hand – that is certainly possible. We will go with you to the harem ourselves; we assume that seeing a female hand will not harm us."

"Seeing a female hand cannot harm the great sovereign," Hodja Nasreddin replied, figuring that he would not be able to see Guljan alone anyway, and, if there had to be a witness, it might as well be the emir himself, so that suspicion would not later creep into his heart.

Chapter 29

Finally, after so many days of fruitless waiting, the doors of the harem had opened before Hodja Nasreddin.

The guards stepped aside, bowing. Hodja Nasreddin followed the emir up the stone staircase, walked through a gate, and saw a beautiful garden: clumps of roses, gillyflowers, and hyacinths, fountains, pools made of white and black marble with light steam rising above them. Morning dew glistened and trembled on the flowers, the grass, and the leaves.

Paleness and color traded places every other moment on Hodja Nasreddin's face. The eunuch flung open the carved chestnut doors. A thick of scent of ambergris, musk, and rose oil came from the dark depths. This was the harem – the sorrowful dwelling of the emir's beautiful prisoners.

Hodja Nasreddin carefully noted all the corners, passageways, and turns, so as not to lose his bearings at a critical moment and doom both himself and Guljan. "Right," he repeated to himself, "Now left. A staircase here. A hag is guarding it. Now, another left…" The passageways were lit with dim blue, green, and pink light breaking through multicolored Chinese glass. The eunuch stopped in front of a small door.

"She is here, sovereign."

Following the emir, Hodja Nasreddin crossed the cherished threshold. Beyond it was a small room with rugs laid on the floor and hanging on the walls. Pearl boxes full of bracelets, earrings, and necklaces stood in niches, and a large silver mirror was hanging on the wall. Poor Guljan had never dreamed of such riches! Hodja Nasreddin trembled when he saw her small, pearl-encrusted slippers. She had already managed to wear down the heels! How much willpower he needed to not betray his excitement!

The eunuch pointed to a silk curtain in the corner. Guljan was lying there. "She is asleep," the eunuch said in a whisper.

Hodja Nasreddin was shaking lightly. His beloved was nearby. "Be strong, take courage!" he said to himself.

But as soon as he approached the curtain and heard the sighs of the sleeping Guljan, as soon as he saw the light fluttering of the silk at the head of her bed, it seemed as if iron fingers had gripped his throat. Tears appeared on his face, and his breath halted.

"Why do you dally, Hussein Huslia?" asked the emir.

"O sovereign, I am listening to her breath. I am trying to hear the heartbeat of your concubine through the curtain. What is her name?"

"Her name is Guljan," the emir replied.

"Guljan," Hodja Nasreddin called out. The curtain, which had been moving regularly near the head of the bed, became still. Guljan woke up and froze, unsure whether she had heard this near, dear voice in her dreams or in reality.

"Guljan!" Hodja Nasreddin repeated. She cried out in a weak voice. Hodja Nasreddin said quickly:

"My name is Hussein Huslia. I am a new sage, astrologer, and healer who has come from Baghdad to serve the emir. Do you understand, Guljan? I am a new sage, astrologer, and healer named Hussein Huslia."

Turning to the emir, Hodja Nasreddin added:

"She became frightened for some reason when she heard my voice. This eunuch probably mistreated her in the sovereign's absence."

The emir glared at the eunuch. The latter began to shake and bowed to the ground, not daring to say a word in his own defense.

"Guljan, you are in danger," Hodja Nasreddin said. "But I will save you, and you must trust me, for my skill can overcome anything."

He fell silent, awaiting her response. Did Guljan not understand, did she not guess? But then her voice came:

"I hear you, Hussein Huslia, sage from Baghdad. I know about you and trust you; I say this here, in the presence of my sovereign, whose legs I can see through a crack in my curtain."

Remembering that he needed to maintain a learned and dignified look in front of the emir, Hodja Nasreddin said sternly:

"Give me your hand, so that I can determine your illness by the color of your nails."

The silk billowed and parted. Gently, Hodja Nasreddin took Guljan's slender hand. He could only express his emotions with a squeeze. Guljan reciprocated faintly. He turned her hand, facing the palm upwards, and looked at it attentively for a long time. "How thin she has grown!" he thought with pain in his heart. The emir leaned over his shoulder and began to wheeze right over his ear. Hodja Nasreddin showed him the nail on Guljan's pinky and shook his head concernedly. Although the nail on the pinky did not look any different from the other nails, the emir managed to see something out of the ordinary. Pursing his lips, he gave Hodja Nasreddin a meaningful, understanding glance.

"Where do you feel pain?" Hodja Nasreddin asked.

"My heart," she replied with a sigh. "My heart hurts from grief and anguish."

"What is the cause of your grief?"

"I am separated from the one I love." Hodja Nasreddin whispered to the emir:

"She is ill because she is separated from the sovereign."

The emir's face lit up with pleasure. He began to wheeze even louder.

"I am separated from my beloved!" Guljan spoke. "And now I can sense that my beloved is here, nearby, but I can neither embrace nor kiss him. O, when will the day come when he will embrace me and bring me closer to him?"

"Almighty Allah!" Hodja Nasreddin exclaimed, feigning amazement. "What mighty passion the sovereign has managed to arouse in her in so short a time!"

The emir was absolutely delighted. He could not even stand still; he began to shift from foot to foot and snicker into his hand stupidly.

"Guljan!" Hodja Nasreddin said. "Calm down. The one who loves you can hear you!"

"Yes, yes!" the emir could not restrain himself. "He hears, Guljan! Your beloved hears you!"

Quiet laughter came from behind the curtain, resembling the babbling of water. Hodja Nasreddin continued:

"You are in danger, Guljan, but you must not be afraid. I, the famous sage, astrologer, and healer Hussein Huslia, will save you!"

"He will save you!" the delighted emir repeated. "He will definitely save you!"

"You heard the sovereign," Hodja Nasreddin concluded. "You must trust me, I will deliver you from danger. The day of your happiness is near. The sovereign cannot visit you right now, for I have warned him that the stars forbid him to touch the veil of a woman. But the stars are beginning to change their arrangement, do you understand, Guljan? Soon they will enter a favorable union, and you will embrace your beloved. The day when I send you your medicine will precede your joy. Do you understand, Guljan? Upon receiving your medicine, you must be ready!"

"Thank you, thank you, Hussein Huslia!" she replied, laughing and weeping from joy. "Thank you, incomparable and wise healer of the sick. My beloved is nearby, I can feel our hearts beating together!…" The emir and Hodja Nasreddin left. The head eunuch caught up with them near the gate.

"O sovereign!" he exclaimed, falling to his knees. "Truly, the world has never seen such a skilled healer. She lay without movement for three days, but now she has left her bed, she is laughing and dancing, and even deigned to slap me when I approached her."

"Sounds familiar," Hodja Nasreddin thought. "She always had quick hands, my Guljan!"

During the morning meal, the emir showered all the courtiers with favors. He gave two purses to Hodja Nasreddin – a large one filled with silver, and a smaller one filled with gold.

"What passion we inspired in her, though!" he said, snickering. "Admit it, Hussein Huslia, it is not often that you get to see such passion, yes? And how her voice was trembling, how she laughed and cried! Imagine what else you will see, Hussein Huslia, when you take the post of head eunuch!"

Whispers spread through the rows of bowing courtiers. A gloating smirk flickered on Bakhtiyar's face. Only now did Hodja Nasreddin understand who had planted the idea to appoint him head eunuch in the emir's head.

"She is better already," the emir continued, "and there are no more reasons to delay with your appointment. We will have some tea now, Hussein Huslia, and then you can sequester yourself with the surgeon. Hey, you!" he said to the surgeon. "Go fetch your knives. Bakhtiyar, give me the decree."

Hodja Nasreddin choked on the hot tea and coughed. Bakhtiyar stepped forward with the prepared decree in his hands, trembling with vengeful delight. The emir was handed a quill; he signed the decree and returned it to Bakhtiyar, who hastily applied a carved copper seal.

All of this happened in less than a minute.

"It seems you have lost your tongue from joy, o esteemed sage Hussein Huslia!" Bakhtiyar said with a triumphant smile. "But the courtly custom demands you thank the emir."

Hodja Nasreddin bent his knees before the emir.

"At last, my wish is granted!" he said. "And imagine my annoyance at the delay which stems from the necessity to prepare medicine for the emir's concubine, so as to strengthen her healing, for otherwise the illness will return to her body."

"Will preparing the medicine really take so much time?" Bakhtiyar asked with concern. "One can prepare medicine in half an hour."

"Exactly," the emir said. "Half an hour is quite enough."

"O sovereign, everything depends on the stars Sad-ad-Zabikh," Hodja Nasreddin replied, using his last and most potent measure. "Depending on their arrangement, I will need from two to five days."

"Five days!" Bakhtiyar exclaimed. "O esteemed Hussein Huslia, I have never heard a medicine taking five days to prepare!"

Hodja Nasreddin turned to the emir:

"Perhaps the illustrious ruler will deign to entrust the further healing of the new concubine to Grand Vizier Bakhtiyar instead of me? Let him try to heal her, but then I do not vouch for her life."

"What are you talking about, Hussein Huslia?" the emir said fearfully. "Bakhtiyar doesn't understand anything about illnesses and, in fact, does not exactly have the sharpest mind, as we had already discussed when I offered you the post of grand vizier."

A slow spasm passed over the entire body of the grand vizier, and he directed a gaze full of insatiable hatred at Hodja Nasreddin.

"Go and prepare the medicine," the emir concluded. "But five days is a long time, Hussein Huslia. Perhaps you could manage to do it sooner, for we can't wait to see you as head eunuch."

"Great ruler, I can't wait for it myself!" Hodja Nasreddin exclaimed. "I will try to finish sooner."

Walking backwards and bowing incessantly, he departed. Bakhtiyar followed him with a gaze which showed clear regret that his enemy and rival was leaving without losing any of his body parts.

"O snake, o devious hyena!" Hodja Nasreddin thought, gnashing his teeth in rage. "But you are too late, Bakhtiyar, now you won't have time to do anything to me because I know all that I needed to know: all the entrances, passageways, and exits in the emir's harem! O, my precious Guljan, you managed to get sick just in time to save Hodja Nasreddin from the palace surgeon's knives. Although, truth be told, you were only looking out for yourself!"

He headed to his tower. Guards were sitting in the shade near its foundation and playing dice; one of them, having already lost everything, was removing his boots in order to bet them. It was very hot, but inside the thick walls of the tower, a damp coolness reigned. Climbing the narrow stone staircase, Hodja Nasreddin passed his own door, heading to the room where the Baghdad sage was kept.

The old man had grown incredibly scruffy over the course of his interment and attained a savage look. His eyes flashed from beneath his overhanging eyebrows. He met Hodja Nasreddin with curses:

"How long will you keep me locked up, o son of sin, may a stone fall on your head and pass right out your foot! O filthy rogue and cheat, who has taken my name, my robe, my turban, and my belt, may maggots eat you alive, may they consume your stomach and your liver!…"

Hodja Nasreddin had grown accustomed to this and did not take offense.

"Esteemed Hussein Huslia, today I have devised a new torture for you, namely: I will squeeze your head using a loop of rope and a staff. Guards are sitting at the foot of the tower, you must scream loudly enough for them to hear."

The old man approached the grated window and began to scream in a weary voice:

"O almighty Allah! O, my suffering is boundless! O, do not squeeze my head using a loop of rope and a staff! O, death would be better than such torments!"

"Wait, esteemed Hussein Huslia," Hodja Nasreddin interrupted. "You are screaming lazily and without a hint of suffering, while the guards, if you recall, are very experienced in such matters. If they detect falseness in your screams and report it to Arslanbek, then you will fall into the hands of a real torturer. Therefore, it is better for you to exert due effort now. Here, I will show you how to scream."

Hodja Nasreddin walked up to the window, filled his chest with air, and wailed so loudly that the old man plugged his ears and shrank away.

"O spawn of the impious!" he exclaimed. "Where am I supposed to obtain a throat like yours, so that my cries may be heard on the opposite end of the city?"

"It is the only way for you to escape the torturer," Hodja Nasreddin countered.

The old man had to make an effort. He screamed and wailed with such woe that the guards at the base of the tower interrupted their game and listened rapturously.

Afterwards, the old man could not stop coughing or catch his breath for a long time.

"Oh!" he spoke. "How can you give such a workout to my old throat? Are you pleased with my screams today, wretched beggar, may you be visited by Azrail?"

"Quite pleased," Hodja Nasreddin replied. "And now, esteemed Hussein Huslia, you will get a reward for your efforts."

He took out the purses given to him by the emir, poured the money out on a tray, and divided it into two equal portions.

The old man would not stop swearing and cursing.

"Why do you curse me?" Hodja Nasreddin asked calmly. "Have I disgraced the name of Hussein Huslia in any way, or shamed his learnedness? Do you see this money? The emir gave it to Hussein Huslia, the famous astrologer and healer, for curing a girl from the harem."

"You cured a girl?" the old man gasped. "But what do you know about illnesses, you know-nothing, you cheat, you beggar?"

"I don't know a thing about illnesses, but I do know a few things about girls," Hodja Nasreddin replied. "And it is therefore fair to split the emir's gift in two – half to you for what you know, and half to me for what I know. Moreover, I must tell you, Hussein Huslia, that I did not go about healing her in any random way, but I first investigated the arrangement of the stars. Last night, I saw that the stars Sad-ad-Suud were in union with the stars Sad-ad-Akhbiya, while the constellation of Scorpio had turned towards the constellation of Capricorn."

"What?" the old man cried and began to run around the room in indignation. "O know-nothing, worthy only of herding donkeys. You do not even know that the stars Sad-ad-Suud cannot be in union with the stars Sad-al-Akhbiya, for they are both in the same constellation! And how could you have seen the constellation of Scorpio this time of year? I myself looked at the sky all night, where the stars Sad-Bula and As-Si-mak were in union, while Al-Djakhba was in descendant; can you hear that, you know-nothing? There is no Scorpio there now! You mixed it all up, o herder of donkeys who has meddled in the business of another, you mistook the stars Al-Haka, which now stand in opposition to the stars Al-Butein, for Scorpio!…"

As he indignantly accused Hodja Nasreddin of ignorance, he spoke of the true arrangement of stars. Hodja Nasreddin listened carefully, trying to remember every word, so as not to make a mistake when speaking to the emir in the presence of the sages.

"O know-nothing, son of a know-nothing, grandson and great-grandson of a know-nothing!" the old man continued. "You do not even know that now, during the nineteenth station of the moon, known as Ash-Shuala and corresponding to the sign of Sagittarius, the fates of men are decided only by the stars of that sign and no other, which is plainly written in the book of the most wise Shikhab-ad-din Mahmoud ibn-Ka-rajah…"

"Shikhab-ad-din Mahmoud ibn-Ka-rajah," Hodja Nasreddin repeated to himself. "No later than tomorrow, I will expose the bearded sage's ignorance of this book in the emir's presence, so as to instill a soul-saving fear of my learnedness in his heart…"

Chapter 30

Jafar the moneylender had twelve sealed pots full of gold in his house, while he wanted desperately to have twenty. But fate, as if deliberately protecting inexperienced and trusting simpletons, had marked Jafar with a look of incredible sleaziness: he had to expend a great deal of effort to lure a new victim into his web; his pots were filling up slower than he would have liked. "Oh, if only I could get rid of my ugliness!" he fantasized. "Then people would not run when they saw me; they would trust me and not suspect any guile in my words. And then I would find it a lot easier to cheat them, and my profits would multiply immeasurably."

When rumors spread through the city that the emir's new sage Hussein Huslia had shown incredible skill in the healing of illnesses, the moneylender Jafar grabbed a basket full of rich gifts and headed to the palace to see Arslanbek.

Glancing inside the basket, Arslanbek expressed his complete desire to help:

"You have come at a good time, esteemed Jafar. Our sovereign is in good spirits today, and I hope he will not refuse you."

The emir listened to the moneylender, accepted the gift – a golden chessboard with the white squares made of ivory – and summoned the sage.

"Hussein Huslia," he said, when Hodja Nasreddin bowed before him. "This man, the moneylender Jafar, is our faithful servant who has served us well. We command you to immediately cure him of his hump, his limp, his walleye, and other disfigurements."

And the emir turned away to signify that he did not wish to hear any objections. Hodja Nasreddin could only bow and leave. The moneylender crawled out after him, dragging his hump along like a tortoise.

"Come quickly, o most wise Hussein Huslia!" he said, not recognizing Hodja Nasreddin beneath the false beard. "Come quickly, the sun has not yet set and I can still be cured before dark… You heard – the emir has commanded you to cure me immediately!"

Hodja Nasreddin inwardly cursed both the moneylender and the emir, and even himself for extolling his own wisdom too much. How would he get out of this one? The moneylender jerked Hodja Nasreddin by the sleeve, insisting they put on speed. The streets were empty, and Hodja Nasreddin's feet were sinking into the hot dust. He walked and wondered: "How will I get out of this?" Suddenly, he stopped. "It seems the time has come for me to keep my oath!" He weighed and planned everything out in an instant. "Yes, the time has come! Moneylender, o merciless tormentor of the poor, today you will be drowned!" He turned away, so the moneylender would not see the sparks in his black eyes.

They turned into an alley where the breeze swept along the road, kicking up dusty whirlwinds. The moneylender opened the gate of his house before Hodja Nasreddin. In the depth of the courtyard, beyond a low fence separating the female quarters of the house, Hodja Nasreddin noticed a motion and heard quiet whispers and laughter. The wives and concubines were happy to see a guest arrive: they had no other joys in their imprisonment. The moneylender stopped and stared menacingly – everything grew quiet… "I will free you today, beautiful prisoners!" Hodja Nasreddin thought.

The room where the moneylender had brought Hodja Nasreddin had no windows, while the door had three locks and a number of other latches whose secret was known only to the master of the house. The moneylender fussed around for a long time, jingling his keys, before all the latches were undone and the door opened. This was where the pots were kept, and this is where the moneylender slept on boards covering the entrance to the cellar.

"Undress!" Hodja Nasreddin commanded. The moneylender threw off his clothes. His nakedness was indescribably hideous. Hodja Nasreddin closed the door and began to pronounce incantations.

Meanwhile, Jafar's numerous relatives had gathered in the courtyard. Many of them owed him money and hoped that he would forgive their debts in celebration of the healing. They hoped in vain: the moneylender could hear the voices of his debtors through the closed door and smirked maliciously to himself. "I will tell them today that I have forgiven their debts," he thought, "but I will not give them back the receipts, the receipts I will keep. They will relax and lead a carefree life, while I will not say anything, but secretly I will continue tallying everything up. And when ten tanga of interest accumulate on every tanga of debt, and the amount of the debt exceeds the cost of the houses, gardens, and vineyards that my debtors presently own, I will call a judge, retract my promise, produce the receipts, sell all their property, leave them impoverished, and fill another pot with gold!" Thus he fantasized, consumed by insatiable greed.

"Stand up and get dressed!" Hodja Nasreddin said. "We will now go to the pond of the holy Ahmed, and you will immerse yourself in its sacred waters. This is necessary to heal you."

"The holy Ahmed's pond!" the moneylender exclaimed fearfully. "I almost drowned in its waters once already. Know, o most wise Hussein Huslia, that I cannot swim."

"You must pronounce prayers incessantly on your way to the pond," Hodja Nasreddin said. "And you must not think of worldly matters. Moreover, you will take a purse of gold and give each person you meet a gold coin."

The moneylender moaned and groaned, but performed everything exactly as told. He met various people along the way – tradesmen, beggars; his face contorting, he gave a gold coin to every one. Numerous relatives walked behind him. Hodja Nasreddin called them on purpose, so as to escape accusations afterwards that the drowning of the moneylender was premeditated.

The sun sank beneath the rooftops, the trees covered the pond with their shadows, and mosquitoes were buzzing in the air. Jafar undressed himself once more and approached the water.

"It is very deep here," he said pitifully. "Hussein Huslia, you did not forget that I cannot swim, did you?"

The relatives watched in silence. Covering his privates with his hand and fidgeting fearfully, the moneylender circled the pond, looking for a shallow spot.

But then Jafar squatted and, taking hold of the overhanging branches, tested the water with his foot.

"It's cold," he complained; his eyes widened.

"You dally too much," Hodja Nasreddin replied, trying to look away so as not to allow unrighteous pity into his heart. But he recalled the suffering of the poor ruined by Jafar, the parched lips of the sick child, he recalled the tears of old Niyaz. Hodja Nasreddin's face lit up with anger, and he looked into the money-lender right in the eyes openly and bravely.

"You dally too much!" he repeated. "If you wish to be cured, get in."

The moneylender went into the water. He entered very slowly, and his belly was still on the shore when his legs were already in up to the knees. Finally, he stood up. Right near the shore, the water came up to his waist. The weeds swayed, tickling his body with their cold touch. His shoulder blades twitching from the chill, he stepped forward and looked back. He made another step, and looked back. His eyes expressed a silent plea, but Hodja Nasreddin did not heed this plea. To take pity on the moneylender would mean dooming thousands of poor people to more suffering.

The water covered the moneylender's hump, but Hodja Nasreddin chased him relentlessly into the depth.

"More, more… Let the water touch your ears, or else I will not undertake to cure you. Come, be brave, esteemed Jafar! Be brave! Another step! Just a little more!"

"Ulp!" the moneylender said suddenly, and his head vanished in the water.

"Ulp!" he repeated again, appearing on the surface a second later.

"He's drowning! He's drowning!" the relatives shouted. Confusion and shoving ensued as they stretched their arms and various sticks out to the moneylender; some were trying sincerely to help him, while others were only doing it for show.

Hodja Nasreddin determined right away exactly who owed the moneylender, and how much. As for him, he was running around and fussing more than anyone else:

"Give me your hand! Give me your hand, esteemed Jafar! Can you hear me? Give me your hand! Give it!"

"Give it! Give it!" the relatives repeated in unison. The moneylender continued to dive, appearing on the surface less and less often. And it was here, in these sacred waters, that he would have met his end, if a barefoot water-bearer had not appeared from somewhere, carrying an empty water-skin on his back.

"Huh!" he shouted upon seeing the drowning man. "Why, it's the moneylender Jafar!"

Not pausing to think, he jumped into the water without removing his clothes, stretched out his hand, and shouted haltingly:

"Take my hand!"

The moneylender grasped it and was extracted successfully from the water. As he came to on the shore, the water-bearer explained loquaciously to the relatives:

"You were not rescuing him properly. You were shouting 'give', while you had to shout: 'take!' Surely you know that the esteemed Jafar had almost drowned in this sacred pond once before, and was saved by a man who was passing by on a gray donkey. The man applied this very method to save the moneylender, and I remembered it. Today, this knowledge came in handy…"

Hodja Nasreddin bit his lips as he listened. It turned out that he had saved the moneylender twice – once with his own hands, and once with the hands of the water-bearer. "No, I will drown him nonetheless, even if I have to spend another year in Bukhara to do so," he thought. Meanwhile, the moneylender caught his breath and began to shout cantankerously:

"O Hussein Huslia, you came to cure me, and instead you almost drowned me! By Allah, I will never come closer than a hundred steps to this pond! What kind of sage are you, Hussein Huslia, if you do not know how to rescue people from the water, while a simple water-bearer exceeds you in knowledge? Give me my robe and my turban; let us go, Hussein Huslia. It is growing dark, and we must finish what we started."

"Water-bearer!" the moneylender added, rising. "Do not forget that you debt is due in a week. But I wish to reward you, and therefore I forgive you half… that is, I meant to say, a quarter… no, one tenth of your debt. This reward is more than adequate, for I could have gotten out without your aid."

"O esteemed Jafar," the water-bearer said timidly. "You could not have gotten out without my aid. Can't you at least forgive a quarter of my debt?"

"Aha! So you were saving me with ulterior motives!" the moneylender shouted. "This means that you were not driven by the feelings of a good Muslim, but by greed alone! For this, water-bearer, you deserve to be punished. I do not forgive any of your debt!"

The water-bearer stepped aside, dejected. Hodja Nasreddin looked at him with pity, then, with hatred and contempt, at Jafar.

"Hussein Huslia, come quickly," the moneylender insisted. "What are you whispering to that greedy water-bearer?"

"Wait," Hodja Nasreddin replied. "You forgot that you must give a gold coin to everyone you meet. Why didn't you give anything to the water-bearer?"

"O woe to me, o ruin!" the moneylender exclaimed. "I have to give money to this contemptible, avaricious knave as well!" He untied his purse and tossed a coin. "Let this be the last one. It is dark, and we will not meet anyone else on the way back."

But Hodja Nasreddin did not whisper to the water-bearer for nothing. They headed back – the moneylender walking first, then Hodja Nasreddin, then the relatives. But before they could even walk fifty steps, a water-bearer emerged from an alley to meet them – the same one they had just left behind on the shore.

The moneylender turned away and wished to keep walking. Hodja Nasreddin stopped him with a stern voice:

"Do not forget Jafar, everyone you meet!" A torturous moan sounded in the night air: Jafar was untying his purse.

After receiving the coin, the water-bearer disappeared in the darkness. But fifty steps later, he came out to meet them again. The moneylender grew white and began to shake.

"Hussein Huslia," he said pitifully. "Look, it's the same one…"

"Everyone you meet," Hodja Nasreddin repeated.

Again, a moan sounded in the quiet air. Jafar was untying his purse.

This continued the whole way. The water-bearer appeared every fifty steps. He was out of breath, panting heavily and haltingly, and sweat was pouring down his face. He did not understand what was going on. He would take the coin and dash madly around, in order to jump onto the road again from behind some bush.

Saving his money, the moneylender kept quickening his pace, and then he started to run. But, with his limp, could he really outrun the crazed water-bearer, who was speeding along like a whirlwind, leaping over fences? The water-bearer managed to meet the moneylender no less than fifteen times, and, finally, right before the house, he jumped from the roof somewhere and blocked the gate. After receiving the last coin, he fell to the ground in exhaustion.

The moneylender jumped through the gate. Hodja Nasreddin followed him inside. The moneylender threw the empty purse to Hodja Nasreddin's feet and shouted in rage:

"Hussein Huslia, my healing is costing me too much! I have already spent over three thousand tanga on the gifts, the charity, and on that accursed water-bearer!"

"Calm down!" Hodja Nasreddin replied. "In half an hour, you will be rewarded. Let a large fire be lit in the middle of the court-yard."

While the servants were bringing the wood and lighting the fire, Hodja Nasreddin thought about how he could fool the money-lender and blame him for the unsuccessful healing. Various ideas came to his head, but he rejected them one after another, deeming them unworthy. Meanwhile, the fire began to burn brighter, and the flames, swaying lightly in the wind, rose high in the air, casting a crimson glow on the leaves of the grapevines.

"Undress, Jafar, and walk around the fire three times," Hodja Nasreddin said. He had not yet devised a plan and hoped to buy time. His face looked concerned.

The relatives observed in silence. The moneylender walked around the fire like a monkey on a chain, dangling his arms, which hung down almost to his knees.

Suddenly, Hodja Nasreddin's face cleared. He sighed in relief and, leaning back, straightened his shoulders.

"Give me a blanket!" he said in a loud voice. "Jafar and every-one else, come closer!"

He arranged the relatives in a circle and sat the moneylender on the ground in the middle. Then he addressed them all with the following words:

"I will now cover Jafar with this blanket and pronounce a prayer. And all of you, including Jafar, must repeat this prayer after me with your eyes closed. And when I take this blanket off, Jafar will already be healed. But I must warn you of a very important condition, and if anyone should break this condition, Jafar will not be healed. Listen carefully and remember."

The relatives fell silent, ready to listen and remember.

"As you are repeating the words of the prayer," Hodja Nasreddin said loudly and distinctly, "none of you, especially Jafar, can think about a monkey! If any of you should think about a monkey, or, worse yet, visualize it in your imagination – its tail, its red behind, its repulsive snout, and its yellow fangs – then, of course, there will not and there cannot be any healing, for such a pious deed is incompatible with thoughts of a creature as vile as a monkey. Do you understand?"

"We understand!" the relatives replied.

"Get ready, Jafar, close your eyes!" Hodja Nasreddin said solemnly, covering the moneylender with the blanket. "Now you close your eyes," he said to the relatives. "And remember my condition: do not think about a monkey."

He pronounced the first words of the prayer in a singsong voice:

"Allah wise and all-knowing, by the power of the sacred signs Aleph, Lam, Mim, and Ra, grant healing to your unworthy slave Jafar."

"Allah wise and all-knowing…" the many-voiced chorus of relatives repeated.

And then Hodja Nasreddin saw worry and embarrassment on the face of one relative; another began to cough, a third mixed up the words, a fourth started shaking his head as if to chase away a nagging vision. And a minute later, Jafar himself began to toss and turn restlessly under the blanket: a repugnant, unspeakably vile monkey, with a long tail and yellow fangs, persisted in his mind's eye and even taunted him, alternating between showing him its tongue and its round, red behind – in other words, the most indecent spots for a Muslim to contemplate.

Hodja Nasreddin continued to say the prayer loudly and then stopped, as if listening carefully. The relatives fell silent as well, some staggered backwards. Jafar gnashed his teeth under the blanket, for his monkey had started to engage in some truly obscene acts.

"What?" Hodja Nasreddin exclaimed in a thunderous voice. "O impious blasphemers! You violated my prohibition, you dared, while saying the prayer, to think of that which I forbade you to think of!" He tore off the blanket and set upon the moneylender:

"Why did you call me? I understand now that you did not wish to be healed at all! You wanted to besmirch my wisdom, you were sent by my enemies! But beware, Jafar! Tomorrow, the emir will know everything! I will tell him that, as you pronounced the prayer, you deliberately, with blasphemous intent, thought of a monkey! Beware, Jafar, and all of you beware: you will not get off easy, you know of the punishment for blasphemy!"

And since blasphemy was indeed punished very severely, all the relatives froze in terror, while the moneylender began to babble something, trying to explain himself. But Hodja Nasreddin would not listen; he turned abruptly and left, slamming the gate behind him…

Soon, the moon rose in the sky, flooding all of Bukhara with soft, warm light. And sounds of shouting and bickering came from the house of the moneylender until late in the night: they were trying to sort out who was the first to think of a monkey…

Chapter 31

After fooling the moneylender, Hodja Nasreddin headed to the palace.

Bukhara was asleep, its daily labors over. A cool darkness enveloped the alleys, water babbled sonorously under the bridges. Hodja Nasreddin smelled wet earth, and his feet slid on the dirt in a couple of spots: this meant that an overzealous street waterer had passed here, moistening the road copiously so that a gust of wind at night would not raise dust and disturb the tired people sleeping in the courtyards and on the roofs. The gardens had sunk into the darkness, their fragrant nighttime freshness breathing over the fences. Distant stars winked at Hodja Nasreddin from above, promising him good fortune. "Yes!" he smirked. "The world is not such a bad place for those who have heads on their shoulders instead of empty pots!"

He passed by the bazaar square on the way and saw bright, welcoming lights in the chaikhana of his friend Ali. Hodja Nasreddin went around the chaikhana and knocked on the door. The master opened it himself. They embraced and went into the warm room. Voices, laughter, and the clatter of dishes could be heard on the other side of the partition. Ali locked the door and lit an oil lamp.

"Everything is ready," he informed. "I will wait for Guljan in the chaikhana. The blacksmith Yusuf has prepared a safe sanctuary for her. The donkey remains saddled night and day; he is healthy, eats well, and has put on quite a lot of weight."

"Thank you, Ali. I do not know if I will ever be able to repay you."

"You will," said the chaikhana keeper. "You can do anything, Hodja Nasreddin, and let us speak of gratitude no more."

They sat and began to whisper to each other. The chaikhana keeper took out a man's robe prepared for Guljan and a large turban to hide her hair braids.

They arranged everything. Hodja Nasreddin was already preparing to leave when he heard a familiar voice through the wall. It was the voice of the pockmarked spy. Hodja Nasreddin opened the door a crack and looked out.

The pockmarked spy, wearing an expensive robe and turban, with a false beard on his face, was sitting in a circle of commoners and bloviating:

"The man who had previously been trying to pass for Hodja Nasreddin was not Hodja Nasreddin at all, but simply an impostor. I am the real Hodja Nasreddin! But I have long since renounced all my errors, having realized their destructiveness and impiety. And I – the real, genuine Hodja Nasreddin – advise all of you to follow my example. I understood at last that Islam is the only righteous faith; I understood that our great, sun-like emir is truly Allah's deputy on earth, which is proven by his incomparable wisdom, his piety, and his kindness. You have heard this from me, the genuine and true Hodja Nasreddin!"

"Hey!" Hodja Nasreddin said quietly, prodding the chaikhana keeper with his elbow. "Take a look at the stunts they pull when they think I am out of town. I'll have to remind them about me. Ali, I am going to leave you my false beard, brocade robe, and turban for a little bit, in exchange for some old rags."

The chaikhana keeper handed him a robe that had long been serving as a floor mat – dirty, torn, and full of fleas.

"Are you breeding them on purpose?" Hodja Nasreddin asked as he put on the robe. "You must be hoping to profit by selling flea meat. But the fleas will eat you first, Ali."

With these words, he walked out onto the street. The chaikhana keeper returned to his guests, waiting impatiently for what would come next. He did not have to wait for long. Hodja Nasreddin emerged from an alley with the tired gait of a man who had been traveling all day. He walked into the chaikhana, sat down in the shadows, and asked for tea. No one paid any attention to Hodja Nasreddin: who knows what different people wander the streets of Bukhara?

The pockmarked spy continued:

"My delusions were countless, but now I, Hodja Nasreddin, have repented and made a vow to always be pious, perform all the directives of Islam, and obey the emir and all of his viziers, governors, and guards. Since then, I have attained peace and bliss, and multiplied my fortune; before, I was a worthless vagrant, while now I live as befitting every good Muslim."

Some camel driver with a whip tucked in his belt handed a bowl of tea respectfully to the pockmarked spy.

"I have come to Bukhara from Kokand, o incomparable Hodja Nasreddin. I have heard much of your wisdom, but never in my life have I thought that I would get to meet you and even speak with you. Now I will tell everyone about my meeting with you and relay your words."

"Good, good!" the pockmarked spy nodded in approval. "Tell everyone that Hodja Nasreddin has reformed and renounced his delusions; he is now a devout Muslim and a faithful slave of the great emir. Let everyone know this."

"I have a question for you, o incomparable Hodja Nasreddin," the camel driver continued. "I am a devout Muslim, and I do not wish to break any laws even out of ignorance. At the same time, I am unsure of how to act when I hear the call of a muezzin while bathing in the river. Where should I direct my eyes at such a time?"

The pockmarked spy smirked condescendingly:

"Towards Mecca, of course…" But then someone said from a dark corner:

"Towards your clothes. That's the best way to make sure you won't have to return home naked."

Despite their respect for the pockmarked spy, all the people lowered their heads, concealing smiles.

The spy stared at Hodja Nasreddin, but did not recognize him in the shadows.

"Who is that croaking from the corner?" he said haughtily. "Hey, beggar, have you taken it in your head to challenge Hodja Nasreddin in wit?"

"I am far too unworthy for that," Hodja Nasreddin replied and began to drink his tea modestly in the corner.

Some peasant addressed the spy:

"Tell me, o devout Hodja Nasreddin: when a Muslim has to participate in a funeral procession, what is the best location for him according to the directives of Islam – in front of the bier, or behind?"

The spy lifted his finger meaningfully, intending to reply, but the voice from the corner interrupted him:

"It really doesn't matter if you are in front or behind, so long as you are not in the bier itself."

The easily amused chaikhana keeper grabbed his belly and sank down in laughter. The others could not restrain themselves either. This man in the corner had a way with words, and could, perhaps, match wits with Hodja Nasreddin himself.

Growing enraged, the spy turned his head slowly:

"Hey, you, what's your face! I see you have a very long tongue, it would be a shame for you to lose it!... It would not pose any difficulty for me to destroy him with my wit," the spy added, turning to the people around him, "but wit does not befit our pious and edifying conversation. There is a proper time for everything, and therefore I will leave the beggar's words without a reply. And so, I, Hodja Nasreddin, call upon you, o Muslims, to follow my example: respect the mullahs, obey the authorities, and good fortune will bless you and your homes. And most importantly, do not listen to any suspicious vagrants who falsely claim to be Hodja Nasreddin, such as the one who terrorized Bukhara recently and then disappeared without a trace as soon as he heard about the arrival of the real Hodja Nasreddin. Seize and capture these impostors, and hand them over to the emir's guards."

"Exactly!" Hodja Nasreddin exclaimed, stepping from the shadows into the light.

Everyone recognized him at once and froze in surprise. The spy turned white. Hodja Nasreddin walked right up to him, while the chaikhana keeper Ali approached unnoticeably from behind, ready to grab the spy at any moment.

"So you are the genuine Hodja Nasreddin?" The spy glanced round, hesitating. His cheeks were trembling, and his eyes were darting. However, he found the strength to respond:

"Yes, I am the genuine, true Hodja Nasreddin, and all the rest are impostors, including you!"

"Muslims, what are you waiting for?" Hodja Nasreddin shouted. "He has confessed it himself! Grab him, hold him, have you not heard the emir's decree, do you not know what you must do with Hodja Nasreddin? Grab him, or you will answer for harboring him!"

He tore off the spy's false beard. Everyone in the chaikhana recognized the hated pockmarked face with a flat nose and darting eyes.

"He has confessed!" Hodja Nasreddin cried out, winking to the right. "Seize Hodja Nasreddin!" He winked to the left.

The chaikhana keeper Ali was the first to grab the spy. The latter made to run away, but water-bearers, peasants, and tradesmen quickly got to him. For a time, nothing was visible except for rising and falling fists. Hodja Nasreddin was working harder than anyone else.

"I was joking!" the spy shouted, moaning. "O Muslims, I was joking, I am not Hodja Nasreddin! Let me go!"

"Liar!" Hodja Nasreddin shouted in response, working his fists like a good dough-maker. "You confessed it yourself, we heard it! O Muslims, we are all endlessly devoted to our emir and must fulfill his decrees exactly, so beat this Hodja Nasreddin, o Muslims! Drag him off to the palace and hand him off to the guards! Beat him for the glory of Allah and for the glory of the emir!"

They dragged the spy off to the palace, beating him with tireless zeal along the way. Giving the spy a farewell kick just below the back, Hodja Nasreddin returned to the chaikhana.

"Oof!" he said, wiping off sweat. "It seems we've done a fine number on him! I think he's still getting it, can you hear, Ali?"

Excited voices and the spy's pitiful cries came from the distance. He had spited everyone, that spy, and today everyone wanted to pay him back under the pretext of the emir's decree.

Pleased and happy, the chaikhana keeper smirked and patted his belly:

"That'll teach him. He will never come to my chaikhana again!"

Hodja Nasreddin changed in the back room, attached his beard, and turned once more into Hussein Huslia, the Baghdad sage.

When he arrived at the palace, he heard moans coming from the guards' quarters. He peeked inside.

The pockmarked spy was lying on a mat, all beat up, swollen, and crumpled, while Arslanbek was standing over him with a torch in his hand.

"Esteemed Arslanbek, what happened?" Hodja Nasreddin asked in an innocent voice.

"A very bad thing, Hussein Huslia. This vagrant Hodja Nasreddin has returned to the city again and already managed to beat up our most skilled spy, who had been passing himself off as Hodja Nasreddin on my orders and pronouncing devout speeches in order to lessen the harmful influence of the real Hodja Nasreddin on the minds of the people. But you can see what happened!"

"Oh, oh!" the spy said, raising his head, which was decorated with bruises and bloodstains. "Never again will I tangle with that accursed vagrant, because the next time, he will kill me. And I do not wish to be a spy any longer. Tomorrow, I will travel somewhere far away, where no one knows me, and take on an honest trade."

"It seems my friends spared no effort!" Hodja Nasreddin thought, looking at the spy and even feeling a certain pity for him. "If the palace had been another two hundred steps away, they would probably not have delivered him alive. We'll see if he puts this lesson to good use."

Sitting by the window of his tower at dawn, Hodja Nasreddin could see the pockmarked spy walk out of the palace gates carrying a small bundle in his hands. Limping sometimes on his right leg and sometimes on his left, clutching his chest, his shoulders, and his sides, and sitting down every other minute to catch his breath, the spy crossed the bazaar square, which was lit up by the first cool rays of the sun, and disappeared in the shade of the covered rows. Morning was coming to replace the dark night – clean, transparent, clear, awash with dew, pierced with sunlight. The birds were clicking, whistling, and twittering; butterflies flew high into the air to warm themselves in the first rays of light; a bee landed on the windowsill in front of Hodja Nasreddin and began to crawl around in search of the smell of honey coming from a ewer near the window.

The sun – Hodja Nasreddin's ancient, unchanging friend – was rising; they met every morning, and every morning Hodja Nasreddin could rejoice at seeing the sun as if he had not seen it for a whole year. The sun was rising like a kind, generous god, pouring its favors unto all equally, and everything in the world rejoiced gratefully, revealing its beauty, burning, sparkling, and shining in the morning rays – fluffy clouds, minaret tiles, wet leaves, water, grass, flowers. Even a simple, grim stone, forgotten and neglected by nature, found a way to decorate itself for the sun: its cracked sides shone and sparkled as if brushed with diamond dust. How could Hodja Nasreddin remain cool before the face of his shining friend at such an hour? The trees trembled beneath the bright rays of the sun, and Hodja Nasreddin trembled with them, as if he, too, was dressed in green leaves; doves were cooing and cleaning their wings atop a nearby minaret, and Hodja Nasreddin also wanted to clean his wing; two butterflies were fluttering near the window, and he wanted to join their airy game. Hodja Nasreddin's eyes were shining with joy. He remembered the pockmarked spy and wished for this morning to grant him a new life – clean and spotless. But immediately he thought, with regret, that the soul of that man was so full of nastiness that he probably would not be able to free himself, and, after recovering, would return to his old ways.

As will be revealed later, Hodja Nasreddin was not mistaken in his predictions. He knew people too well to be wrong. But how he wanted to be wrong, how happy he would have been to see the spy's soul healed! But that which is rotten cannot once again become blooming and fresh, stench cannot turn into fragrance. Hodja Nasreddin sighed dejectedly.

His most cherished dream was a world where all people could live as brothers, without greed, envy, guile, or anger, helping each other in need and sharing the joy of one as the joy of all. But, as he dreamed of such a joyous world, he observed bitterly that people were leading wrongful lives, oppressing and enslaving each other, and desecrating their souls with all kinds of filth. How much time would people need to understand, at last, the laws of a clean and honest life? Hodja Nasreddin did not doubt it in the least that people would one day understand these laws. He believed firmly that there were far more good people in the world than bad; the moneylender Jafar and the pockmarked spy, with their souls rotten to the core, were but ugly exceptions. He believed firmly that nature only endowed man with good, while all the bad in him was a foreign crust, introduced to the human soul from the outside by

a wrongful, unjust order of things. He believed firmly that a time
would come when people would rebuild and clean up their lives,
cleansing their souls of all dirt in the course of this noble work…
The fact that Hodja Nasreddin thought this way, and not some
other way, is proven by the numerous stories that bear the stamp
of his soul, including this book. And while many have tried to
blacken his memory out of greed, or lowly envy, or malice, they
did not succeed in their endeavors, for lies will never triumph over
truth. The memory of Hodja Nasreddin has remained, and will
forever remain, noble and clear, preserving its transparent glow
like a diamond, forever and in spite of everything! And, to this
day, when travelers stop by a modest headstone in the Turkish Ak-
Shekir, they speak fondly of Hodja Nasreddin, the merry tramp
from Bukhara, and repeat the words of a certain poet: "He gave
his heart to the earth, even though he circled the world like the
wind – like the wind, which, after his death, spread the fragrance
of the blooming roses of his soul throughout the universe. Glorious is the life spent on leaving the stamp of one's soul on the
world and on contemplating all the world's beauties!"

Then again, some say that there is no one buried beneath the
headstone; that the sly Hodja Nasreddin placed it there on purpose and, after spreading rumors of his own death everywhere,
went on traveling the world. Did this happen, or did it not? Let us
not engage in fruitless guessing; let us just say that anything can be
expected from Hodja Nasreddin!

Chapter 32

The morning hours flew away to be replaced by a hot, stuffy day. Everything was ready for the escape.

Hodja Nasreddin went up to his prisoner:

"The term of your imprisonment, most wise Hussein Huslia, has ended. I am leaving the palace tonight. I will leave your room unlocked, but on the condition that you do not come out any earlier than two days from now. If you break this condition, you might accidentally run into me in the palace, and then, as you understand, I will have to accuse you of escaping and hand you off to the executioner. Farewell, Baghdad sage Hussein Huslia, and do not think ill of me! I entrust you with revealing the truth to the emir and telling him my name. Listen carefully – I am known as Hodja Nasreddin!"

"O!" the old man exclaimed, shrinking back, so shocked by the name that he could not say another word.

The door creaked as it closed, and Hodja Nasreddin's steps faded downstairs. The old man approached the door carefully and tested it – it was open. The old man peeked out and saw no one. Then he shut the door hastily and bolted it from within. "No!" he muttered. "I would rather sit here for a whole week than tangle with Hodja Nasreddin."

In the evening, when the first stars were already beginning to appear in the greening sky, Hodja Nasreddin, holding a clay ewer in his hands, walked up to the guards watching the entrance to the emir's harem.

The guards, who had not noticed him approaching, continued their conversation.

"Another star just fell," said the lazy, fat guard who could swallow raw eggs. "If they land on earth, as you say, then why don't people ever find them?"

"They probably fall into the sea," the other guard replied.

"Hey you, valiant warriors," Hodja Nasreddin interrupted. "Call the head eunuch, I must give him the medicine for the sick concubine."

The head eunuch appeared and accepted the small ewer reverently with both hands, even though it contained nothing but a bit of chalk mixed with some water from the aryk. He listened to the detailed instructions as to how the medicine should be used, and departed.

"O most wise Hussein Huslia!" the fat guard said ingratiatingly. "You know everything, your wisdom has no bounds! Tell us where stars land when they fall from the sky and why people never find them on earth!"

Hodja Nasreddin could not resist a joke.

"Don't you know?" he said without a trace of mirth. "When the stars fall, they shatter into small silver coins, and then the poor pick them up. I even used to know some people who became rich this way."

The guards looked at each other. Their faces portrayed unspeakable surprise.

Hodja Nasreddin walked away, snickering at the foolish guards. He had no idea how useful his joke would become very shortly.

He waited in his tower until midnight. But then everything grew quiet in the city and in the palace; all the lights were extinguished. He could not delay any further, for summer nights fly on swift wings. Hodja Nasreddin descended and, sneaking and staying in the shadows, headed towards the harem. "The guards must have fallen asleep by now," he thought.

Imagine his disappointment when, as he drew nearer, he heard the quiet voices of the guards.

"If only a star would fall here!" the lazy, fat guard was saying. "We would pick up the silver and become rich at once."

"You know, I don't really believe that stars can shatter into silver coins," the other guard replied.

"But that's what the Baghdad sage told us," countered the first. "His learnedness is known to all, and he cannot be mistaken."

"Curse you two!" Hodja Nasreddin exclaimed silently, hiding in the shadows. "Oh, why did I tell them about the stars; now they will be arguing till dawn! Will I really have to delay the escape?"

Thousands of stars were burning in the unreachable heights above Bukhara with a clean and silent fire: one tiny star slipped off suddenly and took a headlong plunge, slicing the sky diagonally.

Another followed it, leaving behind a momentary, blinding streak. It was the middle of the summer, and the season of shooting stars was fast approaching.

"If they shattered into silver coins..." the second guard began.

Hodja Nasreddin suddenly had an epiphany. He reached into his pocket hastily and took out his purse, full of silver. He had to wait for a very long time, but no stars fell. Finally, one flew by. Hodja Nasreddin tossed a coin at the guards' feet. The silver jingled on the stone path.

The guards froze at first, and then got up, looking straight at each other.

"Did you hear?" the first asked in a trembling voice.

"I heard," the other replied, stuttering. Hodja Nasreddin tossed another coin. It flashed in the moonbeams. With a quick shout, the lazy guard fell onto it, covering it with his stomach.

"Did you ca... catch it?" the second guard asked, his tongue growing numb.

"I ca... caught it," the fat man responded with trembling lips, rising and showing him the coin.

Suddenly, several stars dropped from the sky at once. Hodja Nasreddin began to throw whole handfuls of silver. The silence of the night was filled with high-pitched, melodious ringing. The crazed guards tossed aside their spears and began to feel for the coins along the ground.

"I found a coin!" one of them shouted in a hoarse and stuffy voice. "Here it is!"

The second crawled around in silence and then rumbled as he came upon a whole pile of coins.

Hodja Nasreddin tossed them another handful and slipped through the gate unhindered.

The rest was easy. The soft Persian rugs accepted his footsteps silently. He remembered all the passageways. The eunuchs were asleep...

Guljan met him with a moist, hot kiss, and embraced him, trembling.

"Come quick!" he whispered.

No one stopped them; only a eunuch began to turn and groan

in his sleep. Hodja Nasreddin leaned over him. But it was not the eunuch's time to die: he smacked his lips and began to snore once more… Faint moonlight was breaking through the multicolored panes of glass.

At the gate, Hodja Nasreddin stopped and peeked out. The guards, standing on all fours in the middle of the courtyard, were gazing at the sky and waiting for another star to fall. With a broad swing, Hodja Nasreddin tossed a handful of coins; they landed far away behind some trees. The guards dashed there. They were so crazed that they barely saw anything. Panting heavily and shrieking feverishly, they broke right through a hedge of thorny bushes, leaving scraps of their pants and robes on the branches.

That night, it was possible to steal all the concubines from the harem instead of just one.

"Faster! Faster!" Hodja Nasreddin said, drawing the girl along. They ran to the tower and climbed upstairs. Hodja Nasreddin took a rope he had prepared a long time ago from under the bed.

"It's high… I am afraid," Guljan whispered. He rebuked her sternly, and she obeyed.

Hodja Nasreddin tied a loop around her and removed the sawn-out grating from the window.

Guljan sat on the windowsill. It was very high, and she began to tremble. "Go!" Hodja Nasreddin commanded, prodding her in the back. She closed her eyes, slid down the smooth stones, and was suspended in the air.

She came to on the ground. "Run! Run!" she heard from above. Hodja Nasreddin was leaning out of the window up to his waist, waving his arms, and pulling on the rope. Guljan untied herself hastily and ran through the deserted square.

She did not know that the entire palace was already seized with alarm and confusion. The head eunuch, who had acquired a passionate zeal for serving the emir after the recent lesson with the cane, peeked into the room of the new concubine in the middle of the night and found her bed empty. The eunuch dashed to the emir and woke him up. The emir summoned Arslanbek. Arslanbek raised the palace guard, torches lit up, shields and spears began to jingle.

They sent for the Baghdad sage. The emir met Hodja Nasreddin with loud complaints:

"Hussein Huslia, how far has depravity spread in our country that we, the great emir, cannot even find peace from that tramp Hodja Nasreddin in our own palace? Who has ever heard of a concubine being stolen from the emir's harem?"

"O great emir," Bakhtiyar dared interrupt. "But perhaps it was not Hodja Nasreddin who did this?"

"Who else?" the emir shouted. "In the morning, we received news that he had returned to Bukhara, and at night, the concubine who used to be his bride disappears! Who but Hodja Nasreddin could have done this? Search for him, post triple guards everywhere – he probably has not escaped the palace yet! Remember, Arslanbek – your head is this close to jumping off your shoulders!"

The search began. Guards rummaged through every corner in the palace. Torches shone everywhere, giving off a tremulous glow.

Hodja Nasreddin searched with more zeal than anyone else. He looked under rugs, poked inside marble pools with a stick, fussed, shouted, and peeked into kettles, pitchers, and even mouse holes.

Returning to the emir's bedroom, he reported:

"Great sovereign, Hodja Nasreddin has already managed to leave the palace."

"Hussein Huslia!" the emir replied angrily. "Your carelessness surprises us. What if he is hiding somewhere? He could have snuck into our bedroom. Hey, guards, over here! Guards!" the emir shouted, terrified at the thought.

A cannon fired outside – to frighten the elusive Hodja Nasreddin.

The emir hunched in some corner and kept shouting:

"Guards! Guards!"

He would not calm down until Arslanbek posted thirty guards at the doors to his bedroom and ten guards by every window.

Only then did the emir crawl out of the corner and say pitifully:

"What do you think, Hussein Huslia? Could this tramp be hiding somewhere in our bedroom?"

"The doors and the windows are being guarded," Hodja Nasreddin replied. "There are only two of us here. Where could Hodja Nasreddin be hiding?"

"But he will not get away with stealing our concubine!" the emir shouted. Fear gave way to rage in his soul, and his fingers twisted convulsively as if he were clutching the throat of Hodja Nasreddin. "O Hussein Huslia!" the emir continued. "Our wrath and our indignation are boundless! We have not even visited her once; the thought of this fills our royal heart with sorrow. Your stars are to blame for all of this, Hussein Huslia, and, if we could, we would behead all the stars for such malicious deeds! But this time, Hodja Nasreddin will not escape unpunished! We have already given orders to Arslanbek! We also command you, Hussein Huslia, to apply all your efforts to capturing this vagrant! Remember that your appointment as head eunuch depends on this. Tomorrow you must leave the palace, Hussein Huslia, and not return without Hodja Nasreddin."

Narrowing his sly, bright eyes, Hodja Nasreddin bowed to the ground before the emir.

Chapter 33

For the remainder of the night, Hodja Nasreddin told the emir about his plans to capture Hodja Nasreddin. The plans were very intricate, and the emir was pleased.

In the morning, after receiving a purse of gold to cover his expenses, Hodja Nasreddin went up to his tower for the last time, placed the money in a leather belt, and glanced around with a sigh: he was suddenly sad to leave his dwelling – he had spent so many lonely, sleepless nights here, and thought of so much; he was leaving a part of his soul amid these grim walls.

He shut the door behind him and ran easily down the steep stone staircase towards freedom. The whole world was open to him once more. Roads, passes, and mountain paths were calling him on a long journey, green woods promised him shelter on soft leaves in the shade, the rivers were waiting to offer a drink of cold water, the birds had prepared their very best songs to please him. He had spent too long in his gilded cage, that merry tramp Hodja Nasreddin, and the world had grown bored without him.

But right by the gates, his heart was dealt a terrible blow.

He stopped, grew pale, and leaned against a wall. Led by numerous guards, his friends were entering the open gates with their heads lowered and their hands bound. He saw the old potter Niyaz, the chaikhana keeper Ali, the blacksmith Yusuf, and many others; everyone he had ever met, spoken to, asked for water or some hay for his donkey, they were all here! Arslanbek brought up the rear of the sorrowful procession.

Hodja Nasreddin did not come to his senses for a long time, and when he did, the gates had already closed and the courtyard was empty: everyone had been taken to the dungeon. Hodja Nasreddin dashed off in search of Arslanbek.

"What happened, esteemed Arslanbek? Who were those people? What crimes have they committed?"

"Those people were harborers and accomplices of Hodja Nasreddin!" Arslanbek replied triumphantly. "My spies tracked them down, and they will all be publicly executed today in a most brutal fashion if they do not give up Hodja Nasreddin. But you are pale, Hussein Huslia! You are very upset!"

"Of course!" Hodja Nasreddin replied. "It means the reward is slipping from my hands into yours!"

Hodja Nasreddin had to remain in the palace. And could he really do otherwise when death was threatening innocent people?

At midday, soldiers appeared on the square, surrounding the judgment platform with a triple ring. The people, who had been notified of the impending execution by heralds, were waiting silently. The burning sky breathed down scalding heat.

The palace doors opened, and the heralds ran out, followed, in the usual order, by guards, musicians, elephants, the retinue, and finally the emir's sedan chair. The people prostrated themselves. The sedan was lifted on the platform.

The emir took his place on the throne. The condemned men were led from the palace. The crowd met them with a rumble. The relatives and friends of the condemned were standing in the front rows so they could see better.

The executioners were fussing around, readying axes, sharpened stakes, and ropes. They had a long day today: they would have to put to death sixty people in a row.

Old Niyaz was first in the fateful line. The executioners were holding him by the arms; there was a gallows to his right, the block to his left, and a sharpened stake was sticking from the ground directly in front.

Grand Vizier Bakhtiyar proclaimed loudly and solemnly:

"In the name of Allah, gracious and merciful! The ruler of Bukhara and the sun of the universe, the emir of Bukhara, has weighed on the scales of justice the crimes committed by sixty of his subjects in relation to harboring the blasphemer, disturber of the peace, sower of discord, and purveyor of indecent acts Hodja Nasreddin, and decided the following: the potter Niyaz, as the chief harborer who sheltered the aforementioned tramp named Hodja Nasreddin for a long time, is to be put to death by separating his head from his body. As for the rest of the criminals, their first punishment will be witnessing the execution of Niyaz, so that they may tremble in anticipation of an even worse fate for themselves. The means of execution for each of them will be announced separately…"

The square was so quiet that Bakhtiyar's every word could be heard distinctly even at the back of the crowd.

"And let it be known to all," he continued, raising his voice, "that in the future, every harborer of Hodja Nasreddin will be treated in the same manner, and none will escape the executioner. But if any of the condemned reveals the hiding place of this thief and idler, he will not only be spared from execution, not only receive a reward from the emir and blessings from heaven, but he will also free all the others from punishment. Potter Niyaz, you can spare yourself and others from execution if you reveal the location of Hodja Nasreddin."

Niyaz was silent for a long time, his head lowered. Bakhtiyar repeated his question.

Niyaz responded:

"No, I cannot reveal his location." The executioners dragged the old man to the block. Someone screamed in the crowd. The old man got down on his knees and, extending his neck, placed his gray head on the block.

At that moment, Hodja Nasreddin pushed aside the courtiers, stepped forward, and stood before the emir.

"O sovereign!" he said loudly, so the people would hear. "Stop the execution, I am about to capture Hodja Nasreddin!"

The emir stared at him in surprise. The people in the square stirred. Obeying the emir's sign, the executioner lowered his axe.

"O ruler!" Hodja Nasreddin said loudly. "Would it be just to execute these minor harborers while the chief harborer, who has sheltered Hodja Nasreddin all this time and continues to shelter him now – who has fed, nourished, rewarded him, and cared for him in every way – remains alive?"

"You are right," the emir said grandly. "If such a harborer exists, then it would be fitting to behead him first. But show us this harborer, Hussein Huslia."

A restrained murmur passed through the crowd: those standing in the front were relaying the emir's words to those behind them.

"But if the great emir declines to execute this chief harborer, if the great emir leaves him alive, would it be just to execute these minor harborers?" asked Hodja Nasreddin.

More and more surprised, the emir replied:

"If we decide not to execute the chief harborer, then, of course, we will cancel the execution of the minor harborers. But there is one thing we do not understand, Hussein Huslia: what could possibly cause us to refrain from executing the chief harborer? Where is he? Point him out, and we will immediately separate his head from his body."

Hodja Nasreddin turned to the people:

"You heard the words of the emir. The sovereign of Bukhara said that if he refuses to execute the chief harborer, whom I will name presently, then all these minor harborers who are standing by the block will be freed and released to their families. Did I speak correctly, o sovereign?"

"You spoke correctly, Hussein Huslia," the emir confirmed. "We give our word. But hurry up and point out the chief harborer."

"Did you hear?" Hodja Nasreddin asked, turning to the people. "The emir gave his word!"

He sighed deeply. He could feel thousands of eyes on himself.

"The chief harborer…"

He stumbled and passed his eyes over the square; many noticed sorrow and deathly anguish on his face. He was saying goodbye to his beloved world, to the people, and to the sun.

"Hurry!" the emir exclaimed impatiently. "Speak quickly, Hussein Huslia!"

Hodja Nasreddin said in a firm, ringing voice:

"The chief harborer is you, emir!"

With an abrupt motion, he flung off his turban and tore the false beard from his face.

The crowd gasped and froze. His eyes bulging, the emir moved his lips but no sound came out. The courtiers turned to stone.

The silence did not last long.

"Hodja Nasreddin! Hodja Nasreddin!" people shouted in the crowd.

"Hodja Nasreddin!" whispered the courtiers.

"Hodja Nasreddin!" exclaimed Arslanbek. Finally, the sovereign himself came to his senses. His lips pronounced indistinctly:

"Hodja Nasreddin!"

"Yes, it is I! Well now, emir, order your own head to be chopped off as the chief harborer! I lived in your palace, shared your food, received your rewards. I was your closest and most important advisor in all matters. You are the harborer, emir, have your own head chopped off!"

Hodja Nasreddin was seized. He did not resist, he was shouting:

"The emir promised to free the condemned! You heard the emir's word."

The people began to murmur anxiously. The triple chain of guards could barely hold off the crowd. People were shouting louder and louder:

"Free the condemned!"

"The emir gave his word!"

"Free them!"

The hum in the crowd spread and grew louder. The chains of guards retreated, pushed back by the people. Bakhtiyar leaned to the emir:

"O sovereign, we must free them, or the people will rebel." The emir nodded.

"The emir keeps his word!" Bakhtiyar shouted. The guards stepped aside. The condemned men disappeared immediately in the crowd.

Hodja Nasreddin was led to the palace. Many in the crowd were weeping and shouting after him:

"Farewell, Hodja Nasreddin! Farewell our beloved, noble Hodja Nasreddin, you will live on forever in our hearts."

He walked with his head raised high, and his face showed fearlessness. He turned in front of the gates and waved goodbye. The crowd responded with a powerful rumble.

The emir climbed back onto his sedan chair in a hurry. The palace procession headed back.

Chapter 34

The divan assembled to judge Hodja Nasreddin.

When he walked in – surrounded by guards, his arms and legs bound – the courtiers looked down. They were ashamed to look at one another. The sages frowned and stroked their beards, while the emir, turning away, sighed and cleared his throat.

As for Hodja Nasreddin, he was looking at them with a straightforward and clear gaze, and, were it not for the fact that his hands were tied behind his back, one could have thought that it was not him on trial, but all the people sitting before him.

The real Baghdad sage Hussein Huslia came to the trial along with the other courtiers, having been released at last from his imprisonment. Hodja Nasreddin winked at him amicably. The Baghdad sage jumped on his pillows and hissed in rage.

The trial did not last long. Hodja Nasreddin was sentenced to death. It remained to determine the method of execution.

"O great ruler!" said Arslanbek. "In my opinion, this criminal should be impaled so that he may end his life in horrible suffering."

Hodja Nasreddin did not bat an eyelid; he stood with a serene smile, placing his face beneath a ray of sun which had entered the hall through an open window in the ceiling.

"No!" the emir said decisively. "The Turkish sultan has already impaled this blasphemer, but evidently he knows a means to survive this method of execution without suffering any harm, or else he would not have escaped from the sultan's hands alive."

Bakhtiyar suggested beheading Hodja Nasreddin.

"True, it is one of the easiest forms of death," he added, "but also the most reliable."

"No!" said the emir. "The caliph of Baghdad has beheaded him before, and yet he is alive."

The officials rose one by one and suggested hanging Hodja Nasreddin or skinning him alive. The emir rejected all these options because, as he secretly watched Hodja Nasreddin, he could not detect any sign of fear, which the emir saw as clear proof that the suggested methods were ineffective.

The courtiers fell silent in embarrassment. The emir began to grow angry.

Then the Baghdad sage rose. He was speaking before the emir for the first time, and therefore he thought about his advice carefully so as to distinguish himself in wisdom from the rest.

"O great sovereign of the universe! If this criminal has managed to escape unharmed from all manners of execution, is this not direct proof that he is assisted by evil forces, in particular the spirit of darkness whose name it would not be proper to say here, before the emir?"

As he said these words, the sage blew on his shoulders, and so did everyone else except Hodja Nasreddin.

"Having weighed and considered all that concerns this criminal," the sage continued, "our great emir rejected the proposed methods of putting Hodja Nasreddin to death, fearing that evil forces would once again help the criminal escape just retribution. But there is one more method of execution that the aforementioned criminal Hodja Nasreddin has never been subjected to, namely: drowning!"

Holding his head up high, the Baghdad sage glanced triumphantly at all those present.

Hodja Nasreddin stirred.

The emir noticed his movement. "Aha! So that's his secret!"

Meanwhile, Hodja Nasreddin was thinking: "It is very good that they are speaking of evil forces. That means all hope is not lost for me!"

"I have learned from tales and books," the sage continued in the meantime, "that there is a sacred pond in Bukhara known as the pond of Sheikh Ahmed. It is clear that evil forces would not dare approach this pond, which is why, o sovereign, we must immerse the criminal fully and for a long time into the sacred waters, after which he will die."

"Now here is sage advice worthy of reward!" the emir exclaimed.

Hodja Nasreddin said reproachfully to the Baghdad sage:

"O Hussein Huslia, is this how I treated you when you were in my power? It really goes to show you can't rely on the gratitude of men!"

It was decided to drown Hodja Nasreddin publicly after sunset in the sacred pond of Sheikh Ahmed. And so that Hodja Nasreddin would not be able to escape along the way, it was decided to deliver him there in a leather sack and drown him in the very same sack.

…The sound of axes could be heard by the pond all day: the carpenters were building a platform, but what else could they do when a guard was standing over each one? They worked silently, with grim, embittered faces. Upon finishing, they refused their meager payment and walked away with downcast eyes.

Carpets were laid over the platform and the entire bank around it. The opposite bank was intended for the people.

Spies reported that unrest was brewing in the city. Therefore, Arslanbek brought great numbers of troops to the pond and placed cannons there. Fearing that the people would try to free Hodja Nasreddin along the way, Arslanbek prepared four sacks full of rags: he intended to send these sacks towards the pond in plain view, along populated streets, while the sack containing Hodja Nasreddin would be transported along deserted alleyways. His cunning went even further – each false sack was accompanied by eight guards, while Hodja Nasreddin's had only three.

"I will send a messenger from the pond," Arslanbek said to the guards. "You must carry out the four false sacks immediately, one after the other, while the fifth sack with the criminal should be carried out a little later and inconspicuously, after all the curious around the gates have followed the false sacks. Do you understand me? Remember that you will answer with your heads."

In the evening, drums sounded on the square, announcing the end of the bazaar. Crowds of people headed towards the pond from all directions. Soon, the emir arrived with his retinue. Torches were lit on the platform and all around it. The flames hissed and swayed in the wind, and their crimson reflections trembled on the water. The opposite bank was dark; one could not see the crowd from the platform, which was flooded with lights, but one could hear clearly how it shifted, moved, and breathed, its indistinct, anxious hum blending with the gusts of nightly wind.

In a loud voice, Bakhtiyar read the emir's decree regarding the putting of Hodja Nasreddin to death. Just then, the wind quieted down as well – it grew so quiet that goosebumps ran up the luminous emir's back. The wind sighed again, and thousands of chests in the crowd sighed with it.

"Arslanbek!" said the emir, and his voice trembled. "Why do you delay?"

"I have already sent the messenger, o sovereign." Suddenly, shouting and the clanging of weapons came from the darkness, a fight broke out somewhere. The emir jumped up, looking round. A minute later, eight guards without a sack entered the brightly lit area in front of the platform.

"Where is the criminal?" the emir shouted. "They took him away from the guards, he slipped away! You see, Arslanbek?"

"O sovereign!" Arslanbek replied. "Your lowly slave has foreseen everything; that sack contained old rags."

The sounds of a scuffle came from another direction. Arslanbek hastened to reassure the emir:

"Let them take it away, o sovereign! That sack, too, has nothing but rags."

…The first sack was recovered from the guards by the chaikhana keeper Ali and his friends, the second was captured by the blacksmiths, headed by Yusuf. Soon, the potters claimed the third sack, but found rags inside. The fourth sack was let through to the platform. By the light of the torches, the guards raised the sack above the water with the whole crowd watching and tossed out the contents: rags came pouring out.

The crowd froze in utter confusion. This was exactly the goal of the experienced Arslanbek, who knew that confusion led to inaction.

The time came for the fifth sack to arrive. But the guards who had been entrusted with it had fallen behind somewhere and had not yet delivered the sack to the pond.

Chapter 35

When the guards brought Hodja Nasreddin from the dungeon, he said:

"So you are going to carry me on your own backs? I regret that my donkey is not here, he would have died laughing."

"Silence! Soon you will be weeping!" the guards replied angrily. They could not forgive Hodja Nasreddin for surrendering to the emir directly, bypassing them.

Holding the cramped sack open, they began to stuff Hodja Nasreddin inside.

"O slaves of the shaitan!" Hodja Nasreddin shouted, folded in three. "Could you not have found a roomier sack?"

"Don't worry!" the guards replied, panting and sweating profusely. "You won't have to suffer long. Now stop spreading yourself out, o son of sin, or we'll stuff your knees into your stomach!"

Palace servants came running to the noise. Finally, after a long struggle, the guards managed to stuff Hodja Nasreddin in the sack, which they tied with a rope. The inside of the sack was cramped, dark, and smelly. Hodja Nasreddin's soul became clouded in a black haze: it seemed there would be no salvation for him now. He called out to fate and to the all-powerful chance: "O fate, who has become my mother; o all-powerful chance, who has guarded me until now like a father – where are you now, why do you not hasten to Hodja Nasreddin's aid? O fate, o all-powerful chance!"

Meanwhile the guards had already made it halfway. They switched carrying the sack every two hundred paces; Hodja Nasreddin counted these brief stops mournfully, determining how far they had traveled and how much was left.

He understood very well that fate and chance will never come to the aid of someone who complains and clamors instead of acting. Only the walking man will survive the road; let his legs grow weak and buckle along the way – he must crawl on his arms and knees, and then he will always see the bright flame of a fire in the distance and find a merchant caravan resting there, and the caravan will surely be headed in the same direction, and there will be a spare camel to carry the traveler where he needs to go… But the man sitting on the road and giving in to despair – no matter how much he weeps and laments – will not evoke compassion in the heartless rocks; he will die of thirst in the desert, his corpse will become the prey of foul-smelling hyenas, hot sand will bury his bones. How many people have died prematurely, for the sole reason that their will to live was not strong enough! Hodja Nasreddin considered such a death disgraceful.

"No!" he said to himself and, clenching his teeth, repeated fiercely:

"No! I will not die today! I do not wish to die!"

But what could he do, folded in three and stuffed into a cramped sack, where he could not move a muscle: his knees and elbows seemed stuck to his torso. Only Hodja Nasreddin's tongue remained free.

"O valiant warriors," he said from the sack. "Stop for a second, I wish to recite a prayer before dying, so the all-merciful Allah may admit my soul into his luminous abodes."

The guards placed the sack on the ground.

"Recite it. But we will not let you out of the sack. Recite your prayer in the sack."

"And where are we now?" Hodja Nasreddin asked. "I am asking so that you can turn me towards the nearest mosque."

"We are near the Karshi gates. There are mosques all around, no matter which way we turn you, so recite your prayer quickly. We cannot delay for long."

"Thank you, o valiant warriors," Hodja Nasreddin replied from the sack in a mournful voice.

What was he planning? He barely knew it himself. "I will gain a few minutes. And then we'll see. Maybe something will turn up…"

He began to pray loudly, listening to what the guards were saying.

"And how did we not guess that the new astrologer was Hodja Nasreddin himself?" the guards were lamenting. "If we had recognized and captured him, we would have received a large reward from the emir."

The guards' thoughts took their usual course, for greed was the essence of their lives.

Hodja Nasreddin took advantage of this. "I must try to make them leave the sack, if only for a short time… Perhaps I will be able to tear the rope, or maybe someone will come along and free me."

"Hurry up and finish your prayer!" the guards said, prodding the sack with their feet. "Do you hear? We cannot wait any longer!"

"One moment, valiant warriors! I have one last request for Allah. O almighty, all-merciful Allah, please make it so that the man who finds the ten thousand tanga I buried takes at least one thousand tanga from this sum, brings it to a mosque, and gives it to a mullah, instructing him to pray for me for a whole year…"

Upon hearing of the ten thousand tanga, the guards grew quiet. Although Hodja Nasreddin could not see anything from his sack, he knew exactly how the guards' faces looked at that moment: how they were exchanging glances and prodding each other with their elbows.

"Carry me on," he said in a meek voice. "I surrender my spirit into the hands of Allah." The guards dallied.

"We will rest a while longer," one of them said insinuatingly. "O Hodja Nasreddin, do not think us to be heartless, evil men. Only our duty forces us to treat you in such a cruel manner; if we and our families could only survive without the emir's wages, we would have immediately set you free…"

"What are you talking about?" the second guard whispered fearfully. "If we set him free, the emir will remove our heads."

"Quiet!" the first hissed. "We just need to get the money."

Hodja Nasreddin did not hear the whispers, but he knew that the guards were whispering, and he knew what they were whispering about.

"I bear no anger towards you, o warriors," he said with a pious sigh. "I have sinned too much myself to judge others. If Allah grants me pardon in the next world, I promise to pray for you before his throne. You say that, were it not for the emir's wages, you would have set me free? Think about what you are saying! You would be disobeying the will of the emir and therefore committing a grave sin. No! I do not want you to burden your souls with sin; take the sack and carry me to the pond. Let the will of Allah and the emir be done!"

The guards looked at each other in confusion, cursing the pious repentance that had – at a very bad time, they thought – taken hold of Hodja Nasreddin.

The third guard entered the conversation. Until now, he was silent, trying to think of a ruse.

"How difficult it is to see a man who has begun to repent his sins and delusions before death," he began, winking at his comrades. "No, I am not like that! I have long since repented and now lead a pious life. But piety in word, unaccompanied by deeds that please Allah, is worthless," the guard continued, while his comrades, who knew him to be an incorrigible gambler and debaucher, were clamping their own mouths with their hands so as not to burst out in laughter. "For instance, I am supplement-ing my pious life with a righteous and pious deed: namely, I am building a large mosque in my home village and, in order to raise money for this project, I even have to deny food to myself and my family."

One of the guards could no longer bear it and, choking with laughter, went off into the darkness.

"I put aside every coin," the pious guard continued, "but still the mosque is being built too slowly, which fills my heart with sorrow. A few days ago, I sold my cow. But even if I have to sell my own boots – I am content to go barefoot if I could only finish what I began."

Hodja Nasreddin sniffled from inside the sack. The guards glanced at each other. Their plan was succeeding. They hurried along their resourceful comrade with their elbows.

"O, if only I could find a man who would agree to donate eight or ten thousand tanga to finish the mosque!" he exclaimed. "I would swear to him that for five years, or even ten years, his name would daily ascend, enrobed in the fragrant smoke of prayer, from beneath the roof of this mosque to Allah's throne!" The first guard said:

"O my pious friend! I do not have ten thousand tanga, but perhaps you will agree to accept my last savings – five hundred tanga. Do not refuse my modest gift, for I, too, wish to participate in such a righteous deed."

"Me too," the second guard said, stuttering and shaking from laughter. "I have three hundred tanga..."

"O righteous, pious man!" Hodja Nasreddin exclaimed, sniffling. "How I wish I could press the flap of your robe to my lips! I am a great sinner, but be merciful and do not refuse my gift. I have ten thousand tanga. When, through blasphemous deceit, I was brought close to the emir, I frequently received purses of gold and silver from him as gifts. After collecting ten thousand tanga, I decided to hide them in order to retrieve them as I fled. And since I had decided to flee through the Karshi gates, I buried this money on the Karshi cemetery under one of the old tombstones."

"On the Karshi cemetery!" the guards exclaimed. "That means they are right here, nearby!"

"Yes! We are now on the north end of the cemetery, and if you walk..."

"We are on the east end! Where, where is your money hidden?"

"It is hidden on the west end of the cemetery," Hodja Nasreddin replied. "But first you must swear to me, o pious guard, that my name will really be mentioned in the mosque daily for ten years."

"I swear!" the guard said, trembling with impatience. "I swear to you by the name of Allah and Muhammad his prophet! Now tell us, quickly, where the money is buried!"

Hodja Nasreddin dallied. "What if they decide to carry me to the pond first and search for the money the next day?" he thought. "No, that won't happen. Firstly, they are consumed by greed and impatience, secondly, they are afraid that someone will beat them to the money, and thirdly, they don't trust each other. Now where should I send them so they dig around as long as possible?"

Leaning over the sack, the guards were waiting. Hodja Nasreddin could hear their heavy breathing, as if they had just run a great distance.

"On the west end of the cemetery, there are three old tombstones forming a triangle," Hodja Nasreddin said. "I have buried three thousand three hundred thirty three and one third tanga under each one…"

"Forming a triangle," the guards repeated together like diligent students repeating the words of the Koran after their teacher. "Three thousand three hundred thirty three and one third tanga…"

They agreed that two would go to fetch the money, while the third would stay behind to guard the sack. This could have caused Hodja Nasreddin to lose heart were it not for his ability to guess people's actions in advance: he knew very well that the third guard would not remain by the sack for long. His predictions came true: once left alone, the guard began to sigh anxiously, cough, and pace back and forth on the road, his weapons clanging. From these noises, Hodja Nasreddin guessed all his thoughts: worry about his three thousand three hundred thirty three and one third tanga was gnawing at the guard. Hodja Nasreddin waited patiently.

"They sure are taking their time," the guard said.

"They are probably hiding the money in a different spot, and tomorrow all three of you will come to get it," Hodja Nasreddin replied.

It was a well-calculated blow. The guard began to breathe heavily, and then pretended to yawn.

"How I would love to hear some soul-saving story before my death," Hodja Nasreddin said from the sack. "Perhaps you can recall a story and tell it to me, o kind guard."

"No!" the guard replied angrily. "I do not know any soul-saving stories… Besides, I am tired. I am going to lie down on the grass here for a little bit."

He did not realize that his footsteps would be heard far and wide on the pavement. At first, he walked slowly, but then the sound of rapid footfalls reached Hodja Nasreddin's ears – the guard went running to the cemetery.

It was time to act. But Hodja Nasreddin rolled and tumbled on the ground in vain – he could not break the rope. "A passerby!" Hodja Nasreddin pleaded. "O fate, send me a passerby."

And fate sent him a passerby.

Fate and favorable chance will always come to the aid of someone who is full of resolve and fights to the last (we have said this before, but the truth does not tarnish from repetition). Hodja

Nasreddin fought for his life with all his strength, and fate could not refuse him aid.

The passerby was walking slowly; he was lame, as Hodja Nasreddin determined by the sound of his footsteps, and not very young, for he was short of breath.

The sack was lying right in the middle of the road. The passerby stopped and looked at it for a long time. He prodded it a couple of times with his cane.

"What's this sack? Where did it come from?" the passerby said in a squeaking voice.

O great joy – Hodja Nasreddin recognized the voice of the moneylender Jafar.

Now Hodja Nasreddin did not doubt his impending salvation. If only they would look for the money a little longer…

He coughed quietly from inside the sack, so as not to frighten the moneylender.

"Hey! There is a man in here!" Jafar exclaimed, jumping back.

"Of course there is a man in here," Hodja Nasreddin said calmly, altering his voice. "What is so surprising about it?"

"What do you mean, surprising? Why did you climb into this sack?"

"Since I climbed into the sack, I evidently had a reason. Be on your way, and do not pester me with questions."

Hodja Nasreddin knew that the moneylender's curiosity had been piqued in the extreme, and that now he would never leave.

"Truly, an incredible thing – to find a man tied up in a sack on the road!" the moneylender said. "Perhaps you were put in the sack by force?"

"By force!" Hodja Nasreddin snorted. "As if I would pay six hundred tanga for someone to put me in the sack by force!"

"Six hundred tanga! Why did you pay so much money?"

"O passerby, I will tell you everything if you promise to leave right after and no longer disturb my peace. This sack belongs to a certain Arab living here in Bukhara, and it has the miraculous ability to cure diseases and disfigurements. Its owner lends it out, but not to everyone, and only for a large sum. I used to be lame, hunchbacked, and blind in one eye, and then I decided to get married. The father of my bride, so as not to upset her gaze with my ugliness, brought me to this Arab, where I loaned the sack for four hours after paying the owner six hundred tanga. And since the sack exhibits its healing properties only when brought near a cemetery, I came here, to the Karshi cemetery, after sunset, along with the father of my bride. He tied the sack with a rope and left, for the presence of another man can ruin the whole thing. The Arab – the owner of the sack – had warned me: as soon as I was left alone, three djinns would fly up to me, their copper wings clanging and producing a lot of noise. And the djinns would ask me in human voices where the ten thousand tanga were buried in the cemetery, while I was to reply with the following myste-rious incantation: 'Those who carry copper shields have copper heads. An owl sits in place of the falcon. O djinns, you search where nothing is hidden, so kiss my donkey on the behind!' This is precisely what happened: the djinns arrived and asked me where the ten thousand tanga were buried. Upon hearing my reply, the djinns fell into unspeakable rage and began to beat me, while I, recalling the Arab's instructions, kept shouting: 'Those who carry copper shields have copper heads, kiss my donkey on the behind!' Then the djinns picked up the sack and began to carry me some-where… After that, I don't remember a thing, only that I awoke two hours later on the same spot, completely healed – my hump disappeared, my leg straightened, and my eye can see, as I have ascertained by peeking through a hole someone had made in the sack before me. And now I am sitting in the sack only because I have already paid – I cannot let my money go to waste! Of course, I made a mistake – I should have made an arrangement with an-other man with similar disfigurements as I; we would have split our time in the sack, each taking two hours, and our healing would have only cost us three hundred tanga each. But what's done is done: forget the money, the important thing is that I am healed.

"Now, passerby, you know everything, so keep your promise and depart. I am a little weak after the healing, and it is difficult for me to speak. You are the tenth man bothering me with questions, and I am tired of repeating the same thing."

The moneylender listened to the story with great attention, in-terrupting Hodja Nasreddin's tale now and again with exclama-tions of surprise.

"Listen, o man who is sitting in the sack!" said the money-lender. "We can both derive benefit from our meeting. You regret that you have not made an arrangement with a man with similar disfigurements, in order to split the cost of the sack. But it is not too late, for am I just the man you need: I am hunchbacked, I limp on my right foot, and I am blind in one eye. And I will gladly pay three hundred tanga to spend the remaining two hours in the sack."

"You must be joking," Hodja Nasreddin replied. "Could such a miraculous coincidence be real? If you speak the truth, then praise Allah for such a fortunate chance! I agree, passerby, but I warn you that I paid in advance, and you will have to do the same. I will not trust a debt."

"I will pay in advance," the moneylender said, untying the rope. "Let us not waste time, for the minutes are ticking by, and now they belong to me."

Hodja Nasreddin covered his face with the sleeve of his robe as he emerged from the sack. But the moneylender was too busy to take a good look anyway: he was counting the money hastily, regretting the loss of passing minutes.

Moaning and groaning, he climbed into the sack and bent his head down.

Hodja Nasreddin tightened the knot, ran to the side, and hid in the shadows behind a tree.

He made it just in time. The loud cursing of the guards came from the direction of the cemetery. First their long shadows crawled onto the road from a break in the cemetery wall, and then they appeared, the moon reflecting in their copper shields.

Chapter 36

"You tramp!" the guards shouted, kicking the sack with their feet, their weapons ringing and clanging such that the noise could easily pass for the sound of copper wings. "We searched the entire cemetery and could not find anything. Tell us, o son of sin, where you buried the ten thousand tanga?"

The moneylender remembered the magical incantation firmly.

"Those who carry copper shields have copper heads," he replied from the sack. "An owl sits in place of the falcon. O djinns, you search where nothing is hidden, so kiss my donkey on the behind!"

Hearing these words, the guards became incredibly furious.

"You lied to us like a foul dog, and now you call us fools! Look, look, the entire sack is covered in dust, which means he was rolling and tumbling all over the road trying to escape, while we scraped our hands bloody as we toiled in the cemetery. You will pay dearly for your lie, o filthy spawn of a fox!"

They let loose a hail of heavy blows, and then, unsatisfied, each did a dance on top of the sack in his copper-clad boots. But the moneylender, heeding Hodja Nasreddin's instructions, kept shouting: "Those who carry copper shields have copper heads!" which drove the guards into a complete frenzy. Expressing their displeasure at the fact that they were not permitted to finish off the criminal themselves, they picked up the sack and carried it off to the pond.

Hodja Nasreddin stepped out onto the road from his hiding place, washed his face in an aryk, and threw off his robe, exposing his broad chest to the evening wind. How happy and carefree he felt now, when the black breath of death had passed by without scorching him! He walked aside, draped his robe on the ground, placed a stone under his head, and lay down – he was tired from being in a small, stuffy sack, and he wished to rest. The wind rustled in the dense tops of the trees, hosts of golden stars swam in the heavenly ocean, the water babbled in the aryk: all of it was ten times more precious and nearer to Hodja Nasreddin's heart than before. "Yes! There are too many good things in the world for me to ever agree to die, even if I was firmly promised heaven: one could go mad with boredom in heaven, sitting beneath the same tree for all eternity, surrounded by the same houri."

Thus he thought as lay beneath the stars on the warm ground, listening keenly to the undying and never sleeping life: his heart was beating in his chest, an owl was sending its night call from the cemetery, something was crawling quietly and carefully through the bushes – perhaps a hedgehog. The wilting grass gave off a pleasant scent, and the entire night was filled with secret fussing and unknown shuffling, crawling, and rustling. The world lived and breathed – broad, open to all equally and offering its boundless expanses to the ant, the bird, and man with the same hospitality, requiring only that this welcoming trust not be used for evil. The master of the house banishes a guest in shame if, taking advantage of the celebration, the guest begins to go through the pockets of the other guests – and, like this thief, the foul moneylender was about to be banished from the happy and joyous world. Hodja Nasreddin did not pity him in the least, for how could one pity someone whose disappearance would ease the lives of thousands and thousands of other people? Hodja Nasreddin regretted only that the moneylender was not the only, not the last villain on earth; o, if only it were possible to gather in one sack all the emirs, officials, mullahs, and moneylenders, and drown them all at once in the holy pond of Sheikh Ahmed, so that their foul breath no longer withered the spring flowers on the trees, so that the jingling of their money, the falseness of their sermons, and the clanging of their swords did not drown out the twittering of birds, so that they could not prevent people from enjoying the beauty of the world and performing their chief function on earth – to always be happy in all their endeavors!

Meanwhile, the guards, afraid to be late, were walking more and more quickly, and finally broke into a run. Shaking and bouncing in the sack, the moneylender was humbly awaiting the end of his unusual journey; he could hear the clanging of weapons and the rustling of stones beneath the feet of the guards, and he wondered only why the mighty djinns were not flying through the air but running on foot with their copper wings unfolded and dragging on the ground, like young roosters chasing after hens. Then a rumble sounded in the distance, resembling the distant roar of a mountain stream, and the moneylender at first decided that the djinns had dragged him into the mountains somewhere, perhaps to their abode on Khan Tengri – the Peak of Spirits. But then he began to discern voices and realized that he was at a nightly gathering with many people; thousands, judging by the noise, just like on the bazaar, but since when is the bazaar in Bukhara open at night? Then he felt that he was being lifted upwards: aha, so the djinns had decided to take to the air after all. How could he have known that the guards were bringing him up the steps leading to the platform? They climbed up the steps and threw the sack down. It tumbled down, and the boards shuddered and rumbled beneath it. The moneylender gasped and groaned.

"Hey you, djinns!" he could not restrain himself. "If you are going to toss the sack around like this, you'll injure me even more, whereas you are supposed to do the opposite!"

He received a fierce kick in response.

"You'll find your healing soon enough, o son of sin, at the bottom of the holy Ahmed's pond."

These words confused the moneylender completely: what did the holy Ahmed's pond have to do with anything? His confusion turned into amazement when he heard above him the voice of an old friend, the esteemed Arslanbek (the moneylender could have sworn it was his voice!), the head of the palace guard and the army. Thoughts became jumbled in the moneylender's head: where did Arslanbek come from, why was he berating the djinns for being late, and why did the djinns tremble with fear and servility as they answered? Surely Arslanbek could not also be the head djinn! And what would be the best course of action – to remain silent, or to call to him? Since the moneylender had not received any instructions for this eventuality, he decided to remain silent just in case.

Meanwhile, the rumble of the crowd grew stronger, and a certain word came up ever more frequently and ever more loudly. It seemed as if everything around – the earth, the air, the wind – was saturated with this word; it hummed, rumbled, roared, and reverberated in the distance. The moneylender grew quiet and listened. And then he heard it.

"Hodja Nasreddin!" the crowd hummed in thousands of voices. "Hodja Nasreddin! Hodja Nasreddin!"

Suddenly, everything grew quiet, and in the dead silence the moneylender heard the hissing of lit torches, the rustling of the wind, and the splashing of water. Goosebumps appeared on his ugly back, and black horror began to crawl towards him, chilling him with its icy, immobilizing breath.

A new voice appeared, and the moneylender could have sworn that it belonged to Grand Vizier Bakhtiyar.

"In the name of Allah, all-merciful and all-powerful! By decree of the great and sun-like emir of Bukhara, the criminal Hodja Nasreddin, defiler of faith, disturber of peace, and sower of discord, will now be put to death by drowning in a sack!"

Someone's hands grabbed the sack and lifted it. Then the moneylender realized that he had fallen into a deadly trap.

"Wait! Wait!" he wailed. "What are you doing to me? Wait, I am not Hodja Nasreddin, I am the moneylender Jafar! Let me go! I am the moneylender Jafar, I am not Hodja Nasreddin! Where are you taking me, I say again that I am the moneylender Jafar!"

The emir and his retinue took in these wails silently. The Baghdad sage Hussein Huslia, who was sitting closest to the emir, shook his head ruefully and said:

"Within this criminal lies a veritable abyss of shamelessness. First he called himself Hussein Huslia, the Baghdad sage, and now he is trying to deceive us by calling himself the moneylender Jafar!"

"And he thinks someone here is dumb enough to believe him," Arslanbek added. "Listen, listen how skillfully he alters his voice!"

"Let me go! I am not Hodja Nasreddin, I am Jafar!" the moneylender strained his voice, while two guards who were standing at the edge of the platform were swaying the sack rhythmically back and forth, preparing to toss it in the dark water. "I am not Hodja Nasreddin, how many times must I tell you!"

But then Arslanbek waved his hand and the sack flew down, turning slowly in the air. A loud splash was heard, droplets of water sparkled in the red light of the torches, and the water closed heavily, swallowing the sinful body and sinful soul of the money-lender Jafar...

A single enormous gasp rose and hung over the crowd in the darkness. A horrible silence ensued for several moments, and then everyone was shaken by a piercing scream, full of inexpressible torment.

Screaming and convulsing in her old father's arms was the beautiful Guljan.

Ali the chaikhana keeper turned away, grasping his head in his hands. Yusuf the blacksmith shuddered haltingly...

Chapter 37

After the execution, the emir and his retinue departed for the palace.

Fearing that someone would pull out the criminal before he had drowned, Arslanbek ordered the guards to surround the pond and not let anyone through. The crowd swayed, retreated under the push of the guards, and stood still – a silent, living black hulk. Arslanbek tried to disperse the crowd, but the people only moved from one place to another or hid in the darkness to return later to their spot.

A great rejoicing ensued in the palace. The emir was celebrating his victory over his enemy. Gold and silver shone everywhere, cauldrons were boiling, braziers were smoking, tambourines were ringing, trumpets were roaring, and drums were rumbling and shaking the air. There were so many lights at this celebration that a glow floated over the emir's palace, as if it was on fire.

But the city around the palace was quiet, plunged into darkness and seized with a mournful silence.

The emir gave out gifts generously, and many made a good haul that day. The poets became hoarse from endless praising, and their backs were beginning to feel a gentle but sweet ache, so often did they have to bend down to pick up silver and gold coins.

"Summon a scribe!" the emir commanded; a scribe ran in and began to scribble quickly with a reed pen.

"From the Great and Brilliant and Sun-eclipsing Ruler, Sovereign, and Lawgiver of Bukhara, the Emir of Bukhara – to the Great and Brilliant and Sun-eclipsing Ruler, Sovereign, and Lawgiver of Khiva, the Khivian Khan, We send roses of greeting and lilies of goodwill. We send You, Our Beloved and Regal Brother, a certain piece of news which may warm Your Heart with the flames of joy and sweetly relax Your Liver. Namely: today, on the seventeenth day of the month of Safar, We, the Great Emir of Bukhara, have publicly executed the criminal Hodja Nasreddin, known to the whole world with his blasphemous and indecent acts, may he be cursed by Allah, by drowning him in a sack, which was performed in Our presence and before Our Eyes, so that We can personally vouch with Our regal word that the aforementioned villain, disturber of peace, defiler of faith, and sower of discord, is no longer alive and will no longer be able to trouble You, Our Beloved Brother, with his unholy escapades…"

The emir wrote similar letters to the caliph of Baghdad, the sultan of Turkey, the shah of Iran, the khan of Kokand, the Afghan emir, and many other sovereigns of both neighboring and distant countries. Grand Vizier Bakhtiyar rolled up the letters, attached seals, and handed them to messengers, who were commanded to leave at once. And at that nightly hour, all the eleven gates of Bukhara opened up, their hinges creaking and squealing loudly, and messengers dashed off in all directions along the major roads, spraying ringing debris and striking sparks from their horseshoes – to Khiva, to Teheran, to Istanbul, to Baghdad, to Kabul, and to many other cities.

…Late at night, four hours after the execution, Arslanbek removed the guards from the pond.

"Even if he were the shaitan himself, he could not stay alive after four hours in the water!" Arslanbek said. "And don't take him out, let whoever wants to muck around with his filthy corpse do so."

As soon as the final guardsman vanished in the darkness, the crowd dashed to the shore, humming and rumbling. People lit torches, which had been prepared in advance and lay nearby in the bushes. Women began to cry woefully, mourning Hodja Nasreddin.

"We should bury him like a good Muslim," said old Niyaz.

Guljan stood next to him, leaning on his shoulder; she was motionless and silent.

Ali the chaikhana keeper and Yusuf the blacksmith went into the water with boat-hooks. They rummaged around for a long time until they managed to hook the sack and drag it to shore. When it emerged from the water – black, glittering in the light of the torches, and covered in clingy weeds – the women began to wail even louder, drowning out the sounds of merriment coming from the palace.

Dozens of hands picked up the sack.

"Follow me," said Yusuf, lighting the way with his torch.

They laid the sack on the grass beneath a branchy tree. The people crowding around waited silently.

Yusuf took out a knife, carefully sliced the sack open lengthwise, glanced at the dead man's face, and shrank back suddenly, freezing in place with his eyes bulging out, trying to say something with his disobeying tongue.

Ali the chaikhana keeper dashed to help Yusuf, but the same thing happened to him. He cried out and fell backwards, directing his fat belly at the sky.

"What happened?" the crowd hummed. "Let us through, show us!"

Weeping, Guljan kneeled before the breathless body, but then someone brought up a torch, and she jumped back in great fear and surprise.

Torches came from all directions, the shore was lit brightly, and a powerful communal cry shattered the darkness of the night:

"Jafar!"

"It is the moneylender Jafar!"

"It is not Hodja Nasreddin!"

There was daze, confusion, and then the people began to shout and climb over each others' shoulders. A crowded jam ensued: everyone wanted to see for himself. Guljan was in such a state that the old Niyaz led her hurriedly from the pond, afraid for her sanity: she was laughing and crying, believing and not believing, and she kept trying to take another look.

"Jafar, Jafar!" came joyous cries, which drowned out the palace celebration completely. "It is the moneylender Jafar! It's him! And his bag full of receipts!"

A lot of time passed before someone came to his senses and directed a question to everyone else:

"But then where is Hodja Nasreddin?" The whole crowd began to rumble from end to end:

"But then where is Hodja Nasreddin? Where did he go, our Hodja Nasreddin?"

"He is here!" said a calm, familiar voice, and everyone turned in amazement to see a living Hodja Nasreddin, unaccompanied by guards; he was yawning and stretching lazily, as he had fallen asleep by the cemetery without noticing it and came to the pond too late.

"I am here!" he repeated. "Whoever needs me, come closer! O noble people of Bukhara, why did you gather here by the pond, and what are you doing here at such a late hour?'

"What do you mean, why?" hundreds of voices replied. "We gathered here to bid you farewell, o Hodja Nasreddin, and to mourn and bury you properly."

"Me?" he said. "Mourn? O noble people of Bukhara, you do not know Hodja Nasreddin if you think he ever intends to die! I merely lay down for a quick rest near the cemetery, and you have already decided that I died!"

He did not manage to say anything else, because the fat chai-khana keeper Ali came at him, shouting, and then Yusuf the blacksmith. Hodja Nasreddin nearly suffocated in their passionate embraces. Niyaz ran up, shuffling his feet, but the old man was quickly pushed aside. Hodja Nasreddin ended up at the center of a large crowd, everyone wanted to hug and greet him, while he, going from embrace to embrace, tried to head to where he could hear Guljan's angry, impatient voice. She was trying in vain to get to him through the crowd. When they met at last, Guljan clasped her arms around his neck. Throwing back her veil, Hodja Nasreddin kissed her in front of everyone, and no one, even the most zealous keepers of law and custom, could find any impropriety in this.

Hodja Nasreddin raised his hand, calling for silence and attention.

"You came here to mourn me, o people of Noble Bukhara! But do you not know that I am immortal?

"I, Hodja Nasreddin, always free have I been, and I say – 'tis no lie – that I never shall die."

He stood there, lit up by the bright flames of hissing torches; the crowd picked up his song, and it sounded over nighttime Bukhara, humming, ringing, and rejoicing: "Poor, tattered, and bare, I have never a care. I will live, sing, and praise, at the sun I will gaze!"

How could the palace ever match such merriment and rejoicing?

"Tell us!" someone shouted. "Tell us how you managed to drown the moneylender Jafar in place of yourself!"

"Right!" Hodja Nasreddin remembered. "Yusuf! Do you recall my oath?"

"I do!" Yusuf replied. "You have kept it, Hodja Nasreddin!"

"Where is he?" Hodja Nasreddin asked. "Where is the moneylender? Did you take his bag?"

"No. We did not touch him."

"Ai-ai-ai!" Hodja Nasreddin said reproachfully. "Do you not understand, o people of Bukhara, who are amply supplied with nobleness but a tad short of wits, that if the moneylender's heirs get their hands on this bag, they will squeeze out all your debts to the last coin? Give me his bag!"

Crowding and yelling, dozens of people ran to perform Hodja Nasreddin's command. They brought the wet bag and handed it to him.

He took out a receipt at random.

"Saddle-maker Mamed!" he shouted. "Where is saddle-maker Mamed?"

"Here!" a thin, jittery voice replied; a tiny old man with a wispy-thin beard stepped out from the crowd, wearing a flowery robe which was ragged in the extreme.

"Tomorrow, saddle-maker Mamed, you have to pay five hundred tanga according to this receipt. But I, Hodja Nasreddin, release you from your debt; use this money for your own needs and buy yourself a new robe, for yours is a lot like a ripe cotton field: there is cotton sticking out everywhere!"

With these words, he tore the receipt to shreds. He repeated this with all the other receipts. When the last one was torn, Hodja Nasreddin took a broad swing and tossed the bag into the pond.

"Let this bag lie at the bottom of this pond eternally and forever!" he exclaimed. "And let no one take it up! O noble people of Bukhara, there is no greater shame for a man than to carry such a bag. No matter what happens to each of you, even if one of you grows rich – which is not too likely, of course, as long as our sun-like emir and his tireless viziers are alive and well – but if one of you does become rich, he must never take up this bag, so as not to cover himself and his offspring to the fourteenth generation with eternal shame! And moreover, he must always remember that Hodja Nasreddin is out there, and Hodja Nasreddin does not mess around – you all saw the punishment he inflicted on the moneylender Jafar! And now I bid you farewell, o people of Noble Bukhara, for the time has come for me to take a long journey. Guljan, will you come with me?"

"I will – wherever you want!" she said.

The people of Bukhara gave Hodja Nasreddin a worthy send-off. The caravanserai keepers brought a cotton-white donkey for the bride; he did not have a single dark spot, and he shone proudly as he stood next to his gray cousin, Hodja Nasreddin's ancient and faithful companion in his wanders. But the gray donkey was not at all embarrassed by such a radiant neighbor. He was calmly chewing juicy green clover and even pushing aside the snout of the white donkey, as if telling him that, despite a clear advantage in color, the white donkey did not yet have the same merits in Hodja Nasreddin's eyes as did he, the gray donkey.

The blacksmiths brought a portable forge and had both donkeys shod right away. The saddle-makers gave two expensive saddles: one, decorated with velvet, for Hodja Nasreddin, and another, embellished with silver, for Guljan. The chaikhana keepers brought two teapots and two fine Chinese drinking bowls, the armorer – a sword made of famous gurda steel, so that Hodja Nasreddin could defend himself from bandits along the way; the carpet-makers brought horse-cloths, the rope weavers – a horsehair lasso which, when laid in a ring around a sleeping man, protects him from the bite of venomous snakes, for the snake cannot crawl past its sharp hairs.

The weavers, coppersmiths, and cobblers also brought gifts; all of Bukhara, with the exception of mullahs, officials, and the rich, helped prepare Hodja Nasreddin for his journey.

The potters stood to the side dejectedly; they had nothing to give. Why would a man need a clay pitcher on the road when he already has a copper one, given by the metalworkers?

But then the most ancient of the potters, who was over a hundred years old, raised his voice:

"Who says that we, potters, have not given anything to Hodja Nasreddin? Does not his bride, this beautiful girl, come from the fine and famous clan of Bukharian potters?"

The potters began to shout excitedly, delighted by the words of the old man. Then they gave Guljan firm instructions – to be a faithful and devoted friend to Hodja Nasreddin, so as to uphold the glory and honor of the clan.

"Dawn is approaching," Hodja Nasreddin said to the people. "The city gates will open soon. My bride and I must leave inconspicuously; if all of you come with us to the gate, the guards will imagine that all of the people of Bukhara have decided to leave the city and settle elsewhere, so they will close the gate and let no one out. Therefore, go home, o people of Noble Bukhara. May your sleep be peaceful, may the black wings of trouble never touch your heads, and may your endeavors be successful. Hodja Nasreddin bids you farewell! For how long? I do not know it myself…"

Already, a narrow, barely noticeable band of light began to congeal in the east. Faint steam was rising from the pond. The crowd began to thin, people were extinguishing their torches and shouting their goodbyes:

"Farewell, Hodja Nasreddin! Do not forget your native Bukhara!"

Saying goodbye to the blacksmith Yusuf and the chaikhana keeper Ali was especially touching. The portly chaikhana keeper could not restrain his tears, which were pouring copiously down his plump cheeks.

Hodja Nasreddin stayed in Niyaz's house until the city gates were opened, but as soon as the first muezzin sent out the mournful, ringing thread of his voice over the city, Hodja Nasreddin and Guljan set off. Old Niyaz saw them to the corner – Hodja Nasreddin would not let him go further – and stopped there, looking after them with moist eyes, until they disappeared around the turn. A light morning breeze fluttered by and set to work on the dusty road, blowing away the footprints.

Niyaz ran home in a hurry and climbed up onto his roof, where he could see far beyond the city wall. Straining his old eyes and brushing off uninvited tears, he looked for a long time at the brown, sun-burned hillside where the gray ribbon of a road was winding towards distant lands. He waited for a long time, and worry crept into his heart: could Hodja Nasreddin and Guljan have fallen into the hands of the guards? But then, looking closer, the old man discerned two spots far away – a white one and gray one. They drew further and further away, shrinking, and then the gray spot disappeared as it blended into the hillside, while the white one could be seen for a long time as it disappeared in the valleys and dips, and reappeared again. Finally, it disappeared as well, dissolving in the rising haze. The day had come, and with it came the heat. But the old man sat on the roof in bitter contemplation, without noticing the sun. His gray head was shaking, and a stuffy lump sat in his throat. He did not resent Hodja Nasreddin and his daughter, he wished them lasting happiness, but he felt bitter and sorry for himself. His house had emptied, and no one would brighten his lonely old age with ringing songs and cheerful laughter. A hot wind blew across the roof, disturbing the leaves of the vineyard and kicking up dust. Its wing brushed the pots that were drying on the roof, and they emitted a long, sorrowful, high-pitched ringing, as if they, too, were pining for those who had left the house…

Hearing a noise behind his back, Niyaz came to his senses and turned around: one after another, three brothers were climbing up the ladder onto the roof – all strapping young lads, and all of them potters. They approached and bowed with deepest respect before the old man.

"O esteemed Niyaz!" the oldest of them said. "Your daughter has left you for Hodja Nasreddin, but you must not grieve and complain, for such is the eternal law of this world that the doe cannot live without the buck, the cow without the bull, and the duck without the drake. So, then, can a girl live without a faithful and devoted friend, and did not Allah create all living things in pairs, even separating the shoots of cotton into male and female? But so that your old age is not darkened, o esteemed Niyaz, we three have decided to tell you the following: he who is kin to Hodja Nasreddin is kin to all of Bukhara, and you, o Niyaz, are now our kin. You know that, last fall, with grief and lamentation, we buried our father and your friend, the esteemed Usman Ali. Since then, there has been an empty spot by our fire intended for an elder, and we are deprived of the daily joy of respectfully contemplating a white beard, without which, as without the cry of an infant, a home is half empty – for a man's soul is well and at peace only when he is between the bearded elder, who gave him life, and the infant lying in the crib, whom he has given life. And therefore, o esteemed Niyaz, we ask you to hearken to our words, accept our request, enter our house, and take the place intended for the elder, to be a father to the three of us and a grandfather to our children."

The brothers were so insistent that Niyaz could not refuse: he entered their home and was met with great respect. Thus, in his old age, he received for his honest and straightforward life the greatest reward a Muslim can obtain: he became Niyaz-bobo, or grandfather, the head of a large family with fourteen grandsons, and his gaze could always rejoice as it passed from one set of pink cheeks, smeared with mulberries and grapes, to another, no less dirty. Since then, his hearing was never burdened again by silence, so much so that he even grew tired at times and retreated to his old house to rest and to grieve for the ones so near to his heart and yet so far away, in some unknown place… On bazaar days, he would head to the square and ask the caravaneers, who had come to Bukhara from all corners of the earth, whether they happened to meet two travelers along the way: a man riding a gray donkey, and a woman on a spotless white donkey. The caravaneers would furrow their tanned brows and shake their heads: no, they had not met such people.

Hodja Nasreddin had disappeared without a trace, as always, only to turn up where no one expected him.

Chapter 38,
which could serve as the start of a new book.

> "I have taken seven journeys, and there is an amazing tale,
> which baffles the mind, about each journey."
>
> *A Thousand and One Nights*

And he turned up where no one expected him. He turned up in Istanbul.

It happened three days after the sultan had received the letter from the emir of Bukhara. Hundreds of messengers were passing through the towns and villages of the Sublime Porte[1], informing the people of Hodja Nasreddin's death. Happy mullahs relayed the emir's letter in their mosques twice a day, in the morning and in the evening, and expressed their gratitude to Allah.

The sultan was feasting in the palace garden, in the cool shade of the poplars, amid the wet mist coming from the fountains. Viziers, sages, poets, and various palace servants crowded around him, greedily anticipating handouts.

Black slaves walked one after the other, carrying steaming trays, hookahs, and pitchers. The sultan was in excellent spirits and joked incessantly.

"Why is it that, despite the heat, the air feels sweet, light, and fragrant?" he asked of the sages and poets, squinting slyly. "Who has a worthy answer to this question?"

Casting tender glances at the purse in the sultan's hands, they replied:

"It is the breath of our luminous sovereign which makes the air sweet and light, while the fragrance has spread because the soul of the impious Hodja Nasreddin has finally ceased to emit its foul stench, which poisoned the whole world."

At the side, keeping an eye on the order, stood Istanbul's guardian of peace and piety – the head of the guard, who differed from his Bukharian colleague Arslanbek only by even greater ferocity and by his extreme thinness. The inhabitants of Istanbul

1 *Sublime Porte* – One of the names given to the court of the Ottoman Empire.

had long ago noticed that these two qualities seemed to reinforce each other, and they would anxiously question the palace bath attendants every week about the state of the chief's venerable frame – if the news were grim, then all the people living near the palace would hide in their homes and not leave them unless absolutely necessary until the next bathing day. And so, this terror-inducing chief was standing to the side; his head, adorned by a turban, was sticking on his thin and long neck as if impaled on a post (many inhabitants of Istanbul would have sighed wistfully upon hearing such a comparison).

Everything was going very well, and nothing clouded the celebration or foretold any trouble. No one noticed the palace overseer, who had slipped in between the courtiers in a deft and familiar manner, approached the head of the guard, and whispered something to him. The head of the guard shuddered, his face changed, and he left hurriedly with the overseer. A minute later he returned, pale and with his lips trembling. Pushing aside the courtiers, he approached the sultan and doubled over before him in a bow.

"O great sovereign!"

"What more is there?" the sultan asked in displeasure. "Can you not keep your news about canings and dungeons to yourself even on such a pleasant day? Speak quickly!"

"O great and luminous sultan, my tongue refuses…"

The sultan grew alarmed and moved his eyebrows together. The head of the guard finished in a whisper:

"He is in Istanbul!"

"Who?" the sultan asked in a hollow voice, even though he understood right away.

"Hodja Nasreddin!"

The head of the guard pronounced the name quietly, but the courtiers had sensitive ears, and the whole garden began to rustle:

"Hodja Nasreddin! He is in Istanbul! Hodja Nasreddin is in Istanbul!"

"How do you know this?" the sultan asked. His voice was hoarse. "Who told you? How can this be, when we have in our possession a letter from the emir of Bukhara, wherein he gives us his regal word that Hodja Nasreddin is no longer alive?"

The head of the guard motioned to the palace overseer, and the latter brought in a man with a flat nose and troubled yellow eyes on a pockmarked face.

"O sovereign!" the head of the guard explained. "This man has served in the palace of the emir of Bukhara for a long time and knows Hodja Nasreddin very well. Later, he moved to Istanbul, and I hired him as a spy, which is his present occupation."

"You saw him?" the sultan interrupted, addressing the spy. "You saw him with your own eyes?" The spy replied in the affirmative.

"But perhaps you were mistaken?"

The spy replied in the negative. He could not have been mistaken. And there was a woman riding next to Hodja Nasreddin on a white donkey.

"Why did you not seize him at once?" the sultan exclaimed. "Why did you not hand him off to the guards?"

"O luminous ruler!" the spy replied and fell to his knees, shaking. "In Bukhara, I once fell into Hodja Nasreddin's hands, and, were it not for the grace of Allah, I would not have escaped alive. And when I saw him today on the streets of Istanbul, my vision blurred with fear, and when I had come to, he was gone."

"Some spies you have!" the sultan exclaimed, his eyes flashing at the bowing chief of the guard. "The mere sight of a criminal leaves them trembling!"

He pushed the pockmarked spy away with his foot and retired to his chambers, accompanied by a long line of black slaves.

The viziers, officials, poets, and sages headed towards the exit as a crowd, humming worriedly.

Five minutes later, only the head of the guard remained in the garden. Staring into space with motionless, empty eyes, he lowered himself helplessly onto the marble edge of a basin and sat there for a long time, listening to the quiet splashing and babbling of the fountains in solitude. And he seemed to grow so thin and shriveled that, had the inhabitants of Istanbul seen him just then, they would have dashed every which way, losing their shoes and not stopping to pick them up.

Meanwhile, the pockmarked spy was running through the heated streets, panting, towards the sea. There, he found an Arabian ship about to depart.

The captain of the ship, who had no doubt that the man before him was an escaped bandit, demanded an outrageous price; paying without haggling, the spy ran onto the deck and hid in a dark, dirty corner. Later, when the slender minarets of Istanbul had vanished in the blue haze and a fresh breeze had filled the sails, he crawled out from his sanctuary, walked around the ship, looked every man in the face, and calmed down at last, having made sure that Hodja Nasreddin was not on board.

Since then, the pockmarked spy spent the rest of his life in constant and unceasing fear: no matter where he went, be it Baghdad, Cairo, Teheran, or Damascus, he could not manage to live there for more than three months, because Hodja Nasreddin would invariably appear in the city. Shuddering at the thought of meeting him, the pockmarked spy fled farther and farther. Here, it would be appropriate to compare Hodja Nasreddin to a mighty hurricane chasing a dry yellow leaf, tearing it from the grass and blowing it out of crevices. Thus the pockmarked spy was punished for all the evil he had done!

And on the next day, amazing and unusual events began to transpire in Istanbul! But it does not befit a man to tell of things he had not witnessed and describe lands he had not visited; with these words, we conclude the final chapter of our tale, which could serve as the beginning of a new book about the subsequent adventures of the incomparable and unrivaled Hodja Nasreddin in Istanbul, Baghdad, Teheran, Damascus, and many other famous cities…